ACCLAIM FOR
The Projectionist

"*The Projectionist* is one of those all too rare literary accomplishments. . . . A bodacious beauty readers and writers will savour and cherish." – *Toronto Star*

"Helm has a great sense of both character and place. . . . Finely crafted, perceptive, funny, and moving."

– *Edmonton Journal*

"A sprawling and often funny novel. Helm has a deft touch. His portrayal of small town life is uncanny in its accuracy."

– Saskatoon *StarPhoenix*

"Extraordinary. . . . Genuinely remarkable is the maturity, sophistication, wit, and critical intelligence that is everywhere apparent in the writing of this novel."

– *Canadian Literature*

"Helm is a gifted raconteur. . . . *The Projectionist* is a novel of ideas, written in spirited language and evoking the over-the-back-fence-conviviality of home. . . . Immensely rewarding. Its horizons are bountiful." – *Ottawa Citizen*

BOOKS BY MICHAEL HELM

The Projectionist (1997)
In the Place of Last Things (2004)

MICHAEL HELM

THE PROJECTIONIST

EMBLEM EDITIONS
Published by McClelland & Stewart

First Emblem Editions publication 2006

Library and Archives Canada Cataloguing in Publication

Helm, Michael, date
The projectionist / Michael Helm.

First published: Vancouver : Douglas & McIntyre, 1997.
ISBN-13: 978-0-7710-4062-7
ISBN-10: 0-7710-4062-8

I. Title.

PS8565.E4593P76 2006 C813'.54 C2005-907271-7

We acknowledge the financial support of the Government of Canada through the Book Publishing Industry Development Program and that of the Government of Ontario through the Ontario Media Development Corporation's Ontario Book Initiative. We further acknowledge the support of the Canada Council for the Arts and the Ontario Arts Council for our publishing program.

My thanks to the Ontario Arts Council and the Explorations Program of the Canada Council for their generous support, and to Dr. Gerald Conaty of the Glenbow Museum in Calgary. A prolonged howl of appreciation for my friends.

SERIES EDITOR: ELLEN SELIGMAN

Cover design: Terri Nimmo
Cover photograph: Volker Seding
Series logo design: Brian Bean

Printed and bound in Canada

This book is printed on acid-free paper that is 100% recycled, ancient-forest friendly (40% post-consumer recycled).

EMBLEM EDITIONS
McClelland & Stewart Ltd.
75 Sherbourne Street
Toronto, Ontario
M5A 2P9
www.mcclelland.com/emblem

1 2 3 4 5 10 09 08 07 06

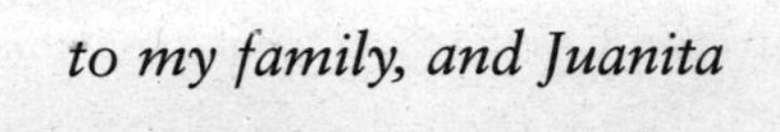

to my family, and Juanita

". . . every one was so positive of their having seen what they pretended to see, that there was no contradicting them without breach of friendship, or being accounted rude and unmannerly on the one hand, and profane and impenetrable on the other."

Daniel Defoe,
A Journal of the Plague Year

THE PROJECTIONIST

1988

I

BREAKUP TIME

1

NOW PAST the valley flats and the rolling climb to level prairie I turn east and then north, pulling a funnel of earth towards town, twelve miles ahead and edged into the morning like blade teeth above a saw table. Kill the a.m. news and roll down the window to the wingsounds of escaping grasshoppers. Every few miles the sunny side of a Westeel-Rosco gleams from just off the road, the bins empty from three years of drought that have punished to near ruin the best farmland in the country. The few inches of unbroken green in late-seeded flax don't yet convince anyone of a comeback. So early in the day and my mouth is dry, the blood's response to another night of strong bourbon proof levelled against me, so I reach over and open the glove compartment and out fall a postcard and an open three-day-old bag of strawberry licorice sticks. I pull one out, insert it into my mouth at the usual slick angle. Not that anyone can see me. On a windless morning in a prairie June you can expect to see tractors or farm trucks pulling sprayers along the road, but there's no one in sight.

Unless you count Walt Sandor, flailing a wave from his barn roof. Likely oiling the weathervane, an elephant this month, his showpiece from the stock of zoological compositions he works up in his yard from scrap metal. The sideline caused his daughter Arla no end of ridicule before she left town last year to land a Home Economics degree. People called her "Shapes," short for "Animal Shapes," a mnemonic clue I myself came up with to remember her real name when it first appeared on my attendance sheet and which not only located her farm (I never forget which name belongs to which place) but was true to her initials. I give Walt a good-morning horn blast.

The card came yesterday from Maracaibo, a place I know nothing about. It's from my estranged, Marcie. I prop it on the speedometer glass and look again at the poorly recoloured view of the city, the buildings a scattering of teeth and broken bones. I remember the first and last lines—"Bet you wonder how I got here" and "It seems important that no one I know has ever been this far south." There's not much between them but I've spent more time thinking about this card than I did about the other three since Christmas. In the last line alone she's more reflective than I've ever given her credit for being. And there's a sense she's writing the card not for me but for herself as an act of recording interiors as she discovers them. Keeping in mind, this is hardly *my* most reflective time of year. Summer tends to run a tab on my dark, prelogical side, and then skip town before I can settle the accounts.

In the fall, I revert to being a teacher. It's roundly understood, though the point's not actually been put to me, that I'd have been fired by now if Mayford weren't my home town. Given my perceived failings—the unorthodox pedagogy, the rumours of bad exampling and an untidy home life—I may not have long anyway, and though my reasons to stay are too personal for me to admit even to myself, at least I share with my accusers the general sense of doom here in a drought-sieged grain town.

Indulging a new habit, I stop in at the Prairie Heritage Museum at the edge of town to say hi to Karen Shaulter, the woman I've been "seeing" for a few weeks, as the euphemism goes, if not exactly "knowing" yet. She's local stock, a few years my senior. She moved to British Columbia after high school and gave birth to someone named Wendy, now eighteen, and was more or less forgotten until she returned this past January to live with her mother. The museum had been without a caretaker since the fall so no one objected to her filling the position of curator, though she refuses the title, saying, "It sounds fake or something, pretentious." Instead she calls herself "Collector and Keeper," which suggests to me that if the stuff of your life doesn't survive into the museum, you end up on the wrong end of that impudent children's rhyme as a "loser, weeper." I've heard these rhymes everywhere in the few years since Marcie told me she didn't want children.

The museum building is the old United Church manse, a huge white house dominated by the steep peaks of a black, gabled roof. I park in front of the veranda. Karen appears in the doorway. Her bemused smile as usual wins her some immediate leverage by suggesting she's heard something about me and she hasn't yet decided whether she believes it or not. It's easy to read too much into an expression, but she has a face very obviously assembled with intent to charm, even if it isn't *her* intent. Her hair is loose and covers her shoulders in a lovely dark brown that she calls chestnut but I don't because chestnut is a horse colour, just as tan is a dog colour. She's holding two cups of coffee and brings them out to my truck and stands at my window in a blue summer dress.

"No thanks, it makes my stick go limp."

She sets one of the cups on top of my roof.

"I've been meaning to tell you, you look a little dumb with that thing in your mouth."

"Only up close. From a distance I look real smooth."

"And it makes you talk funny."

"Sounds pretty sexy on the phone, I'm told."

"I wouldn't know," she says. I won't call her at home because her mother might answer and present me with my record or ask my intentions though I'm thirty-two years old or what I'm doing calling her daughter when I'm still a married man. I admit a failure of nerve but there it is.

"And how was your night? How's your mom?"

A solitary look discloses itself in her features.

"She was fine." She looks over the roof and into town, sips her coffee and grimaces. "I'll never get used to this water. What about your night? Drinking alone again?"

"I invited you. We might've drunk alone together."

"I shouldn't leave Mother at night, and from what she tells me I wouldn't want to be out in the middle of nowhere with you anyway."

I pretend to regard her I-know-you act as good fun but there's always the sense of a blunt probe being shoved in.

"Well then, if not in the middle of nowhere, where are we, exactly?"

"She says she trusts my judgement but there aren't many in town who trust yours."

"I see."

"She says aspersions attach to you like you're the Devil in scripture. You sound to me like one of those natural innocent suspect people who need a lot of alibis. If anyone asks, you can say I was with you all night."

"In this town, that would be the charge, not the alibi."

"You haven't heard the latest thing, I guess. Last night some guy from across the river found a dead cow all scrambled and torn up down in the ditchlands."

"Where'd you hear this one?"

"Kid at the gas station, three or four at the post office, and probably anyone who comes by today. There's all sorts of wild theories."

Launching wild theories is the favourite local sport. I used to find it charming.

"Yeah, well, we live in a hot spot of UFOs, satanic cults, world conspiracy troubles. They manipulate the weather, you know."

"Even a nice morning like this?"

"They beam mind-control signals from satellites."

"I see no evidence of well-controlled thought—last night Mother told me the same story for the third time this week.... Sorry, we were having fun."

"Okay." The matter darts between us every few seconds and seems to want itself collared. Even the town doctor has assured Karen that she's not likely witnessing the onset of her mother's senility—there is such a thing as common forgetfulness. "But I don't mind talking about her, Karen. What was the story she told?"

She bends down and kisses me on the cheek. She's never done this before. By some rude habit I find myself picturing her in a few intimate postures. A kind of preparatory thought, out of place here, if not out of season.

"She said when she was a girl her father used to go walking with her at night, and they'd leave the farmyard and go into the fields. It would always seem they walked too far to ever go back, she said, but they did, of course, and they never took a lantern because he said they could trust in God and each other. He told her she was learning a rule to live by. He never explained the rule beyond that but she said she always called it 'the moonlight rule.' She thought it was pretty, I guess. She's lived by that rule. Which as far as I can see means do everything the hard way."

"At least she's got a pretty name for it."

"What's a name count for? It's just what's left over when you've lost track of what day it is or where you are in the world."

"Maybe it counts for a lot, Karen. I wouldn't pretend to know." The morning's first breeze blows a skein of hair across her face, and she runs a finger along her hairline to set it back in place.

"I shouldn't dramatize, she's not that far gone. Yet."

She sips the coffee again, squints at it, then dumps it into the gravel and does the same to the cup she brought me.

"She's nailed me pretty straight, anyway. Here, have a stick of licorice."

"You can't lure me with candy, I'm older than you. Mother's right, you know. A few minutes with you and I just wanna... I don't know, skip church or something."

"That's me, all right, Godless Toss Raymond. Be careful or I'll charm you into an open road, nation-wide church-skipping spree. Large denominations only."

"I should've known you're probably evil. I bet we'll have a wax figure of you here in the museum in another ten years." And just like that she takes her cups and walks back to the doorway, offering no more than a killing little smile over her shoulder as she disappears inside and leaves me in her aftermath.

Farther into town the outward appearances are somehow maintained at great cost, a few fresh coats here and there, and even the weathered places are most often fronted by dry but neatly cut creeping red fescue and Kentucky bluegrass. Low trees and hedgerows border wide streets, imparting a sense of flat openness that invites the eye to magnificent distances that will not be taken for granted. It's still beautiful to me. Karen makes the place sound slightly more pernicious than it is. I have my supporters, but sometimes even the blue-sky faithful get bored and look hopefully upward for the approach of lightning or funnel clouds.

I twist the rearview and check myself out. The licorice stick does perhaps put the wrong emphasis on my perky cheekbones and horseshoe jaw. There are already a few too many sharp angles, too much up front. I've always thought my face gives people the wrong impression of meanness. Who knows what loves or troubles have passed me by because of it?

Outside the post office a group of farmers in dealers' caps.

"Open season for you, ain't it?" asks Wayne Walker.

"Sorry?"

"The kids. You got licence to bring a few down, a few of the weak ones." He grins forth some pretty astonishing tobacco stains.

"I guess I don't think of it that way. What about you, Wayne? Who're you taking aim at these days?" We both know our parts. I hint I know the story of his latest sexual adventures—and sometimes I do, and never has he had them—and he adopts a sort of sly humility.

"It's that time of year all year for us single guys. Dig your holes and sharpen your augers."

"And clean your decoys," I add, by way of toppling the analogies.

"Eh?"

"It's a sex hygiene thing, right, Toss?" his brother-in-law Bill explains. Bill never lets me indulge myself at anyone's expense and that's one reason I like him.

"That's it," I say.

"That's a helluva thing about that yearling at the ditch, eh?" Wayne says. "They don't even know whose it was."

"They're not even sure it was a yearling, is what I heard," says Bill.

"I heard yearling," I say. "I heard yearling, definitely."

They nod, then Bill announces they're off to the lumberyard to get a kitchen deck's worth of supplies before the place goes under. Some have heard tell of a betting pool of predictions as to the exact dates of announcements for business closings. I myself have money on late August for the lumberyard, hoping for some repayment at least towards a $500 promissory note I signed a few weeks back when ten or twelve of us, Bill included, got together to try to keep a couple of essential businesses afloat. We didn't really expect any returns.

Inside the post office I find two elderly ladies peering at a large yellow message taped to my box. When one of them notices me she taps the other on the elbow and says to me, "We wondered if there wasn't a sale." I smile and they clear off. The note reads: "Dewey Beyer requests an audience." I remove it, collect my mail and drive off into my workday, wondering how any man might come to be quite so counter-custom as my friend Dewey.

Besides a good turnout for tonight's movie, what the note asks for is my company for about thirty minutes as he prepares the Palace Theatre for the eight o'clock and only show. This is fast becoming a routine for us. On Mondays and Thursdays, not long after the new movie and trailers have been delivered, we sip from

Dewey's stock of sour-mash whiskey while I lend him a hand by changing the marquee (far too late to serve any purpose) and loading the popcorn machine. By this arrangement I can keep any movie poster I want, no small reward for a bug of what my cousin Perry once thought was called "the silver scream." When the counter girl comes to work—a graduating student of mine trippingly named Zinvalena Wall—we finish the drinks, ready the cash and open the doors to the rest of the world, all but ten or twelve of whom never show.

Dewey is an enigma brought to town this past winter by a meatcutting job at the Co-op store, and whatever his motive, boredom or ambition, he also took Jasper Payne's long-standing offer for someone to manage the Palace. Jasper trained him as a projectionist, trusted him as a businessman, put him in charge, and then moved to the Okanagan Valley. Owing to the popularity of satellite dishes and VCR machines the Palace is slumping and might well have gone under months ago had Dewey not tapped into the distribution circuit of first-run films instead of the usual year-old fare. But now word on the vine is that minors have seen things they shouldn't have, and—worse in a town running dry of cash—Dewey has admitted them at adult rates. The matter escalated into an open letter exchange in the *Mayford Weekly News*, with the anonymous Concerned Citizens Alliance of Mayford (Coca May) accusing "the proprietor" of "obscene taste and moral looseness," and Dewey shooting back (with my editorial help), "Can I suggest that the Coca May, whoever they are, just avoid the Palace themselves and perhaps tag their teens with some distinctive shirt pin, a blindfolded monkey if you like, so I'll know who to send home to another night of watching the farm beasts and wondering why there aren't more two-headed calves in the world?" The letter ended, "As for the so-called 'gruesome and unrealistic violence,' let me remind you of the difference between a good makeup job and real blood and guts. Do you know what goes on during my afternoon meatcuttings?"

Dewey somehow maintains an enviable measure of loft above the rest of us, and he's resented for it by the many here who, unlike me, don't value diversions from the usual course of things and variations on the same old saw.

The two of us are held in mutual regard, of course, proving the existence of the small-town misfit as a personality type, I suppose. Dewey is the only unhistoried friend I have—neither of us talks much about our pasts—but we share more than overlarge imaginations. He is by nature an extravagant bullshitter and prefers the loop to the line and the rusted weathervane pointing west to the radio report that swears a southerly.

And I, a history and geography teacher (by day, in season), tell my students lies. Or that's what I'm accused of. I've taken as sound pedagogy the old Renaissance notions about the art of memory, that if anything important exists in the cold narrative accounts we cover in class, it might find its way into the students' minds through distortions, the principle being that tortured or twisted shapes are more suggestive of original forms than the more naturalistic renderings of our national yarn. In my class the word "cartoon" is a verb, and I cartoon history, with pictures to match the stories (Mackenzie King with broken crown representing his landing the country's dominion status and, by way of a pun, his role as a political broker of renown; the War of 1812 as two lumberjacks on a double saw— "it was a saw-off," I tell them).

The students don't mind, their parents do, people used to living in a part of the world where all things are viewed at right angles, where we can define our location in mathematical terms, the towns and roads set out in grids, designed with the same impulse that lines a globe—the world in a net shell.

My point, and maybe it's Dewey's too, is that though we may work with accuracies, we can't pretend to live by them. Regret gets in the way. And loss.

I might say, "It hurts to lose the people you love," but, as anyone comes to know sooner or later, that hardly gets at it, does it?

2

IN 1911 my grandfather Eudoras filed title on land and was granted section 13, township 29, range 19, west of the third meridian, and settled there in the cold clean heart of what John Palliser called the "Central Desert," and within a year he'd built a modest cattle ranch—the Square H, initialled after his wife, Helen—along a string of such spreads lining the river all the way to Alberta. Most of the land and all the cattle are gone now but the house still stands on the north bank of the South Saskatchewan River, fifteen miles south of Mayford, and it's where I grew up and have lived most of my thirty-few years.

The difference between living as we imagine and living as we do is that one allows for compromise. Unless you value your imaginings there's a coldness to this fact, and maybe there's a coldness to it anyway, so I wonder sometimes how Eudoras felt when it became obvious he'd erred in claiming too little pasture and no farmland, a concession to the comfort of limitation in the face of boundless opportunity. Marius inherited the entire parcel at a time when small ranches were selling to larger operations or, more commonly around here, converting to farms, but because he revered provisions for times ahead he hung on until the times themselves were gone. Lucky for me I have no taste for sad retrospectives.

But whatever the complex and contradictory reasons we tell stories for—to make sense or escape it—and whether or not the stories are letter-true, once an order of events has been worked through, there's no losing the simple consoling fact of our having it to carry with us and, maybe just this once, to lay down for someone else.

When I was four the neighbour's eight-year-old, Alan Nash, ventured into our yard with a .22 rifle and shot the windows out of a huge old Dodge sedan we had sitting on blocks in our yard. What he didn't know was that the night before, my dad, Marius, had come home drunk and been locked out of the house by my mother, and was sleeping off the drunk inside the car when the bullets arrived. He scrambled out, still drunk, I suppose, and now bleeding from glass cuts, and saw Alan hightailing for home, and took after him. Alan was naturally scared out of his few wits and when it was quite apparent he'd never make it home, he turned and levelled the rifle on Marius and told him to stop. But Marius didn't stop, and Alan pulled the trigger—I remember this point came up several times in my brother Eugene's retelling over the next weeks—but the rifle was spent and Marius caught him and laid a beating on him that I frankly can't imagine, for he never once struck me or Eugene, and when he stopped, Alan was unconscious. After a moment of surely terrible revelation, Marius lifted him in his arms and turned to take him back to our house and found my mother running towards him. She'd heard the shots and been watching the rest from the house. And it was my mother who carried Alan back to our house and called the doctor in town and Alan's dad, Mike.

Eugene and I heard the rest from the top of the stairs and put together the picture of the scene from what we could guess and what we found. Blood on the chesterfield where Alan came to consciousness before his dad arrived, and where he cried almost silently while my mother sat with him and held her hand to his head and said "thank you dear Lord" when he woke. Blood on the kitchen chair where Marius sat wordless. A lone button torn loose from a dress in the front doorway from some rough handling between my mother and Mike when he arrived and collected Alan while she pleaded for him to wait for the doctor. There was no confrontation with Marius. When the doctor came, my mother sent him over to the Nash house.

Life between Marius and Mike seemed to go on as usual. No one spoke of the event, at least not around Eugene or me. Within a few weeks, the two families had even agreed upon a land transaction that saw most of our best pasture land, little though it was, sold to Mike for an undisclosed price.

And that could be the end of the story. Or it could lead to another, though there is not enough known cause in these matters alone for the effects that follow.

One afternoon in the February after Alan's beating my mother sent Eugene and me to our naps, got into the newest family car, a rusting old Buick Marius had bought from some farmer, and drove it out onto the river and through the ice. Most people around here still believe she had some place to go that day. People drove across the river every winter—they still do—but it had been strangely warm for ten days and no one had tried a crossing in a week.

I spent a few days in my room with Eugene, and the morning he went back to school I was allowed on the bus with him. The two of us lived in town with our Aunt Cora for a few weeks. Marius didn't visit us. Years later Cora told me that he just disappeared for a while, and she wasn't sure at the time whether he'd ever show up again.

Only last year I asked Cora if she had any idea why her sister had driven onto that river and she asked, "Why would you think there was any one reason?" and I have come to think there really is nothing to be recovered from my mother's death. It's one of those large events that we are best not to find precise terms for. It's both a secret and a mystery, and those are terms enough.

Before me is the one-storey, two-winged brickwork, the two wings squared hard as a bad rhyme. I haven't worn a watch in years but

I know I'm late again in that no one's hanging around outside the school. By now my classes know enough to go where they're supposed to, and cover for me if the weaselturd Principal Basso comes by. I sneak in through the industrial arts shop entrance and breeze down the hall to the last pre-exam class of the absurdly broad Grade 12 history: Europe to North America—1750-1950.

The students, occupied with their study groups, barely notice me when I come in.

There are questions.

"Is it 'Riel Rebellion' or 'Red River Rebellion' or 'Red River Riel Rebellion'?"

"Have you told us everything?"

We spend a few minutes straightening out names and marrying facts. When I went to school here June exams didn't matter quite so much—the end of a school year was a twilight season of wandering devotions—but these students have become outright fearful, none of the expected roosting. For me, their dread is all that staves off the usual term-end screaming boredom. Right now it doesn't matter where we might find history's heart, or whether history is best thought of as a continuum or an ongoing shtick or some high drollery in bad taste. What matters is each kid whose future now suddenly lies away from the farm, away from town. Thirty years back, the graduating classes were sixty students deep. Fifteen years ago my class was thirty-five. The last three years there have been exactly fourteen and I'm looking at twelve, every one of whom will go on to university or trade school in Saskatoon or Medicine Hat, though most or all would rather stay home on the farm or in town. Even so, they have learned enough to know there are many worse times and places to begin a life. Frankly, they are better prepared for whatever lies ahead than I was at their age. By now there is not much these kids need to be told about the sad ironies of history.

When they are back at work I take a minute to read the morning's other piece of mail, a letter from Dr. Lucas of the University of Alberta. He notes with great interest my findings and observations about native peoples in the South Saskatchewan River valley. Of course, areas of activity are common throughout the valley. They are surprisingly easy to find and, in fact, are more often found accidentally by farmers and gamesmen than by so-called "experts" such as himself.

> Please believe me when I say that your knowledge of Plains Indian culture is impressive, but unless you are willing to be specific as to your reasons for suspecting a burial ground is identifiable, I cannot, I am afraid, lend you my expertise. Either one has evidence or one does not. Perhaps you should keep in mind that such valleys were wintering areas for various tribes over hundreds of years. If you have an artifact, it is likely valuable and of interest to me, but it is also likely not unique or particularly early in terms of the time scheme with which we are dealing. Thank you for writing, but please tell me more.

Precisely my appeal to the grasslands and cliff walls, please tell me more or lead me to luck—not to good fortune—but luck. I talk to you to charm you so you might charm me.

Not long before he left home for good, Eugene told me about an Indian burial ground he'd found somewhere in the river hills near our home in the valley, and he gave me a pendant he said he'd found beside the completely intact skeleton. Only a couple of years ago I started looking for the grave. That it should be in the hills is unusual. The Plains Indian tribes usually practised tree-perch burials or flatland burials in the ground or cairns, or in the few hills they might be near, but if it is in the valley hills then it makes sense no one's found it. No one looks there. Deer hunters stake the draws, people look down from buffalo jumps, but only I systematically scale the walls and search each bluff. I've suffered startled badgers and skunks, diving hawks, cloudbursts with no cover, hundreds of deep cactus wounds, more than one bullsnake.

I've found so many arrowheads and shards of stonehammers that I don't even pick them up any more. I've mapped the variant folds, marked the safest routes and the yet untried ones. These were nomadic people. Impermanence was their natural state. Nothing bound them—no place, no shared languages, no written words. But earth itself locates the dead and unless I see the grave or a trace of it, even Eugene will inevitably become as transitory to me as the Plains tribes are to the rest of us. The ground I look for is his because he told me about it.

"Have you told us everything?"

It's the only question left for them. The honest answer is no.

"Of course not. And no one ever will, get used to it."

It's occurred to them, I'm sure, that I withhold certain accountings, namely those of local and recent history. But what could I tell, or how?

A shoetree sits on my bedroom windowsill, blind to the southern view that Marcie, a city girl, never appreciated. Just visible from the window is the place where I would stand fishing every fine Saturday from May to August on the eastern tip of the sandbar. I'd wade to the island through a small channel, usually about chest-deep, and walk through a dense strip of seven-foot saplings, coming then to a long stretch of dark brown sand broken cleanly in places by bluffs and less certainly by deer and coyote tracks. I'd keep my tackle in a cropping of weeds. There is something ritualistic in all this, of course, but it wasn't as if I found solace in the routine, I just enjoyed fishing. Around four p.m. I would go home, and sometimes return in the evening to watch the birds. In the fall they touch down by the thousands, all around.

The first time I got drunk enough to fall asleep on the island Marcie guessed I'd been swept away, and when I hadn't returned by sunset she phoned our neighbour, Alan Nash. I remember him waking me from one of the deepest sleeps I'd ever had. I don't recall him saying anything at first, though I guess he must have called out, but he was leaning over me, the folds in his jacket holding silver against the night sky. When I came to, he stood, and above him was the Great Bear, and for a moment I wasn't sure which one had wakened me.

As we waded back across the channel I was struck by the drunken strangeness of the moment. Alan's presence had revealed to me a contrary absence in the black above, and beneath the river's surface, and between the two of us, and I knew something important was upon me, a near understanding of life's insuperables. Out there was a great landscape lit only by the desperate light that shines on the walls of prairie homes, some of it escaping through windows and out into impossible odds. But Alan wasn't the sort you'd reveal thoughts like that to, and we didn't say much until we got to his truck. Then he slapped his hand on the hood and said, "This is stupid, Toss. I can't let this happen to any of us. I know what's being said but we didn't *do* anything. I don't love Marcie, Toss. It's not something that happened." My condition exempted me from any vocal response, though I understood that something nasty was loose in the universe. The question was whether or not this news should surprise me.

He dropped me off and I went straight upstairs to my room. I heard Marcie phoning to thank him, the dial's recoil spelling out his name, and I thought of circles, of how they are essentially meaningless. Of how, when measured against the flight of the sun, the river can be seen to run counter-clockwise, exactly the sort of loaded abstraction that takes hold in me for a long time.

Ten miles east of my place the loam soils below the hills give way to scrubland that has flooded since the river was dammed and the flats east of town were drained, the water having slowed into narrow channels, shallow and good for no one but water-skiers and cattle, both mosquito-bitten from head to mudcrust. It's the single best place I know of to find deer or gamebirds or coyote tracks. I once saw a water-skier in an orange wetsuit spray water from a snigh into low-cropped trees near the bank and send up five nervous Hungarian partridges. I knew the skier but didn't tell him about the birds because from then on he would likely have carried a gun while in tow. The place wouldn't normally afford so much of a sporting chance given the numbers of animals but because of the water there isn't much hunting in the area. Each summer it seems more of a preserve. Everyone calls it the ditch, and it's the setting for last night's finding.

"What I heard, it was wolfkill," Colin Blizanken tells everyone gathered outside the main entrance at recess. "Except," he pauses portentously, "there's no wolves."

"Right, Colin," says the mocking Zinvalena, "so it must've been a werewolf. Don't be so thick."

Kevin McCormac thinks maybe a few small grey aliens pulled another mutilation stunt like they did back in '79. Kevin is the seventeen-year-old father of a son who will one day be visited by poor study skills and a fascination with the bra lines on the girl in front of him.

"You think it was the bug-eyed Martians, Mr. Ray?" asks Colin. My name is Mr. Raymond but they take liberties.

"Makes sense. We haven't had wolves around here in sixty years."

The bell rings and we go back in for our day's final duty, the last pre-exam class of English—Today's Writing, my third of a course improvised when a newly hired teacher left town at Christmas never to return. Though I don't prefer them, I've taught English classes in past years and even proposed that the school acquire a stock of translated classics, an idea vetoed because the principal, Milt Basso, had never heard of the writers and couldn't pronounce most of their names. I once had dinner with a priest new to town who was openly astonished that I seemed to be a literate man, my very existence somehow lessening his sense of mission. A teacher is one thing, he probably thought, but penny-ante, two-bit stuff. His own tastes leaned towards the nineteenth century, Russian and French. We found ourselves playing match-the-name-to-the-title. I convinced him that Gogol had never written a story called "The Overshoe" but he became so disheartened that I confessed my troubles with Tolstoy's longer novels. The fact is, I've been reading good books since I myself was in high school. There was a period of about six months one year when the American book club I belonged to consistently sent me the wrong items, from Kerouac to Billy Graham. I sent them back but read them first, all except one implausibly titled *A Popular History of Northern Pelts,* which got me thinking I was being used as a remainder bin and prompted me to write a nasty letter.

The class moves by almost without incident, except that Laura (The Pleader) McGreater glares at me for as long as she can without blinking or rolling her eyes. She still hasn't forgiven me for awarding her a B on her last paper, something to do with "poetry" in country lyrics. When I pointed out certain weaknesses in her prose, namely a lack of actual sentences, she replied that no one else had ever thought they were weaknesses and her "real" English teachers had graded her higher. "They said there were many plus factors." She and her brother Morris should be sold into slavery and made to sell grave-heisted flowers at bus terminals. With five minutes left, a few of the students break down and begin asking me what I know about the stories that the school board may be thinking of "cutting back" a teacher or two for next year. I tell them they probably know more about what's in the works than I do, but not to worry because I certainly won't. Another lie.

The bell rings. They've all filed out when one reappears in the doorway. It's Laura. She says, "We liked having you," and then turns and leaves before things get mushy or I can make a smartass remark. And so we are friends again, sort of, and I think differently of her and admit I might have misread her attention. Despite appearances, none of us inhabits an inevitable world. We are always taking stock, reassessing. We brace against shock waves others might not feel and could never predict. They don't come sometimes, and sometimes they lay us out.

The bind is that while precautions must be taken they can never be relied upon. The lesson of scarecrows—they don't work any more. One autumn my farming neighbours used cannons that every twenty minutes blasted a warning to hungry geese made wise by the effects of hunters' rifles. (Crows were never much of a problem.) Before long the cannons didn't work either, and eventually the crops were just given over to the birds, and they ingested so much chemical and died in such great numbers that the farmers' problem was solved. Though there's less for them to eat now, the birds are coming back because three successive years of drought have dried up the chemical money, and most of us are more aware than we once were, and the farmers have stopped spraying on sheer principle. I consider it a hopeful sign that we haven't yet buggered up the magic of homing instincts.

3

SHE COMES through the door waving a two-dollar bill and smiling at Roger, the bartender and table hop. The players at the pool table pause to watch. Roger places a roll of packing tape on the bar and she sits on a stool and puts the bill before her and begins folding the paper with precision, as if wrapping a small, precious gift. She bends close to her work. She says goodbye to the queen. Roger spreads his hands on the bar and she measures the package against his thumbnail. When she looks to him he nods and pulls two inches of tape. She seals the bill. Roger moves a mickey of Smirnoff that partially hides the terracotta apple behind it. The apple is bigger than life, the size of a pumpkin. He slides it into the open. She runs her finger along the top until she finds the crevice and flicks the bill like a cigarette ash into the fruit. The players clap and one lets out a howl. Roger puts up a Blue and she takes it and joins me at our usual table beneath Lenny, the mounted bull moose who stares steady as a cadet at a dead neon Molson's sign on the opposite wall.

"You'll ruin the economy."

"It's just bad luck and eastern money." It isn't that Karen has bought into the western Canadian superstition about two-dollar bills, only that she appreciates local rituals as much as the rest of us. "I always trade bad luck for loons when I can. It's my only philosophy about life. Who are those guys playing pool?"

"Don't know. They sure wouldn't be oil riggers."

"They look nasty."

"How is that? You mean they look nasty or they look nasty for oil riggers?"

"It isn't that complicated." She slices a fingernail through the coaster. "Tell me something," she says. "Why are we here?"

"Goddamn homesteaders."

"You mean we're here out of sheer family." I can see she is about to launch more of her Burning Questions. She tends them all day and can't wait to see me and fire them off. "Do you think your aunt needs you as much as Mother needs me?"

"Karen, there's more to the custom here than the age-old two-dollar ritual. You've been away too long. You forget we don't casually ask questions about anything that matters."

"But does she need you?"

"Perry's alot for Cora to handle, but then I guess I don't help out much either, no."

"So what, I wonder?"

"Will you quit this? People are just... trying to make a go of the family project. Christ, don't start doubting the premise."

She puts the bottle to her lips, stares at me down its neck. She sets the beer down and nods. "And how's the go turning out?"

"It's been a bad few years but, lately, I have my hopes."

It's my turn to ask what her plans are, but frankly I'm a little afraid to know. Or maybe I already do know and don't want a confirmation. Maybe all I really need to know is why she hasn't been a little more physical with me in all the time we've spent together. Maybe she can't afford certain kinds of attachments, given her long-term plans.

One of the riggers misses a shot and yells "cocksucker!" and I acknowledge to myself the reliability of sixth senses. It's too early in the day, the bar is too empty for shouted obscenities. Maybe they really are nasty.

"Karen, I know you can't come down to the river at night but there's time right now. Why not come out and see my place? It seems a bit strange you still haven't been there."

"Now why would I put myself in that kind of jeopardy?"

"You're willing to be seen with me, that's about the only damage I can do you. Let's us head down to the river."

"Not just now but I'll keep it in mind. It's one of the directions we could go."

The pool players leave and a few locals come in and give us waves. At exactly three minutes past five Dewey appears in his customary white t-shirt and jeans and bounces on over to our table. At the end of a day's butchering he looks especially thin but strong—vascular arms, the veins visible from knuckles to deltoid, and a long, hungry, articulated face.

"You get my message?"

"I hope to be busy, otherwise I'll drop by."

"Dewey," says Karen, "you know I'm fond of you, and if this hadn't happened before I wouldn't mention it.…" She looks to me for help.

"She wants to tell you you stink. You smell like you've been wrangling dead animals all day."

"Not really 'stink,'" she says.

He grins at her. "Well you smell like dead people's underwear, sweetie. Where's my drink?"

"What's he mean?"

"He means those pioneer corsets."

"Oh. All right, but you better quit asking me to find you a date until you get a little more… self-conscious, like Toss here."

"I don't think of myself quite that way," I say.

"Uh-huh."

We watch Dewey receive and down his shot of whiskey in one motion as Roger produces the second shot and sets it in front of him. He is about to enter one of his free-associative riffing states and, unless we leave first, Karen and I won't exchange another serious word until Dewey's had his fun and gone off to set up the Palace.

"Question number one," he begins, "a startup bonus for five

dollars: In the 1973 movie *The Sting,* what's the betting information that Robert Shaw misinterprets?"

"Not Shaw. Newman plays Shaw."

"He plays Gandorph. I'm talking about Robert Shaw, the actor."

"That's Gandorph's con name. Newman is Gandorph and then Shaw. Redford is Hooker. I don't know this other Shaw."

"I used to know a hooker named Candy Shaw in Vancouver," Karen adds.

"He's the bad guy," says Dewey. "Robert Shaw! He plays Quint in *Jaws.* The 'Y'folla' guy."

"*Jaws*? Oh, him? His information is to 'place it on Lucky Dan, third race, Riverside Park.'"

"That's incredible. Nobody knows that."

"You drink too much. Your memory's bad."

"If we've done this before the bet's off."

"No legal grounds," Karen explains. Dewey buys our next round.

"I don't suppose you heard about this werewolf affair." He over-enunciates when he's being sardonic.

"By the sounds of it, pretty much the whole town will be blasting away down at the ditch tonight."

"It's gonna eat into my gate at the Palace." Dewey explains that when he first heard the story he planned to phone the RCMP station and offer himself as an expert witness to help identify the species of the carcass in exchange for information the police might have as to the identities of those involved in the Coca May. Then someone at work told him that a lot of people wanted to know how to go about joining up with the Coca May. "So I say fuck Coca May," he announces. He's getting louder and a little toped and Karen will leave soon.

She says, "Sorry guys—"

"I'm coming too."

"I just got here," says Dewey.

"I might drop by tonight," I say. "Meanwhile, see if you can't exert a little moral judgement when an eight-year-old flashes a twenty."

As we get to our feet he looks up to long-jawed Lenny and asks him what he makes of this werewolf stuff. We leave him staring at the moose, waiting for a response.

Outside, in the late-afternoon light, I see just exactly how well tanned are Karen's arms, a deep brown like leather rubbed with mink oil. Then I look up and see my truck has been stolen.

"Oh, Christ."

"Your cousin Perry again."

"Jesus."

"That kid's a real delinquent, isn't he?"

"He's too old, he's an actual criminal now."

"I guess charges aren't an option."

"He always makes like it's a joke but the fact is he wants a truck for the night and he knows I won't lend it if he asks."

"You better start locking it. What's the town coming to?"

She leans in and administers another one of her pecks on the cheek, right there scandalously on Main Street, and then gets into her car and drives off, leaving me stranded in a vague, nameless between state, blinded by the memory of the shapes revealed as the light did a turn on her blue summer dress.

4

GIVEN THAT Karen seems set on avoiding my place, even if Perry hadn't stolen my truck I would still have spent the night in Aunt Cora's spare room. I often stay late nights here rather than drive home and then back again for school the next morning. Cora mothers me. My reserve clothes are always clean and ironed. Towels laid out on the upstairs banister. Hot breakfast. But my verbal sluggishness at this time of day is unfailing. Though neat beginnings are comfortable I will never get used to them. I require a slow and solitary gathering of my senses before the world is too much with me. Cora has never understood this condition and her loud "Good-day, Mr. Ray" almost keeps me from the kitchen.

One place setting has already been cleared, washed and set on the rack to dry. Perry is well into his workday, which in summer means driving tractor for the Rural Municipality. The idea of real work—who knows what the job means to him, what he has to worry about and what he looks forward to, if he can keep focused or if the time alone makes his mind wander, and if it wanders, then where to? Living alone has its perks but there is no freedom in working alone, for too much quiet makes you talk to yourself, questions and answers and catcalls from the gallery, and eventually you get trapped in the lines of those voices. Maybe he premeditates his misdemeanours, for the most part vehicle and bylaw violations. Or maybe his thoughts aren't long enough.

"Did Perry ask to borrow your truck last night?" Cora asks, spooning some garishly green barley powder into a glass of water.

As she stirs, the green deepens and sets off the highlights in the flowered apron she's wearing over her nurse's uniform.

"I oversalted the hashbrowns but this is a real breakfast."

"Thank you. Now did he?"

"Some things go unspoken between us."

"I'm sorry, Wesley. I don't know why he's so inconsiderate sometimes." Cora's the only person who calls me by my given name, Wesley, rather than Toss, a name I won as a kid because I couldn't stay on a horse. Owing to his childhood lisp and our twelve-year age difference, Perry used to call me "Uncle Thoth" or "Uncle Toth." For a while I was "Cousin" and now I'm just Toss, more of a brother than anything, I suppose.

"The truck doesn't matter to me but I'll pretend it does by way of leverage on him."

"It shouldn't take leverage." When she's done mixing, she drinks the thing in two tilts, then rinses the glass. "He's getting to be old enough by now." However it was intended, the comment strikes me as an admonishment. I always feel I've provided Perry less guidance than I might have over the nearly twenty years since his dad died in a fall from a rotted grain elevator platform. "Did you have a good night anyway?"

I pretend she's not asking about Karen.

"I had another tornado dream. Actually I was standing in your garden watching the thing approach, and I thought, 'This is strange. They usually come from the southwest.'"

"If you have the same dream a few times it must mean something."

"Stress. Time of year. It's not always the same. The last tornado caught me on a paddle boat and landed me in 1930s China, which I knew because a guy on shore gave me an English-language newspaper by way of explanation. He looked confused, not at all inscrutable."

"I can't make sense of that. But then I haven't asked lately about Marcie." She turns from the sink and offers a look of lingering scrutiny. So much for standard mode. There's that name again, not twenty minutes into the day.

"I got a card this week from Venezuela. That's all she ever sends and she doesn't say much. Don't think the separation will repair itself, Cora. Marcie and I...we're over." Saying as much is somehow banal. A mysterious perceptual closing has occurred, and yet what bothered me most a year ago was having been shut off from all the sound judgement I'd gained in the years of university and teaching. I was shaken to learn that the confidence of an open and analytical mind is not a true possession but only something we own for as long as we can keep it. When the world turns over we can lose all surety like coins from our pockets on a carnival ride. The sky can fall. But that is water under the bridge. Water passed. Time pissed away.

Cora knows all about the local inevitability of falsehoods and embellishments, but she also believes that, in small matters at least, if you ask the right person you can learn what happened and sometimes make some pretty good headway on the question of why.

She sits down across from me.

"Evidently, Perry's taken over the role of the angry young man from the last one who played it." I have the feeling she wants me to stop counting the tines on my fork and look her in the eye. I keep counting.

"He's not angry, and I was never angry at anyone in particular, I was angry at the town. There's no one person to blame."

"But you do blame the town for making you angry?" She wants me to say that I am to blame, that I was angry with no one but myself, and that I took out my anger on my own reputation.

"The town is narrow-minded and vindictive. And I feel especially fond of everyone in it 'cause we all have to put up with the son-of-a-bitch." Normally out of bounds in this house, the strong language is intended to make *her* angry and throw her off this line of questioning.

"What I'm asking, is whether you think Perry will ever pick a fight with someone on Main Street."

"That was a year ago. I didn't know you'd heard about that."

"Everyone heard about it."

"It's usually said I attacked a defenceless man with a weapon."

"Are you still that mad?"

"I thought we were talking about Perry. But, no I'm not. It's not so . . . physical now."

"It always ends up physical with men, one way or another."

"Well, these days I have . . . an outlet. You should meet Karen sometime."

"Oh, Wesley. An *outlet.* Honestly." She gets up and removes the apron, hangs it on the back of the chair. She absolves and cautions me, "Perry watches you, dear. He learns things." She passes by and tousles my hair. "Radio says it's another scorcher. No end in sight." Just as she opens the back screen door she asks, "What weapon?"

"Sorry?"

"You had a weapon?"

"Not really. It was a . . . a toy boat."

"A toy boat."

"Yes."

"Well, I suppose." And she disappears on her way to her half-day shift at the hospital.

I wonder if she knows that I've lied to her—it wasn't a toy boat, though that is what people call it. The morning after Alan found me on the island and offered his plea I got up and left the house without so much as looking at Marcie or saying a word, and all the way to town I tried to remember what it was she and I had ever talked about. Then I found myself trying to imagine her voice, and before long I was having trouble even picturing her face. I said aloud to myself, "I'm having a spell. It will go away." But another mile on the only point I could be sure of was that somewhere, somehow I'd misplaced my wife. I'd lost the details. The previous night had sifted over her and Marcie had become a stranger to me. Even then I must have known that the loss itself had been gradual and only the revelation was sudden, but all that mattered to me there in the truck was that I couldn't hear her or see her. I simply couldn't imagine the woman.

I found myself in Willard's Hardware staring at an artist's rendering of a toddler fitted into an inflatable creature named Arthur the Safety Dragon. A voice balloon floating above Arthur allowed him to say, "Thafety firtht!" Someone had pulled Arthur's head out of the box and it lolled over the shelf, one-eyed, grinning, flat as five-day road kill. I decided I hated Arthur. I moved a couple of aisles over and found a bin of roofing nails and took one, then returned to Arthur and poked him in the eye four times. Up at the front of the store Willard and two older men, Fred and Eddy Chapdelaine, were leaning conspiratorially towards one another over the checkout counter. They seemed to be pretending I wasn't there. With their voices just out of earshot, the three of them described something but I wasn't sure just what until Fred, finding one of Willard's asides especially funny, reared back and bawled like a calf. To my way of seeing, they were, the three of them, a little town.

By now I'd drifted a few aisles over and had my hand around a headless axe handle. I thought for a second that maybe that was what I'd come in there for. Willard muttered another witticism and this time both brothers lit up. I raised the handle above my head and, taking aim at a role of tarpaper, brought it down hard, with a thwacking sound that caused the men to turn and regard me.

"You need a hand with somethin', Toss?" asked Willard.

Eddy leaned in and commented and his brother struggled to hold his mirth.

"Doesn't my good neighbour make his rounds in here about this time of day?" The brothers straightened up, looked out at the street.

“He’s not a regular.”

“But you sell his carpentry out front, right? His dumb planters and yard ornaments?”

“This isn’t the place to meet him. Why don’t you go to his house? We don’t need a spectacle, Toss.”

“You’d love a spectacle, you old buzzards.”

The brothers turned in unison and Fred said, reasonably enough, “Don’t act like such a goddamn Yankee.”

And thusly, for the moment, I was disarmed. I dropped the axe handle, picked it up again, set it neatly on a shelf. When I looked back up front, Willard was involved in some subterfuge in the doorway and I heard him say “keep walking” to someone out on the sidewalk. By the time I cleared the entrance Alan had a half block on me. I looked down at the load of creations he’d just dropped off, decided on an empty planter in the likeness of a galley ship, the oars louvered with the prevailing wind. I lifted it off its mount. My forearm fit quite snugly into the ship’s hollow. As I ran, holding the thing out to the side as if I were about to chuck a spear, the oars rattled and everywhere people turned to watch me with expressions that suggested I had, in fact, produced a spectacle.

Alan took in my approach with a sort of pained bafflement, as if I’d already brained him. He made no move to defend himself, except to take a few steps back, and I had no clear sense of what I was doing, so rather than strike him I simply ran into him and butted him to the sidewalk. Then I kneeled on his arms in the manner of a schoolyard bully and brandished the ship over his skull.

“Jesus Christ, Toss.”

“You stupid prick. You started those rumours yourself, didn’t you?”

“Jesus.”

“Didn’t you?”

“Christ, I made a joke about her helping me with an oil change. People took it wrong.”

"Where'd you tell it?"

"There at Willard's. It got a laugh so I went over and told it on coffee row. It got a laugh there too. But people took it.... Everyone's taking it wrong. You hit me with that ship and you're just . . . giving pre-tence."

"The word is 'credence.' And you 'lend' it, you fucking illiterate."

"Don't act smart with me, Toss."

I looked up to see around us about a dozen people, including Willard and the Chapdelaines and old Mrs. Collinsworth, widely considered an important personage in the local branch of the Eastern Star, and her daughter Lilly, just now extracting her glasses from her purse and deploying them, everyone keeping their distance, apparently not wanting to interfere and pretty much dumbfounded with curiosity.

"How is Wanda taking this?"

"'Bout the same as you, looks like. But she's been taking me that way all our life. You gonna hit me or what?"

"I don't know."

"Well hit me or let me up but do something. We must look pretty stupid."

Knowing he was right, and that the fear of looking stupid had entirely lost its sway, I felt liberated.

"You like the ship?" he asked, looking admiringly at his work. "It floats."

I took my first good look at it. There were some intricacies I wouldn't have guessed. "What gave you the idea for this?" I thrust my elbow and waved the stern before him.

"One of them Saturday morning movies. The one where they're after the fleece."

It was the word "fleece." In just one elbow smash I shattered the thing on the concrete beside Alan's head (to his credit, he flinched but didn't buck), and as the crowd moved in I had time to grab one of the oars and get off three clean smacks to his face (now he was bucking) before being lifted away.

That Alan chose not to press charges did, I suppose, lend credence. People assumed he knew he had it coming.

For a moment I consider giving Karen a good-morning call at the museum, but I decide not to; I hope she misses me and doesn't smell a ploy. My truck's out front but I choose to walk the eight blocks to school. In front of the new manse the United Church minister's young wife is out watering her bedding plants before the heat gets a chokehold on the morning. I wave and she nods at me dubiously, as if she knows exactly who I am. On past the watertower, workers are laying new sod in the park, pressing the seams down with their boots. The grass looks a little dry already and the whole enterprise seems a touch desperate. Ty Williams spots me and tips his cap with an exaggerated motion. Small and unexamined communities cradle their peculiarities, novel codes of address and conduct. Repeated courtesy sometimes gives ground to pernicious nuance. As if anything were so simple I'm tempted to add that my own regular and outward departures from custom are likely therapeutic or preventive measures. Hence my sometimes elliptical expressions, stupid smiles, an out-of-place sense of irony which has recently taken note of the hard times settled here like a defoliate. But, as I say, things don't add up quite so easily, and self-analysis is itself a dangerous business, wherein the tendency is towards short titles for big pictures.

Last night after Karen left me I walked down to the Reliable Café and had a plate of gummy Chinese food, then headed over to the movie house. The Palace Theatre is an immense orange stucco building a half block off Fourth Avenue, on Second Street, concealed on both sides by rows of elm trees. It's open year round because the man who long ago cornered the movie market in town, Jasper Payne, came to believe the drive-in screen had seen too many windstorms and was likely to fall over one night and effect the sort of protest usually reserved for hockey refs thought to be in the visiting team's pocket. Not a man to take risks, he sold the drive-in property on the west side of town to a farm implements dealership (since gone under) and put some of the money into restoring the Palace. The floor in the lobby has been recently carpeted and the seats in the hall have been replaced, though nothing has been done about the swell in the lower right corner of the screen, and the walls have retained the grease spots they've acquired from the resting heads of generations. Time in the Palace is forgetful and I always look forward to being there, but until Dewey began working the place I didn't know it could be intimate.

When I arrived the door was open, Dewey was somewhere unseen and my drink was waiting for me atop the concession counter. The new movie posters had been delivered so I changed the boards outside and in the entranceway. When Dewey came down the stairs from the projection booth I'd just rolled Sly Stallone and was holding him in my fist.

"Like I said, no gate. There are unhappy people in this town who haven't been out to a movie in thirty years, I just know it."

"My Aunt Cora thinks nothing will top *Double Indemnity.*"

He reached below the ticket window and then held up the book I'd lent Zinvalena to read during the frequent lulls at the snack bar. *Lines of Discovery* by Arthur Hopkins is a seminal work of historical geography.

"I stash bottles, you stash books. You've got a real problem but you hide it well. Your actuality bears no resemblance to what you seem." It occurs to me that Dewey likely has no idea exactly what it is I teach. The fact I teach anything at all is a notion he hasn't quite reconciled with his sense of me. He once accused me of "playing dumb" but I argued to be seen as having a horse-sensical simplicity, a degree of wisdom somewhere between hayseed and sage. Yet he knows he has the drop on me in any conversation, and unlike most people he doesn't mistakenly assume that teachers are by definition thoughtful and knowledgeable. I'm sure he finds me a slow learner, easily swayed by a thousand varieties of false evidence.

"I've looked into this book," he said. "If only someone had given it to me when I was Zinvalena's age, I could've made something of myself."

"Will you so testify?"

"All that food for thought. Explorers, maps. Most people go through life unaware that the word 'maps' spelled backwards is 'spam.' Have you thought about what that suggests?" The man's orbits have strange loops. I enjoy watching him and waiting for his to-the-heart-of-the-matter skewers of conversation and consistently out-of-place viewpoints. I can't help but wonder where he's from. He is rumoured to be an American landed up here long ago as a draft resister, but he isn't old enough. I know for sure only that he's been a moviegoer for a long time.

Zinvalena appeared and announced that she hoped she wasn't expected to work much because her last exams were in the morning, so I offered to help her study up in the projection booth while Dewey manned the counter. And so, finding our voices somewhere between the whirring projector and the screen sound, we did our work, she with her eyes closed, remembering, and I looking into the projected beam at what might as well have been chalkdust floating in the air.

"You know the provinces and capitals. You know territories. Tell me about maps themselves and how they've messed up the road system around here."

"We don't have to know that. Do history."

"It all relates. What's an isopleth?"

"It doesn't matter. Do history."

"An isopleth, Zinvalena, is a line representing values which cannot exist at any particular point."

"Does that make sense? I've got social studies tomorrow and my own teacher won't help me study. Can't we please let's do history?" And so we did history, Zinvalena and I. Yes, she knew what it meant to rise and fall, and I had a dirty mind, and indeed, as I myself had noted in class, Canadian history has few great rises and falls, so instead we spent thirty minutes covering the subtle undulations from the Family Compact to the Quiet Revolution. She knew her facts but her regurgitation of the exact contents of the lesson notes—my own words offered back to me—left a doubt as to whether she'd actually learned anything. We finished in time to watch the American journalist woman escape the yacht of the anonymously Arab terrorists and thus ensure the just demise of the corrupt senator.

Towards the end I noticed someone on the theatre floor walking up and down the two aisles, stopping and peering at the six or seven customers. The yellow stripe running down each leg picked up the screen light and gave him away as Corporal Alvin Hall of the local detachment. He was obviously checking for minors. He leaned in and chatted briefly with someone, then turned and feigned interest in the movie for a few seconds before waving goodbye and leaving. Hall is an infuriatingly polite man whom I've confronted from time to time about his ongoing attempt to nail Perry with any charge he can dream up. He coached a peewee hockey team this winter and the town is generally on good terms with him, which explains why he was there, following upon an old complaint, rather than out keeping the wolf hunters from shooting each other.

Zinvalena said she had a serious question.

"All right."

"Tell me the truth. Do you think I'd do okay at university?"

"I'm pretty sure you would, yes."

"I'd have to take a loan and my dad said I'd better be sure I'd do okay. The whole thought of... well, it's a little scary putting us further in debt."

"All I can say is, if you go, you'll do fine."

"You have to think of the whole family picture sometimes."

"That's exactly right."

She gathered up her books and started out of the booth and I said, "And Zinvalena. Don't marry the first farmer who can get the question together. Get what you want out of the next ten years."

"I'll be sure to clear anyone with you first, Mr. Ray."

Outside the theatre Eldon Kay told me he liked the movie. He never fails to be satisfied by "big smoke" pictures and the lead actress had an especially "barnfire ass." Eldon and I went to school together and since graduating have maintained an easy friendship. We caught up on springtime news: spraying isn't finished (we could, as usual, use a large spot of rain), there are monsters running around down by the river, people are saying I've led my job into an ambush, the Bucks look promising. Depending on the time of year, the Bucks are either the local men's hockey team or the local senior semi-semi-pro baseball team, of which Eldon is playing manager. Every year the team imports three American college players and pays them to shore up the local unpaid talent. The city teams that make up the rest of the league can by charter import only two Americans. The team with the best Americans usually wins. Ours are most often from California, places like San Mateo and Berkeley, and some have even gone on to the majors, though the Mayford Bucks have yet to be mentioned on bubblegum cards. This year, Eldon informed me, we would have three new Americans. He asked if I'd like to drive into Saskatoon with him tonight to pick them up at the airport.

"Always a fun time. You know they like welcoming parties. Guaranteed they'll know zero about where they are, like all the other dumb tits we get. Were you there the year we told them the girls in town only spoke French?" I remember we spent the trip home practising phrases they could use. *Qu'est-ce que vous voulez comme plat de viande?* The offer tempted me but I had other plans. I told him I'd come round to practise next week, with a case of beer. After he left I wondered if he still gave the new players a welcoming gift of Canadian Club.

Without my noticing, Zinvalena had gone and I'd missed the sight of her climbing into her Mustang and driving away, something she does so simply you wonder why, when watching her, it seems everyone else gets it wrong. Back inside, Dewey was counting his take. He zipped the money bag, I collected my poster and book and the two of us locked up.

"I don't know what you told her, but I said to get the hell out of town. There's no future here," he said.

"Sure there is. It's just a different kind of future. Lives go on. We're both here."

"It's hard to think we're setting examples. Besides, who knows where we'll be a year from now."

And I almost said, "But this is home," but then I realized I didn't know what I meant in saying as much any more.

When they have their exam papers I go over the test with the students, a spoon-feeder for the most part, but the last two questions are zingers. First, an omnibus tour of the centuries: "Considering what you know about so-called Western civilization over the last few centuries, write a history of the idea of 'the end of the world.' How has this notion been conceived of in the past and what does it mean today? (No more than 500 words.)" Second: "With reference to specific conflicts, examine Canada's role as an international peacekeeper since the end of the Second World War. Be sure to mention Canada's role within the United Nations. (Again, be brief.)" We spent some time on the clumsy or muddled symbolism of international politics, my point being that figurative gestures are by nature equivocal. Letters of concern, diplomatic consultations, the presumably limited options of third parties and middle powers. The catch is that such symbols are rooted in nothing but literal thought. The players can say what they like but we all know diplomacy is mostly bad art.

A glaze covers the class.

"Do you believe in omens, Mr. Ray?" Colin asks.

"They're not hard to find when you feel a bit jittery."

"You heard about that meteor strike south of town last night?"

"I thought you said it was a spaceship that crashed," says Zinvalena. "Let's do the test before I forget everything."

"Well, something blew up, anyway—"

"Maybe it was a cow," says Kevin.

"But whatever, you read the test, you think it was an omen blew up out there."

I say, "The clock starts now. Get to it."

It's the last time I'll see this group. For just a moment I feel a sharp pang of absolute dread for all their futures, but I'm good at ignoring dread and regret, and pretty soon I'm focused on thoughts of Karen, and imagining our summer just ahead. I'd like to think that our time, Karen's and mine, is just beginning, but we've stalled a bit over this trouble of finding time to be alone together and I don't know much more about her now than I did a few weeks ago. My suspicion is that she misses indulging her interests out here—she studied fine arts at UBC—and maybe I'm just boring to her. If only she knew the measures I'm capable of taking.

Knock knock. Principal Basso walks in and leans over to whisper in my ear that there's a Mountie in his office who wants a word with me. Basso's a short man with a large stomach, so when he stands straight and attempts with some authority to tell me he'll look after the students until I'm back, the delivery comes off less meaningfully than he'd like.

"Seems like you've thought this through pretty well, Milt. Just don't fumble any questions now."

"I'm sure you've prepared them really good and there won't be any questions." He takes my seat and looks out at the class with a kind of wonderment that they aren't smartassing the way they do in the accounting course he teaches. You'd swear he was lost.

"That's really good of you to say. Really."

In Basso's office Vice-Principal Bill Chalmers is showing Alvin Hall the principal's collection of eight big-league hockey pucks, each on its own pedestal. Hall sees me and steps forward to shake my hand, a habit he can't seem to break.

"Corporal."

"Mr. Raymond. We've just been admiring the pucks. I had no idea."

Chalmers looks searchingly at me, as if to find out what this is all about and maybe justify an outright incident report. My failing status has been a kind of project of his since the day he caught me siphoning the gas from Basso's car so the kids in the shop lab could run the badly dated Briggs and Strattons. Chalmers said right to my face that he considered me "a strange and dangerous egg." He leaves us with the arrayed pucks and exits to the outer office, where he lingers and pretends an interest in the summer plans of the secretary, Marleen. She'll be staying in town but dreams of Reno.

"This is normally the sort of chat we'd have down at the station, I think you know that."

"I'm not sure I follow, corporal."

"Well, that doesn't surprise me. I was the one following you last night."

For a moment I think he means he followed me to the Palace for some reason and it was me he was looking for on the floor of the theatre. Then I twig.

"Yes, well, I thought I saw you back there."

"You know it's an offence not to heed an officer of the law."

Marleen has started to say something in the outer office but Chalmers cuts her off with a nasty "Shhh!" She says, "Well I nev—" and he cuts her off again.

"Could you run through the offences, all of them?"

"Wilful destruction of property, speeding and undue care and attention, damaging the property of whoever owns that field you cut across, illegal transport of a dangerous substance." It seems Perry has won me some pretty deep trouble and for his sake I have no choice but to make Hall think his angles are the right ones.

"I guess there's a charge, then?"

The charge in question turns out to be the one set into the ventilation duct of Alan Nash's house. "Rather than track you down last night, I thought I'd better go back and see what it was you were leading me away from."

"I should've known I couldn't outsmart you, corporal. It's your damn intelligence training."

"Now, I'm not saying a man shouldn't even the score in a limited way when it comes to his wife. But blowing up the man's house? And a year too late?" Only now does he step over and close the office door. The doorknob entirely disappears in his enormous hand. He's taller than I am, about six foot three, I'd say, but his hands belong on some mountain primate. When he's not using them they hang at his sides like spadeheads. "You might wonder why I'm pausing over laying charges of my own in this matter."

"Sorry to interrupt but, why do you talk like that?"

"Pardon?"

"Why so formal? You and I are about the same age. Does it come with the getup or does it figure into the selection process?"

"Now listen here!" He detects some obscure posturing and it makes him testy. "It's my understanding that you've had a hand in helping Mr. Dewey Beyer with his letters to the paper. Now alot of people are upset about those letters and about who sees what in that theatre, and I'm sure he'll go right on without you if I start an official process here, so what I want instead is for you to turn you and your friend—and your cousin, while you're at it—into model citizens. I don't want trouble around here and what I see now is a way of getting rid of it."

"I see." I turn my back to him and look out Basso's window across the dirt football field, deadblack, to the last row of units at the old folks' lodge, retrimmed in blues and greens. "All right, but just one thing. What exactly was I going to use to blow up the Nashes' house?"

"I could show you the evidence, if you don't believe I've got it."

"That's fine. Just describe it."

"Dynamite."

"And now tell me how you managed to move capped and

nitro-sensitive dynamite to town, where there's no safe place to store it and there's no place to dump it."

He pauses a second. Picks up Basso's souvenir from the '85 All-Star Game in Calgary and roughly fingers the edge.

"I don't have to show you anything," he says. "Maybe I'll just go ahead and lay the charge. But it wouldn't do your professional life any good, now would it?"

"You got me there, corporal. I'll see what I can do about all these troublemakers."

"Good," he says. "It's best for everyone."

"Just before you go—you get reports of a meteor strike south of town last night? Someone was saying they saw an explosion out there somewhere. Near the gravel pit, it sounds like."

He nods and pretends to concede nothing. "Just more stories. You'd think people would have more on their minds."

"I guess so." He offers his hand and squeezes a touch harder now as we shake. "It's exam week," I say. "Try not to jangle in the halls on your way out."

The Inuit made maps in the snow. The northern landscape is constantly changing through shifting ice and melting snow. And faulty memory. No doubt more stories about me are spreading, as they do easily in this landscape, and today's news probably runs at least as fast as the story taken to town a few years back by Murray Reddick, who was on the river island spotting deer one day when he came upon an etching in the sand. While I'd gone to no great lengths to conceal it, it wasn't visible from either bank or the widest stretch of clearing. As far as Murray was concerned, the story goes, someone had drawn an obscenity, a scene of two human figures, about ten feet long, engaging in an unnatural union. And I don't doubt that this is exactly what Murray saw, though in fact what I'd drawn was six miles of the river valley rendered into the general shape, or so I thought, of a horse and rider. I've tried a few of these over the years, for interest's sake, but none has turned out very well. My best effort was a deer buck version of the ditch lands on which I marked the various property lines. These maps are of a kind most popular before science got the best of cartography, a field of study now dominated by literal-minded people like Murray, aware only of their own suppositionless landscapes. Of course the horse and rider drawing was unsigned, but I was accused and, given my bird-watching penchant, the label of "hornythologist" inevitably stuck for a few weeks. I wonder what clever tag they'll come up with now that I'm apparently a house bomber.

In a roadside ditch five miles north of town, Perry sits parked in his cabless Case tractor, his legs propped on the steering wheel and his head resting on the hydraulics, angelic babyface tilted to the sun, asleep. When he hears me pull up, he starts and almost falls off, no doubt thinking his foreman's nabbed him again. No such luck. Within a minute he's fessing up.

"I was out at Matthew Short's farm and we were planning to go find the bastards who killed that cow. We figured some weirdos and thought they might've taken up an abandoned house somewhere. That's why we checked the Nash place. When they weren't there, Matthew started talking about what a prick Nash was to do that to you and Marcie."

"You know those stories aren't true."

"That's what I was telling him but he got me all turned around. And we'd been drinking."

"Where'd you get the dynamite?"

"Matthew's coop. His dad has this stash of weapons and explosives out in an old coop 'cause he thinks the Yanks are gonna take us from the south real soon for our water, so he orders this stuff from Arizona or somewhere they're worried about Mexicans—and we just lifted it. Matthew knows about handling the stuff."

"Just one stick?"

"Yeah."

"You were driving drunk with a stick of wet dynamite?"

"Yeah. That's what we did." He tries to laugh. "Stupid, huh?"

"In my truck?"

"With you in mind, Toss. At least after the cult guys weren't around."

"Bullshit," I say levelly. "You're just a couple of pisshounds. You get reverse hard-ons, they stretch up inside you and poke the sense out of your brains." He's looking down like a scolded puppy. I decide to leave him that way and head back to my truck. I had to walk back to Cora's to pick it up and find him.

"I got you something," he calls. "Did you see what I got you?"

"On top of all this shit I'm in?"

He runs up and past me to the truck, where he opens the glove box and takes out a bundled cloth which he unwraps. Inside is his gift. It's a Plains Indian artifact, a catlinite pendant that looks very much like the one Eugene gave me when I was a kid. The markings are almost identical.

"What I guess Hall doesn't know is, we looked around inside the house a bit before we planted the stick, just in case anyone was in there or anything real valuable would get blown up."

"You mean besides the house."

"Yeah, well, maybe we were gonna steal some stuff but there wasn't much left inside. I found a room in the basement with all this Indian junk in it and I saw this stone was like the one you already got. I knew you'd be interested so I took it."

"What else did you take?"

"Nothing. I swear."

"And Matthew?"

"Nothing. We were in a hurry to get it done. We knew no one was around, that you'd be in town for the night, but Matthew said he saw a car drive into your yard. We went out and planted the stick and waited for the car to leave but it just sat there for a while, like someone was waiting for you to show. Then Hall must've seen your truck over in Nash's yard. Then as it got close we saw it was the cop's ghost car, so we ran for it. At least we pulled that off okay."

I want to believe that whatever happened last night is over, but I can't be sure, and I tell Perry as much. I say, "One of us might get charged with something here. For Cora's sake I'll take the rap, but you just tell your friend to keep his mouth shut about your parts in this. If I hear your name associated with this trouble I'll turn you in myself. Did anyone see you in my truck last night?"

"I don't think so. I just headed out to Matthew's. You're not really gonna get charged, are you?"

"Depends."

"What on?"

"I don't know. Maybe on just how bad Dewey gets under Alvin Hall's skin."

5

SUMMER'S EARLY mornings in Saskatoon I'd walk midway across the train bridge and watch the steam rise off the river until the first old man appeared and cast his line from the bank, my signal to move on and find breakfast before the eight o'clock train trapped me above the water. And so I've seen river steam, not uncommon but strange. Even stranger is the sight of the dry steam I saw last summer, and before that not since I was a kid. If a drought takes hold and the air is dry enough the fine sand on the river islands moves skyward in filaments, a natural inversion of the kind that leads to dirt rain or, in other parts of the country, frogs falling from stormclouds. People who don't find these things wonderful spend a lot of money in amusement parks. Their insides are geared wrong. They move steadily through all parts of the day. More sensitive types like myself are always on the lookout for mystery and the secret heart of every small thing. We are inquisitive. We ponder and search. We even trespass, and are not above a harmless break and enter.

Before Perry and his crew broke in, Alan's house had been closed up since Wanda left in March, seven months after her husband (whereabouts unknown), eight months after Marcie. On request of the police (small irony) I've kept a watch for thieves and vandals and have visited the yard a few times to look in the windows and examine the doors, though I don't really know what good I could possibly be doing. The green aluminum siding with simulated wood grain. Steel retaining walls around basement windows. The sheer drapes half closed behind the picture window, and the shag carpet and plaid upholstered couch and matching recliner angled outside a lacquered coffee table made from a large spruce stump. Nothing else was visible from the porch steps, nothing to invite investigation. The screen door is locked. I check the windows. The bedroom and kitchen frames are silicone-sealed and bolted from the inside. The picture window is a double-paned thermal. Only by crawling on hands and knees do I find the point of access, a cellar window held shut by nothing more than dried paint, which I do violence upon with a well-aimed boot heel. Without so much as cracking the glass I separate the window from its hinges, lift it out, place it on the ground, and lower myself down feet first and ass backwards.

The musk of a closed room is caused not by airlessness but rather by the minute issuance of each ignored object. The basement is almost empty of light but I make out a floor freezer, a throw rug. A shelf of books and magazines stands opposite the freezer. Between the quartz owl-face bookends are back issues of *Time* and *Western Report* and several paperback espionage thrillers. The thought of Alan sitting on his front-room couch reading anything more than photo captions is beyond imagining. This must be Wanda's shelf, and whatever it is I'm looking for won't concern her.

I head upstairs for Alan's workshop, an addition he built off the tv room so he could work year-round on his hobby, the crafting of decorative waterfowl. He claimed to have gotten the knack from his dad, Mike, who had learned carving as a boy from his uncle, Cole, though Alan had nothing good to say about Mike or Cole as artists, ignoring the fact that Cole made crude black lies for functional purposes and had no market for them. Mike sold to hunters. Alan made ridiculous profits at craft shows. To me the birds are just more of Alan's handiwork. For tangible reasons, a small scar on my brow ridge and a marvellous if painful image, they connect me to him. Marcie and I broke up without much thunder directed at one another until her last exit. Picture a flying duck, or rather a duck moving through space with its wings furled, its feet invisible, and its entire body somersaulting wildly, a motion unresponsive to the subtle changes in air currents that even I can detect from time to time in my living-room. At flight's end, the target reached and the bird unharmed but for a hairline fissure along its cape and an unnatural recolouring of its crown, now beaded red, it sat at my feet, upright on the carpet, my view of it giving way to more red, the interceding streams from my forehead flooding my right eye and threatening my left, though I saw Marcie's departure through the front door and could take some satisfaction in her successful execution of a once-in-a-lifetime slap in the face. I'd commented that she was taking this so well maybe she could tell me where she'd stashed the better-sex book I'd bought us for my birthday (she paused by the door). I said, "It used to be with your potions and things in the bathroom closet" (she eyed the decoy). I said, "Maybe it's mixed up with your New Age shit. You always thought it was strictly a self-help guide" (she hucked the duck).

The decoy was a gift to us from Alan. It is now a shoe tree.

I'm unprepared for the sheer number of birds that await me, three walls' worth shelved from floor to ceiling, lined up like toy soldiers, each in the same uncomplicated repose. I wonder if they float. Though some are more intricately feathered than others, from a short distance they look remarkably lifelike, not least of all their plastic red eyes. Hitchcock comes to mind, the stuffed birds on Anthony Perkins' motel walls. I check behind me on the off-chance there's a knife-wielding multiple personality, but all I see is an armchair with a tv remote control propped on the back. The real weapons are at the other end of the room. Under Alan's work-table is a galley ship exactly like the one I hit him with. On the table are a hatchet, a spokeshave, an assortment of sandpapers and chisels, a drawknife, and—pushed to one side—jars of brushes and paints and an open book with colour photos of pintails.

There's not a single unfinished bird on the table and not even any wood left to be carved. He didn't leave Wanda on impulse. His was a planned escape.

In the rest of the house it's the rooms themselves that seem petrified. Much of the furniture and many of the personal oddments have been removed but of what remains, nothing is out of place, as if while she was preparing to vacate, Wanda was expecting company. And here I am. The only room I hesitate in entering is the one I've never seen before, the bedroom. Though I don't believe I'm a cuckold, the persistent stories have left a small part of me suspicious of every natural concealment for miles around.

The bed is flawlessly made, the sheets and patterned quilt drawn over the pillows to form what I've always called a blind bed, one where the face has been covered like that of someone recently dead. I don't make my bed this way. The four-posted oak frame matches the night table. I draw the curtains and watch how the room changes in the light. The dresser has braces for a triptych mirror that's not there, which may explain why, even in a land of conservative fashion where the only marks of a sharply dressed man are an unbuttoned neck and a well-rolled sleeve, Alan didn't dress well. The outside view surprises me. The riverbank below my house is visible, the ground anchored by the familiar tree roots that are cauterized each winter and then exposed in the spring. From my house I can see nothing of this yard.

I'll leave where I came in. I've saved for last the room Perry told me about, the one where he found the pendant, the closest thing I've had to a clue in all the months of searching for Eugene's secret place. At the foot of the stairs the window light reveals no more than it did a few minutes ago, the shelf and freezer and rug, but I see now that the darkness extends behind the furnace. I sit on the stairs for a moment with my eyes closed so they can adjust to the dark. Then I rise and step, almost blindly, into the shadow.

II

THE PROJECTIONIST

6

DEWEY LIVES in a 1970s nine-bedroom, three-bathroom, thoroughly dated monstrosity with two south-facing decks, a basement shooting range, a main floor atrium and an indoor swimming-pool. All this he rents for two-fifty a month from a once successful farmer named Bill Pratz, now bereft of everything and tending fairways in northern British Columbia. Bill was the youngest of eleven goldshit grain kings who decided to make a kind of millionaire's row they called Harvest Lane on the south edge of town. Seven of these farmers are still there, hanging on. They are Dewey's neighbours. Unlike him, they have to pay huge property taxes. Unlike anyone else, Dewey had the gall to rent the place. Some people really hate him.

A Sunday mid-morning, about half an hour before service for the church-goers, I pull into Dewey's four-car garage and emerge to see Old Norm Reynolds regarding me from across the street. He's a hard man, Old Norm. He's fixed me now, cradles his watering hose like a rifle. Wattled face, his eyes strafe across the house and he calls out, "He let them plants go dead in there, didn' he."

"Not too sure, Norm. I think he's taking care of things pretty straight."

"Like hell," he says, and stoops off stalking the perennials.

It was once possible to search for Dewey in this place and not find him—he moved his mattress just about anywhere and once actually slept out on the roof—but he seems to have settled on the empty pool as the spot he can most fully inhabit, his reason being that it most resembles the kinds of places he's used to living in. The rest of the house is fully furnished in the Pratz family manner, right down to the pinup blessings, but Dewey has a hard time feeling comfortable anywhere inside. The place makes him feel like a ghost.

Electrical cords feed into the pool to service a couple of standing lamps in the shallow end, where Dewey has a table and small shelf and three folding chairs sociably angled towards one another. The mattress lies precariously near the edge where the bottom drops off to the deep end, which features a wire strung between the opposing ladders and sagging with clothes.

He's on a fold-up chair, reading the paper in his underwear. I stand on deck. Our voices echo.

"Some people really hate me."

"You don't have to live in this place."

"No one else would. Here I thought I was helping a man out."

"Sure, that'll wash." I produce a page from my inside jacket pocket. "I have a draft."

He's distracted. "Fine, fine, come on down the little ladder there." At the foot of the little ladder is a badly frayed welcome mat reading "Bless This."

The Coca May letter in Friday's *Weekly News* made an issue of a poster Dewey had worked up with a green marker pen and placed in his front window to appease the neighbours. Under a rather approximate drawing of a plant was the caption "Say Nope to Wild Oats." It had garnered him, if not praise, then at least some neutrality, until one of the schoolkids pointed out that the plant was a dead ringer for cannabis. This reading was widely accepted as typical of Dewey, and was received none too well by farmers suspicious even of what is locally called "ethnic diversity" in their crops—shunning the few wingnuts who give coriander, anise or garbanzo beans a run.

The letter brought up the spectre of "the druggy culture." It declared that "The man responsible for the sign"—they never use

Dewey's name—"should know that his habits are not just wrong, they are evil. We will not now, at a time when our children are especially vulnerable to the temptations of Satan, allow anyone to influence them to take up dark practices."

I hand him my response. It's an apology. He reads it and looks at me uncomprehendingly.

"Aren't you having fun any more? Where's that spirit I once knew? And why are you so dollied up today?"

"I'm goin a-courtin'. I just think we should show a willingness to allow them their opinion."

"What on sunbaked earth are you talking about?"

"Corporal Hall asked me to rein you in."

A look of wild expectancy comes over him.

"Now why would he do that?"

"He seems to be feeling pressured to do something about you."

"I see."

"And he has something on me." I tell him about Perry's misadventure.

"Your cousin sounds like he has the right idea. Don't you worry about Hall. He won't touch either of us if we just maintain the right amount of ambiguity in all of this."

"Sometimes I don't know what you mean. Maybe I should've mentioned as much before now."

"Hall is a haunted man, you can see it in his eyes. I truly think we scare him a little bit."

Dewey gets up and climbs the little ladder and wanders off to the kitchen. I see that he's set up a small bookshelf beside the mattress. An unlikely assortment of titles: *The Prairie Nocturnal, Science and the Common Understanding, The Life of Mary Shelley, A History of Tennessee Stills*, books on revolution, rhetoric and riddles. It's easy to think of him as the true autodidact, harbouring all sorts of random knowledge.

He returns with a paper and pen and writes as we speak.

"I was wondering if I could use this place some afternoons," I say.

"Ahem." He cocks a brow. "People will see you."

"No cost to you."

"It will do neither of us any good."

"I don't care who sees what."

"Karen still has good heiferweight in this town."

"That's only because nobody knows her yet."

" . . . You included."

When he's finished he reads it to himself, humming a single note in no particular rhythm. He hands it over.

> This millennium thing is getting out of hand. Could you please train your indignation on what's actually happening in the world? I don't know how to tell you, but it's a pretty terrible place any place you go and we are not, on this little ground of ours, waging a battle for souls. Most days, God can't find us with a map.

"That last's a bit risky."

"It oughta keep up the free and frank exchange." He has an idea, takes back the paper and adds a line asking the Coca May to define their principles in forty words or less. "Where do they meet, I wonder. I bet that old Reynolds bastard across the street is one of them."

"He doesn't strike me as the group action type."

"And Bonny in the Co-op, she's one. She announced to us yesterday that her daughter had 'yielded' a child. My God, they have euphemisms for *giving birth*. It boggles. It—"

"Ah Christ, what time is it?" I spring up and make for the ladder, then pause. "So I can bring Karen here?"

"It seems not right somehow," he says. "Me so lonely and her a fine woman, and you so willing to compromise."

"Okay, I'm sorry. I didn't expect you to fold up over this feeble little gesture."

"Good. Yes bring her. The place needs some livening up."

Last night Karen suggested I drive her and her mother, Kate, to church today as a way of introducing myself in a small, well-controlled dose. I was so happy she'd decided to move us along that I resolved to surprise her and go the whole hog and dudded up, ready to sit with them, drop a twenty into the offering tray, belt out a few hymns.

The note taped on her front door reads, "I built you up for hours as a man of substance, then opened the door to a swarm of gnats. Don't bother putting any more effort into this than you have already."

In two minutes I'm parked outside the United Church. According to the radio I'm seventeen minutes late. Only a complete asshole would make an entrance now, but it takes some doing to keep myself put and wait for the service to let out.

A life lived out on paper—I draft another letter, this one to Dr. Lucas, explaining that I do in fact have evidence he might be interested in. What I found in the dark of Alan's basement was an earth-chilled room and a table headed with a buffalo skull probably meant to startle intruders but looking less like a menacing ghost than the front end of some Cadillac parody. Behind it on the table lay the shapes of a prairie archaeologist's dreams. My fingers identified what my eyes couldn't: flint blades and arrowheads, stone shards with worn grooves, three trade axes, a crooked knife, a firesteel, and what felt like small shale carvings, though I couldn't be sure and so pocketed them for a closer look outside. I considered bumping around in the dark a little longer but thought I might damage some part of the collection, or some part of me. And there was something else in the room. A hanging blackness deeper than the rest was shaped into the far wall, an area with a distinct character of no-light. I couldn't guess at this and, while my hands might have identified the texture, it was something I didn't yet care to know. A little spooked, I left, pulling myself to daylight with an embarrassing urgency. In the light I examined the three shale pieces. They were more pendants, artifacts rare enough that even sketches and photos of them are hard to come by—the northern Plains tribes didn't often use stone as a personal adornment. Each was tapered and grooved and depicted human figures, two to each pendant and all of them apparently hunters. A typical geometry suggested these might be Sioux pictographs. The bodies and mouths were rectangular, the faces were circles, the most common clothing designs were triangles, as were the spear tips and arrowheads. They are almost identical to the pendant Eugene gave me from the grave he found.

I'm sitting in the sun, sweating. I take off my jacket but keep my collar buttoned in case Karen and her mother see me before I can get the jacket back on.

I describe the pendants for Dr. Lucas and imply that the artifacts are mine and I may want to sell them. If he's interested Lucas will do some investigation of his own, and if their origins can be traced the pendants and tools will speak a little more story into the faint and much-ignored indigenous history. I end the letter by asking, "Aren't these items the kinds of personal possessions sometimes included in burial grounds?" Why ask the question unless I hadn't found them in the field? So what if I'm a scavenger? At least I scavenge my own turf, or close to it. Admittedly there are legal complications I'm ignoring, but as long as the items haven't been catalogued—a safe bet—I see no reason why I shouldn't ask questions.

By the time I've finished the letter and a poorly representational drawing, people in Sunday dress have begun to stream in front of the truck. I recognize many of them and prop my hand on the steering wheel at twelve o'clock so it can jerk away in greeting. I'm sweating so much my hair is damp. I don't see Karen. As the crowd thins I catch a glimpse of activity in the rearview and see the Anglican church across the street letting out, and suddenly I realize I don't know which church they attend. I mean, I supposed it wasn't Full Gospel or Catholic, but the rest was all assumption. Sure enough, Karen emerges beside a sturdy-looking woman who looks vaguely familiar, and younger than I'd have guessed. The traffic behind me is steady by now so I can't back out. I could run across to them but I'd have to say my hellos to everyone on this side and that would put them out of reach. I opt to sit in my window and give the horn a quick blast.

Along with everyone, they look over at me with my head and shoulders above my truck roof, which is when I detect damp sweat stains very possibly the size of catcher's mitts butterflied out from my armpits. Then I realize I have a licorice stick protruding from my mouth. I suppose I look pretty silly. I smile.

Her mother asks Karen something.

Karen nods and leads her away to their car.

"What in hell was that all about?" I twist around to see Wayne Walker. His hair is creased where his cap usually sits. "You shoulda been in there, Toss. The minister had a thing or two to say about bearing false witness. The idea was how evil forces aren't the sort of thing you go after with Dad's rifle and alot of skunk dope."

"He said 'skunk dope'?"

"It was one of those 'he said, God said' deals. You're never sure who's telling you what."

"You want scripture, Wayne?" I get back in my seat. "God said he wished to hell people would stop bringing his name into every little thing."

Plainly the best strategy was not to call Karen but to let her cool a bit. I dropped by Cora's instead, and sat with Perry watching a tv show in which people in gaudy spandex shot plastic balls at one another. One of them was a champion at this sort of thing and in the post-match interview said he wanted his years of training acknowledged by the International Olympic Committee. By the end of it all you couldn't feel much more like offing yourself. I invited Perry to bring his mom down to my place for dinner, but his friends were coming by soon to take him to a mud fling somewhere. Perry looked over at me slouched in my chair and must have recognized the signs of a drunk coming on. He dialled the phone and passed it to me.

"Hello?"

"Hello?"

"Please don't call. I won't say please again." Then she hung up.

I more or less staggered out without a word and drove myself home. Indulging a maudlin impulse, I reread Marcie's cards and found I didn't feel any worse, so I shot for the moon and got out the family papers, including a couple of newspapers, and these have come together in a way I haven't connected before.

Among my father's papers is a 1953 edition of *The Powder River County Examiner* sent to us by some American relative of ours named Gray, from a branch of the family I've never met. The lead story quotes a livestock expert who rates the Gray ranch as the most efficient cow outfit in the state, and includes an interview with Bud Gray wherein he spills five or six beans about running cattle. One tenet I remember for its tenacious rhythm: "Never move cattle to feed—move to market instead." Marius had at least as much sense as old Bud, is my guess, he just didn't have the range. If he had had it, Eugene might not have studied that paper so much when he was a kid and then taken the first opportunity to leave us and poke cows for some American rancher with too much land to know where all his animals were.

I was thirteen when he left. It was late summer. I hadn't seen much of him since the spring. He hired himself out during calving season and often spent three or four days at a time in some distant place where he could earn a few bucks as a short-stint hired hand. There wasn't much work left at home—Marius grew feed and sold it locally, but most of his work was in one farmyard or another as a heavy machinery repairman. One day Eugene showed out of nowhere to collect his talisman from home and load it into his truck. The charm was a large buffalo-rubbing stone from a circle across the river, the animal oil still dark on the surface. Though he never said so, he surely took the stone to the same place he took his girls, somewhere he said no one knew about. Some place you could get to by truck and maybe a short walk or climb, at night, in 1968. A place to be alone. Even on some winter days he'd spend his afternoons there and come home tracking snow inside, his steps sounding upstairs just long enough for him to change into dry clothes and then come back down and into the kitchen to the fridge and back out again before the prints had melted or he answered the question from Marius, "What's her name tonight?" This scene repeated throughout his last year in the house, after he'd resolved to leave some day, though in fact he left at night and sooner than he might have guessed, before a sixteen-year-old out-of-towner spread the lie that she was pregnant.

I was shining my Sunday shoes in our room. To cover the floor I'd laid out a couple of pages of the Saskatoon daily and was looking at pictures—pictures I've saved here—of the new prime minister and of angry soldiers in Cleveland and Prague. I remember a moment of sweet curiosity about the names Cleveland and Prague, and I remember that when Eugene came in I said, "People keep shooting people everywhere." He said, "It's a good thing for both of us we aren't much the same. I'm just telling you I'm going now. So, here I go." He was around then always wearing the black and yellow checkered shirt Marius kept hanging in the shed, the one coloured like a field of mustard against a thunderhead. He left Marius asleep but made a point to get the shirt from the shed, all the while saying, "Don't believe what you hear. It doesn't matter anyway 'cause anyway I was leaving." He walked the yard fast and loaded up. "Things blow over," he said. "And nothing here is your fault. Maybe he'll need looking after but don't let him get on you about things. You'll need something to keep from going crazy out here." He tied the canvas over the truck box and said nothing when the cord pinched a blood blister into his finger. "If he asks I have enough money to get where I plan, and I can always make a few bucks. I hope to fuck the road's open." He left then without hesitation, as if he'd see me again soon enough, though in fact we never saw each other again and I heard no news of him until fourteen years later, when I learned he was dead. The night ended with a gun rack in the back, going away. With animal shadows on the bedroom wall and the shapes you can see in a rag and shoe.

7

BY THE time I reach the museum in the morning I've rehearsed my apology so many times and worked myself into such a heightened state of preparedness that when I come through the door to find, quite unexpectedly, two museum-goers, and they say hello, I can manage no more than a grunt. It's Mrs. Lorne Marleyfoot, Eunice to some, school trustee and mother of Donald Marleyfoot, the local Conservative Party M.L.A. Eunice is with her daughter Altha, last year's Gopher Days Queen, elected in a classic come-through-the-middle manoeuvre when her two rivals fell into disfavour for privately making dirty accusations about one another involving, in the case of Mary Loots, sympathetic connections with "eastern anti-beef groups," and in that of Mary Elkins, questionable sexual orientation. The Marys denied both the accusations and the making of them. Neither knew what had hit her, they used to be such friends. What had hit them, of course, was Eunice Marleyfoot.

"Well, let's try again," says Eunice. "Good morning, Mr. Raymond."

"Yes. Good morning to you Marleyfeet." I leave them with the historical photo albums and stride on into the "Homesteader's Kitchen," looking for Karen. Her purse sits on top of the wood stove. When I hear footsteps coming up the basement stairwell, I lean casually against a table laid out with twine-tied bundles of dried plants and flowers "used in making teas and remedies," as the sign says, and as she appears in the kitchen I reach back and grab one of the bundles and offer it, bouquet-like.

She ignores it, stares fiercely at me.

"I knew you'd show up. In your own time."

"Can we speak, Karen?"

"I'm just a little busy now." She makes her way out to say hello to the guests. I follow.

Eunice has a question about one of the photos. She's tapping her finger on a seventy-year-old shot of the pool hall on Main.

"You've written here that this building is the only original building still standing in town, which would make it the earliest, but in fact the earliest is the little building attached to the Pioneer elevator. It used to be the government titles building."

"I see," says Karen.

"But it's been moved and built onto," I say. "It doesn't count."

"It certainly *does* count," says Eunice. "We don't want a pool hall as our oldest building."

"Essentially what you're talking about is oldest original lumber, not building."

"Well, I won't pretend to see any sense in *that* statement."

"Of course not," says Karen. "I'll look into the dates and change the text if there's been a mistake. Thank you for pointing it out."

Through all of this, Altha has stood by, looking practised, if a bit tired. Now she announces she's going upstairs to look at the "Early Wares" display. Her mother completely ignores her and she heads on up the stairs.

"I'll come by next week to see how you've made out." Eunice inclines slightly to Karen, whom she no doubt sees as a shirker.

"It'll be nice to see you."

"That pool hall has been trouble all these years," she says. Then, as if looking for something she's misplaced, she begins bobbing her head in several directions.

"There's an original spittoon upstairs," I offer. Karen glares at me.

"Where's my Altha?"

"She went upstairs." As Eunice turns away, I point to the stairway with the dried flowers I'm still holding for some reason. Several dozen little yellow seeds fall into Eunice's hair. She doesn't notice. I don't point it out. Karen massages her brow with her index finger.

"Those tar soaps up there are still the best thing for psoriasis," I say. Eunice casts back a look as if to say she doesn't know how something like me could have been produced in this town. When she's disappeared Karen asks me to leave.

"I thought we'd agreed to talk."

"I have a job to do. I don't need you to complicate things here."

"You haven't even let me say I'm sorry yet."

"You have a professional suicide wish, you know that?"

"I huh?"

"Eunice is on the school board, you know."

"Yes?"

"There's a pattern to your behaviour."

"What behaviour? Look, Dewey said it would be okay if we used his house at lunch."

"Used it for what?" She doesn't alter her bearing an inch. She's gonna blow any second.

"I'll fix you up some lunch."

Now she stabs her finger towards the front door, then heads upstairs.

I follow again.

Straight past the roped off "Bathing Room" with its tub partially hiding the pretty much unmentionable chamber-pots and on by the "Child's Bedroom" with its assorted and ghastly-eyed wooden dolls, I find the three of them in a room cluttered with a miscellany of collected house junk. They're gathered around a table.

Eunice and Altha are looking with genuine curiosity at a mystery display. Karen studies their faces and smiles, even after I pull up. The sign beside the table asks, "Do You Know What These

Are? Many of our exhibit pieces are donated by the families of original prairiemen and women. Often, even the families of these western developers don't know what they've had passed down to them, and neither do we at the museum. If you have any idea what these objects might be, please tell us so we can tag the pieces accurately."

On the table are a miniature winch device the size of a belt buckle, what looks like a few feet of yarn wrapped around what looks like a large wooden elf's shoe, and a piece of torn and stretched leather on top of which are four variously sized metal rings.

"I know what this is," I say, pointing to the rings.

Karen detects danger and says, "Toss."

"Can you guess, Altha?"

She studies the rings.

"Can I touch them?" she asks Karen.

"Of course."

She picks up the smallest ring and rubs it.

"Any guesses?" I ask.

"It's smooth," she says. "Maybe they're earrings."

"They're solid though, and a little big for earrings. What about you, Mrs. Marleyfoot? I bet you know."

"They might not be earrings but they're certainly some sort of... adornments."

"Go ahead and pick one up."

"No."

I pick up the whole arrangement and spill the rings into my hand, then hold up the leather.

"It's a condom!" I announce. "An early-days one!"

Eunice looks at the leather and opens her mouth but nothing emerges.

"You mean for a horse?" asks Altha.

"No."

Karen says, "You're making this up. He's making this up."

"I guess you've never known a true prairieman, Karen."

"Stop," she says.

"They used it thusly." I pick up the elf's shoe and poke it into the leather, which does, in fact, form quite naturally into a long, roomy pouch. To my surprise, the thing looks as though it might actually do the job. "Then you slip the ring on like this to hold it down. It's loose here but then things would tighten up some. I can't really show you with a shoe."

Eunice is quite obviously in need of something. Karen takes her by the elbow and ushers her to the stairs, which they negotiate together. Altha stays behind a second and reaches over to give the sheathed elf shoe a little squeeze. She smiles.

"I feel like Mother doesn't always tell me things," she says. "I still don't know what happened with that Gopher Queen stuff."

"That was just too bad. I don't think anyone blames you, Altha."

"Yes they do," she says. "But I'm glad we came by this morning. I don't think Mother expected to . . . learn anything."

I listen to her go downstairs and out to the car. I hear Karen saying goodbye. I hear her come back in and shout up, "Get out of here *now*." I think momentarily of Marcie. When I don't respond, she comes up and I tell her I'll hang around all day venturing opinions unless she agrees to make time for us to be alone. I brandish the shoe, and we make an arrangement.

Around four-thirty I hear car tires move over the Texas gate and from the window I watch her turn into the laneway, stop her little Maverick and unfold herself from the seat. She's changed into jeans and a white cotton shirt. She looks west down the river and into the hills, where the shadows are growing. The engine will be ticking, and then it will stop and she'll think to herself, This is the quietest place in the world. I leave enough time, then go out to meet her.

"I suppose you expect me to comment on the view."

"I'd invite you for a walk but the mosquitoes would suck your eyeballs."

"Is that pleasant?"

"After a certain point. Come on in." She fetches a leather case from the front seat. As I turn to the door she moves in behind me and pulls me around by the elbow, skipping her focus up from my t-shirt collar to my eyes.

"I'm really glad I could come," she says, but she doesn't look glad. She looks scared.

"Okay," I say. "Good."

We tacitly settle on the kitchen table as neutral ground. I have something I want to show her. Last night I hit a short stretch of despair and a half bottle of corn mash and drove back over to the Nash house, this time with a flashlight. I came back with a natural buzz and a little drawing I'd made.

I show Karen the spiral pattern. From centre to outside it moves counter-clockwise. The lines are formed by pictographs.

"The next question is, whose pictures?"

"I don't get it. This is a drawing of a drawing?"

"It's a Plains Indian calendar drawn on a skin of some sort, probably a buffalo skin. Certain tribes marked the passage of time by noting a single event each year in story or pictures, a memorable event. But there might be a few count-makers in any tribe and they wouldn't necessarily record the same events. The result is a sort of unofficial tribal history."

"Is it valuable?"

"As an artifact it would be. I just want to know who made it, who it belongs to."

"And why it's in your neighbour's basement."

"That might be hoping for too much."

"Aren't there any natives or archaeologists around here who'd know?"

"I'm the local expert. And that, as you see, is a sad matter."

Without occasion she gets up and goes into the living-room

and I find myself staring at her jeans. They're old and a bit frayed, and serviceable in every way that counts. She angles out of view and next I hear her rummaging through my cassettes. I'm left with my little drawing. I guess I expected she'd be a bit more charmed by it.

She returns as Neil Young starts up in the next room.

"You think the calendar's connected to your brother somehow?"

"Maybe. That pendant sure seems likely to be. I'd just like to find his hideaway, that grave he talked about."

"Whatever for? There won't be anything magical about it."

"Except it's a specific place to be. It gives location to things. I don't have much connection to him."

"Well, if you're so determined to get a fix on your family, then I have something for you."

She pulls her briefcase up onto the table. It's an executive model. I can think of no reason why Karen should own one. Gold lettering. Genuine cowhide. What we make of things.

Inside the case is a small box she found in the museum's basement containing photos from the town's early years. They haven't been tagged or identified in any way but she showed them to her mother, who recognized herself in a schoolclass shot as a girl of eight or nine. Karen points out her mother. There's more.

"She says this one over here is your mother." A little girl with thickish features, smiling at me. "I thought you might like to keep this. Keep the whole box if you want. She said your dad would be in that picture too somewhere, and your Aunt Cora, but she can't remember who's who. Why don't you ask your aunt?... Toss?"

It's the smile I'm unprepared for. In the few photos I've seen of her, my mother is never smiling, and beyond that, is curiously expressionless. Although I might have attributed her countenance to any number of things, I always imagined the cause was a great, coursing sorrow, what might have been called melancholy at the time, a state pre-existing her life with Marius. All of this surmised from a few of Cora's old photos and the one picture of her I own. It was taken on her wedding day, on the steps of the Anglican church. She's standing just ahead of a black-suited Marius. She looks entirely alone. Nothing about her except her dress suggests she's a bride. The date is scratched into the negative in a childlike scrawl in the bottom right corner—1946.

"Thank you. I will keep this. Thanks."

"Are you upset?"

"It's just . . . you wonder what happens to a person, a little girl."

"Your aunt doesn't know what happened?"

"No. My dad might've had some idea but I didn't know how to ask him."

I get up and open the fridge and stare inside for a few moments. I thought my drawing might interest her, but mostly it was a conversation piece, and that's how she may have intended the photo. But it occurs to me that it could be an avoidance tactic, though I don't know what it is she wants us to avoid, unless it's sex. Then I realize what a boob I can be when left to my own thoughts.

I bring two bottles of beer back to the table.

"Toss, don't mind me but sometimes it seems like you let your past matter more to you than your future."

"Did you want a glass with that?"

"It's just, I don't know where you're heading. Long term or even minute to minute."

"You know what I think is the saddest thing in the world, Karen? It's that lives come and go and nothing marks them and no one remembers."

"So you're trying to recover lives. There's a lot of . . . the forgotten around here."

"And in a few years, Mayford will be gone and we won't matter to anyone either."

"I suppose you're right," she says. "Cheers."

Things lighten for us a bit when I field what is now the third phone call since I got home this afternoon from people asking me if I want to join their "search party" tonight, and wanting clearance to be on my land. This time it's Morely Pearson, the gym teacher. He says he knows there's no monster but he feels better after unloading at the wind a few times. I tell him no thanks and please stay off my land though it's nothing personal. A few days ago I would have said the only common feeling around here was desperation, but now something else has taken hold. Lucky for me I have another pursuit.

Karen's now positioned herself on the living-room floor with her back on the couch.

I say, "It used to be safe to howl at the moon down here. Now it's likely to get you killed."

"People are just generally scared."

I sit above and beside her. Something awakens in me for the first time in years, not just attraction but a kind of scheming intention. This is both shameful and amusing.

My hand ventures forth onto her hair. She leans her head back against it and we exchange pressures. She tilts straight back and smiles up at me.

"What happens when this happens?" she asks.

"Just familiar blood principles taking over, I guess. Diastolic, I believe."

"You know, when you don't have something stuck in your mouth you're not a completely unattractive man, Toss."

"Yeah, well, same goes."

"You have a nice body."

"I'm not real good at this compliment thing."

"Aren't there any features you like?"

"Okay, um. Your posterior can really turn a phrase."

She's laughing by now so I start to try again but she puts her finger to her lips and silences me. She turns and sits on her knees and runs her hands up to my back pockets and pulls me down with her onto the floor. Mr. Young earnestly believes a man needs a maid. I feel I should turn him down but there's no leaving now. She rolls me onto my back and raises herself on top of me in a kind of coming-attraction move and I feel the weight of knowing what can happen in a short time away from voices. Then our mouths are together. I'm vaguely aware that I'm holding her too tight. Hands run up my shoulders to my hair and she leads me by pulling lightly one way or another. We move ever further from words and the descriptions of things, almost from an awareness of the shapes we take.

I was thinking that sex is more powerful when it's not a foregone conclusion and then I dozed and now I hear her frying something in the kitchen. It's the top of some hour or other because the CBC is bringing me other-worldly news when I least want it. In Peru the Shining Path has taken to shooting tourists to kill the trade and weaken the economy, such as it is. It's hard to imagine Marcie's life leading to any such end, but she does tend to go out of her way to find trouble. I telepath her a warning and wish her the protection of a jungle's worth of wood-carved animals.

Grub turns out to be blade steak I'd been planning to marinate. When the chewing gets tough for us I blame the cut on Dewey and praise the sustenance to be had from simply not eating alone. Half-way through I think to haul out a Burgundy and rinse the dust from two wine glasses.

"I never knew anyone who talked like that during sex," she says.

"Like what?"

"All that explorer's journal stuff—all that 'mighty river' and 'God's paradise' and 'behold the curious humped beast' stuff."

"Very funny. I must've flashed on the Parry Expedition." God help us where we learn our love talk. One winter night outside a high-school dance I found myself in the back of a friend's Charger with an out-of-town girl who shared with me the tender age of sixteen and all the charms she had so far gathered, and though her name escaped me even then I remember that in mid pitch and sway she sang out a chant of "Tossy, Tossy, hot and saucy," reducing me to a burger-joint menu item. This was more distracting than offensive, but she almost ruined our moment.

In my reverie I catch only the end of Karen saying something about "coming up with some intentions."

"I'm sorry, I missed that."

"Please stay with me, Toss. I'm just working up to this." She focuses behind me, a few seconds on something, a few on something else. We shunted onto another track here when I wasn't paying attention. And we're barely moving, it seems. Little of the loverly world so abrades me as slow revelation when I know the full disclosure will likely hurt. It's like having to watch a striptease of the living dead.

She stands and collects our plates, though I haven't finished yet, takes them to the kitchen counter and returns.

"What's the biggest secret you've ever kept?" she asks.

"This won't be easy, will it?"

"You've never asked me why I didn't come back home all those years."

"Some people don't. It's not that unusual."

"Don't you want to know why?"

"I do now."

"All right." She dips her head once, then looks at me point-blank and begins. "You know I went to university in Vancouver. That's where I met a guy named Kenneth. He was friends with a girlfriend of mine and her gang. They used to run drugs back and forth across the border, or that's what they said, and it made sense, but Kenneth wasn't really a part of that. I think he just bought a lot of stuff. But anyway we started up together and were pretty hot for a while, travelling all over on his parents' money, he was a FURK, a fucked-up rich kid from Toronto, and then after two years we came to our senses about each other. I realized he was a jerk and he realized I knew it. By the time I started my third year we'd definitely split up, though I still saw him once in a while, but only maybe three or four times all summer. And then, of course, I found out I was pregnant. I knew I'd have the child and that I didn't want anything to do with Kenneth, that it was my baby and not his because he didn't want one or care about raising one.

"When I told him he threw a tantrum and practically got violent when I said I was going ahead with it and I didn't want to give it away. Eventually his solution was to set up a little fund I could draw on for as many years as I didn't hassle him. This was the best I could hope for, so I agreed and dropped out of school to find work and then have her. I wasn't even nineteen years old. Mother came out for a few weeks after the baby to help me with her and to tell me my dad didn't want me coming home any more. He didn't want anything to do with me, and he didn't want anyone in town knowing about Wendy.

"At first I was willing to go along with his wishes, he was the kind of man who would be absolutely crushed by shame, though I wasn't completely stupid—I knew it meant I'd have to cut myself off from Mayford and my friends here—but I was young and thought I didn't have a choice. Anyway, Mother did have a choice. She and Dad—it was like this huge crisis in their marriage—but she stood up for me and told him I was coming home sooner or later and better not to show up in town some day with a ten-year-old daughter nobody knew about. And so I sent out birth notices. I put some friends up in Vancouver and they met my little girl, and Wendy and me made a life there. I brought her out once when Dad was alive, and for his funeral, and once since."

"How did he take her being here?"

"He was ashamed."

"Even—"

"Not of me or Wendy. He knew Wendy by then, they'd been out to visit us, but when we came here, one day the four of us were downtown and he went out of his way to introduce Wendy to everyone he could, like he could never make up for how he used to feel about her, and me."

"How did she handle all the attention?"

"If she didn't know how to feel, she watched me, and I acted like I couldn't be happier. And a year later he was dead and I hadn't found a way to tell him I forgave him."

By the end of her story she's almost convinced me she can speak dispassionately about this part of herself, but the truth is that she has kept a secret for years. Not her daughter, but her regret. I can't help but wonder why she's telling me, or at least why she's telling me now.

"You haven't mentioned her much, Karen. You told me she was eighteen and lived with her boyfriend. I'd like to know more."

"Yeah, but it's like... it's not just as easy as describing her. I'd have to describe our whole world out there, and I just don't know how." She hurries these last words to get to a point. "But that isn't why I've told you all this."

"You want me to know how much you owe your mother."

She nods slowly. Apparently I've drawn the right lesson.

I get up to make some coffee. If I were to be honest with her, I'd say her whole story has the feel of an ultramontane fable, for though I know all about elaborately guarded secrets and regrets, I stupidly and selfishly pretended Karen didn't have an impassioned, peopled history. And one so far from my imagining. I've never known drug runners or anyone who wanted to be called Kenneth instead of Ken or Kenny.

As I bring our coffees to the table she produces one more photo and sets it before me. It's another school picture, this one a standard head-and-shoulders shot. The girl's blonde and bright-eyed, with a gap in her front teeth.

"She's looks . . . alert. Why not bring her out again?"

"It's not really her sort of place. She likes meeting people but I don't have many friends here. Everyone's either left or, you know, they think of me as sort of an outsider. We're just sort of polite. We catch up on each other in about ten seconds."

From where I'm sitting I can see into the living-room. The bottom two-thirds of the stairway is visible. It occurs to me I'm sitting just where Marius sat bleeding the day Alan shot out the car windows.

"So Karen."

"Yes?"

"What does it mean?"

"What does my telling you this mean? It means I've confided in you about my dad. It means I must trust you. Surprise."

"No. We've never talked about what your having a daughter means. For us."

"We haven't been an 'us' yet, Toss. We're working on 'us' now, tonight."

"Now that we've had sex?"

"*No.* Now that you know about . . . *me.*" She returns Wendy's photo to her wallet and drops the wallet into her case. She stares at the handle. "Do you have any secrets, Toss?"

"Is there something you expect me to confess here?"

"Oh Christ." She gets up and heads for the door. I don't know how we ended up here but there's no looking back on our alexandrine path.

As she leaves I call out, "I'm sorry! I just don't get this whole sharing deal!" and I detect an exasperated sound before the door closes.

So the day ends badly, but then what is the reason we overvalue endings? Even minor departures stir a fear of finality, every leaving a small death. We seem to be rehearsing something. When I'm laid out on the couch with the CBC fading in the background, I calmly perceive that I'm only a little worried about Karen and our spat, and in fact, due to a law of counterbalance, would rather disturb some older ground. I think about forced exits. They're everywhere around me and, just now, I understand how someone might come to believe a heart shows well in its surviving a life of narrow escapes. Anyone my age has witnessed and been party to much hardship, and some of it is very nearly unbearable, though if we're lucky it is so only for a short time, but I've never understood what exactly a breakdown is, for instance, and I'm not sure if I've ever witnessed one. I remember feeling in control of myself in the days after Marcie left, but there's no denying that my behaviour changed in a quiet sort of way. I quit fishing. I took a road trip on impulse. But my condition then was a case of common sorrow, an affliction that excluded all others. If anyone had broken, it was Marcie, with her crying and her duck toss. And yet even violent destruction can pertain to a coherent pattern. She was a victim of attrition. She wanted to move to a city because she feared a mundane life. She could bear children but not the thought of raising them. She had learned from her mother's mistakes. She feared regret and contentment equally. She had found the age and place of extreme removal. She tried to escape without leaving, and then she left.

Some nights you can hear a car move miles away and the sound of geese far above.

8

FROM ALMOST anywhere in town, in one direction or another you can see open prairie. For my taste too much is made of the great western expanses and their powers to shape the rural consciousness. I have no quarrel with what is common, only with what is thought to be. Someone, I forget who, once told me about a Polish sailor who for some reason was travelling across Saskatchewan and though he spoke little English managed with gestures and nouns to express his clichéd observation that the wheatfields were like the sea in that they moved in waves and rolls. This sort of story gets retold because even farmers who've never been to sea have long believed they could but for their roots as easily be fishermen, and for that matter Christ's first-chosen disciples might as easily have been farmers and Christ himself might have walked on wheat rather than water, which after all isn't so remarkable in Saskatchewan at certain times of the year. But that's the original Polish-sailor story, and every such tale ever told to me that I accept as true for a long time afterward, and eventually recall without knowing its origin, I consider a Polish-sailor story. The stuff of personal apocrypha. Too many Polish sailors and we are left not with a lovely view but with a view of the view, a degree of self-awareness that removes us from the landscape, or turns us into multi-eyed aliens who see in every direction at once but can't drink from a bottle or pet a dog. When I start to think this way I go into the hills or bounce around the gym until I work up a sweat. I then remember only my surfaces, and so reclaim the immediate world of them.

I lace on my baseball spikes and look out at the empty diamond and grandstand that mark the west edge of town. I mean to make something of the last few hours of otherwise wasted Tuesday sunshine, most of my day so far having been spent in sleep and the states orbiting it. The honest labour of an overnight exam-grading binge gave way to the disagreeable combination of drink and a methodical analysis of the drawings on the animal skin in Alan's basement. I made notes, but from today's perspective, though they begin well enough, they seem to become a touch too clever, connected to nothing outside themselves, and now as I wait for the Bucks to show for practice—they always need extra bodies—I take them from the dash and read them over again:

> This is from my rendering of what is on the skin. The skin itself I'll consider a winter count calendar, probably of a Plains tribe (Sioux? Blackfoot?)
>
> Most of the figures are immediately identifiable, from what I know, from what I have gathered
>
> horse = the year of their appearance?
> deer
> fortified lodges = the year they were built
> calumet exchange (white man suggested by hat)
> hoof prints = horse stealing
> a tally of graves (those killed in battle?)
> celestial events?
> gun
> pemmican hung to dry = a good buffalo year
> raven
> tipi
>
> Other figures are variations on these or else are uninterpretable. There are 74 pictures altogether

> I'm troubled most by an "I" shape. What is it a picture of? My interpretive instincts get in the way here by leading me to Roman numerals and English pronouns. And my knowledge that this is a story in the collective first person. *Check* if I have drawn this accurately
>
> The spiral should likely be read inside to outside, like the spiral calendars of the Toltecs. It should not be read while driving
>
> Insiders who help us interpret what we see are called "informants." Like spies. Is there any way of knowing if they're double agents?
>
> The spiral should not be read while drinking. Q: Where is all this water coming from? A: The ice inside the glass has beaded the outside and the beads have run together and dripped. Note: It's taken me years to notice this phenomenon

Which proves I'm over my head with any problem requiring deep thought. So why not bead my brow tonight and throw out my first arm of the year?

At the moment all that matters is a Rawlings infielder's glove with an "Edge-U-Cated Heel" (the swampishly named Wade Boggs model), bought for less than eighty dollars two years back when I came out of a ten-year retirement and actually played a season with the Bucks. And the shoes (black Nikes, never polished) and the Bucks team cap and even the protective cup I'm wearing. My talents as a third baseman are that I have quick hands and for some reason was born with an arm capable of throwing a ball through the shell of a Quonset hut. In fact every year I could throw four balls this hard, but then my shoulder and elbow get all humble and my arm becomes useless for two months. My weaknesses are that I can't hit a curveball and can barely see a fastball. Tonight is my season.

My last year with the Bucks was intended as therapy. Having played half-seasons for two summers while I was in university, I thought I knew what I was getting into, but at that time the Bucks were a winning team and a happy one. Happy teams are all alike, but unhappy teams provide us a more accurate metaphor for our existence: loss breeds desperation breeds extremity breeds violence breeds violence. At first we lost close games and no one was too discouraged because our Americans hadn't yet arrived, but that year we had a bad shipment. Everyone's favourite was Tim, an unassuming kid from somewhere in the west who seemed genuinely pleased to be here. As is the lot of nice guys, his fastball didn't move and he was shelled all season long. We invited him back the next year only because he converted to middle infield and the unpaid local players consistently won money from him in poker. The other imports were an alcoholic who disappeared after a road game in Regina and was next reported in Los Angeles, and a drawling redneck named Don who pitched twice a week and began each game with a beanball to the leadoff hitter. There were many brawls that year but no one was killed. We won four games, lost fourteen.

But numbers alone, as sports analysts say, do not tell the whole story. As embarrassing practice ran into disgraceful game a sort of nihilism grew over us, eclipsing even the light usually surrounding the buckle-up farm boys used to the occasional bad yields and unhappy prospects. Eldon and I actually had serious if short discussions about the point of it all, not just baseball but everything. We all drank and shook our heads a lot. The whole process was stupefying. I'm just thankful I never once suggested there were lessons to be learned from our circumstance. In the end all we had were practical measures. Look inward and find some small thing to love (in my case a ground-ball hit to my left) and commit to it. And chew Red Man or bubble-gum because it's hard to be anguished while doing so.

Two trucks I can't recognize from this distance are stopped on the highway north of me, the drivers leaning out and talking to one another. They both turn into the ditch and ride up into the fairgrounds, making their way here, and then decide to make a race of it and cut across a little-league diamond, leaving much of it hanging a few feet in the air. They've taken direct aim so I duck inside my cab and close the door to avoid the dirtstorm. They skid to a stop on either side of me. Even before the light is back I can recognize the driver on my right by his cackle howl. It's Two-Four Wright, as always with his spaniel mutt Randy in the passenger seat. In the other truck are Keith Sidoryk and Stew Gates, who opens his door smiling. "Drought," he says.

"Hey Toss," Two-Four yells, "who'd we give up to get you?"

"Gave up on the season," I say. Keith hasn't said anything but waves and smiles. He wasn't on the team when I last played, in fact was in high school at the time. When everyone's ready Keith hauls out the equipment bags from the bed of his truck and we start playing catch.

"If anyone asks, we did our windsprints," says Two-Four.

Within ten minutes the rest of the team has straggled together and Two-Four has recounted his uneventful and deflationary previous evening in "Party D." Eldon has actually co-ordinated the search groups under letter designations. I find myself nodding a lot, disbelief no longer a functional response to the world.

I wonder who among the players I don't know are kids from places nearby and who are Americans. Eldon calls everyone together and introduces us to the two imports he collected just last night from the Saskatoon airport.

"Michael Lacousiere comes to us from Georgia," he explains. A tall kid in white spikes doffs his cap and glances at everyone, looking squarely only at the short, dark-skinned man standing next to him, who turns out to be mystery American number two. Lacousiere whispers something and laughs but the short man seems to ignore him.

Eldon continues, "And John Murphy is from Arizona, and

both of them claim they can play infield and pitch, though we don't know that yet"—our turn to laugh, but they don't look worried—"and our other import won't show for ten days so it's nice to see Toss out here to carry us over. You men who don't know Toss can call him Boom-Boom." No laughter.

During hitting practice a group of us shag in the outfield. I drift near Eldon and he tells me he's a little worried because Lacousiere is a smartass and Murphy doesn't seem to like him, but Murphy doesn't say much and that may mean something too. "He's a Navajo Indian," says Eldon. "I'd never guessed from the name." If troubles are brewing, it hasn't effected their swings. Lacousiere laces line drives to all fields and Murphy launches six or seven balls well over the left-centre fence.

No sooner do I secure a position at deep third than Wingnut Peters, a dead-pull hitter, steps into the box to take his cuts. The first four balls are hit right at me and three of them go through to the outfield, where Gunner Lawson and his cousin Gerald start to hoot and jeer. "Get outta the chute." "It's chewing you up. Don't make me watch." The chatter is of course part of the fun, but it doesn't remove the possibility of imminent death if I don't sharpen up. A nasty good luck transforms my flight reaction to a fight instinct when Lacousiere calls from shortstop, "Back home they call you a fetal boy." He smiles at me. What an asshole. I cheat to the left and manage to steal a couple of balls from him. After Gunner lays down his bunts he goes through a simulated at-bat and Lacousiere moves to second to practise his double-play pivot. By this time I want the ball, determined that nothing will get by me and if I get a chance I'll gun Lacousiere in the teeth. The count is two and one and for some reason I know the ball is coming my way on the next pitch. It's hit to my left. I sweep it up and pass it to my right hand in one motion, and then, while stepping towards the target, I unload.

There goes my arm.

Lacousiere catches the ball at throat level and relays it to first while turning a beautiful pirouette. He is grace without manners, one of those first impressions you know will last a long time.

"Nice throw," he says.

"Nice shoes," I say.

"We got something in them two." There are no lights over the field so practice ends at medium dusk. I sit exhausted, looking through my windshield and the backstop screen, trying to see a single and unbroken third base line. Stew and Eldon lean on my truck.

"Murphy looks good," I concede. "He seems to mean business."

"The other guy too. How bad a guy could he be if he plays like that?" Stew does his logical best. I nod for him.

"We'll see you two at the party then? It'll be a real bang-up time." Eldon leers.

"Which two and which party?"

"I thought you'd know about it. There's a party tomorrow night at Earl Shavers'. Marleen said Karen knows. Didn't she tell you?"

"Her plans don't seem to include me at the moment." To their credit neither of them raises his eyebrows at this news, but as I put the truck in gear Stew pats me on the shoulder and it means more than it should, coming from someone I'm not especially close to. Then he says, "See you, stud buddy," burning off any bonding residue.

Over to Cora's house to see if she has a flash Polaroid. Though it's dark she's standing in her garden mumbling at her plants. I don't intend to stay long but feel ridiculous in two-tone cowboy boots and grey sweats, so I head upstairs and change into some cottons. I make it out back again in time to help her roll up a garden hose onto an old wheel rim we've mounted onto the back of the house. My right arm feels like it's trying to change species.

"We've got one somewhere if the flash still works. That's two or three cameras ago." She frowns at the hose. "The tomatoes needed a good soaking."

"I'll take your word for it. I can't see them. How're the bedding plants?"

"They all took pretty well but everything looks nervous to me this year. The third generation of drought-grown plants can probably smell rain five hundred miles away." As if on cue a wind kicks up and blows shut the latch gate in the neighbour's yard. Though it's full dark now we both instinctively look west to see what's brewing. The windstorms last summer literally blew some buildings away, some people too if you count the farm families that went the way of their topsoil. There are clouds but no lightning. Only the flies amassed on the back screen door promise rain. I get a beer from the fridge as Cora goes into her room to shut a window.

"You know something we never do any more is barbecue. Why don't we plan one for next week?" I ask.

"Did you say barbecue?" She returns and sits with me at the table. "Perry claims he doesn't like them. That's his excuse for not going to his class reunion on July first. I think it's nice they invited him. I mean he didn't graduate so they didn't have to, but he got an invitation and then got moody. I told him not to be a spoilsport, which you probably think is unkind. It's not."

"Do you want me to get on him about it?"

"Would you? I should've asked before now. It might be too late anyway."

"I'll remind him he owes me some favours." I could also remind him he owes me money from the last time I sat in on a game of High Chicago, in that he's not the kind to distinguish between clean debts and corrupt ones.

I can smell the approaching rain and could feel it in my knee too if my legs weren't already aching. The moments before rain are as close as we can get to making the physical world a minded thing. This apart from hallucinatory wanderings. If I'm left alone in a certain chair in a certain room my focus invariably moves to the same spot time after time, and I imagine seeing on the wall or ceiling or cupboard door the movement of any number of figures, usually human. The perspectives are sometimes my own and other times those of a tv or movie shot. On Cora's yellowed lily wallpaper I often see a few seconds of hockey from the centre-ice camera, but now there is only pattern on paper on wall. All those moments I catch myself in my father's postures, those attitudes of his I hadn't realized I'd taken notice of until I assumed them. Fingertips to forehead, with thumb under cheekbone. Whenever was he still enough to make this impression? But then memory asks little of time.

"Do you know that it doesn't bother him to swear in front of me any more? Today he came home at lunch and said, 'You won't believe the f-ing story that's going around now.' It disturbed me so much I almost didn't hear the story."

"Did it have something to do with an animal carcass, by any chance?"

"Something like that."

"Are you telling me you were more disturbed by his language than by the slaughter, or are you trying to find a way to ask me what I know?" This is a cruel device but the direct approach still has its uses. Perry wouldn't have volunteered the dynamite rumour and my guess is she hasn't heard it. She scowls and I continue, "I'm just prodding you, Cora. Perry hasn't done a good job of softening you up for me. You know better than to worry about him, though I don't remember when it's ever stopped you."

"A mother's concern is my prerogative. But what would I need softening for?"

"It's just a few things have lined up against me lately and now I can feel this latest round of misinformation moving in."

"Apparently the evidence is."

"The evidence was ten miles from me."

"That was earlier. This morning someone found a carcass on

the east island. Some people would call that your back yard."

"I'm sure they are."

"Yes, well, that's what's got him so upset. For a while it went around that you were the one who found it. Now most people are saying it was someone from across the river. Not that it makes any difference."

"I can see how it might make a lot of difference depending on the rest of the details. But these things don't cling to me much any more. They shouldn't bother Perry either. Tell him he has to learn how to laugh at bad intentions. It's the only appropriate response."

"I don't agree with you there."

"But that's what he needs to think." A moth beats against the plastic shade of the ceiling fluorescent. "At his age. Now let's hunt up that camera."

What unruly truths live inaccessibly beyond our best efforts at straightening the record. Cora's last words as I go out the door. "Those boots don't go with what you're wearing. Not that anyone cares."

The night turns gothic with overhead lightning and a gutter-flood of rain that washes over the high-speed wiper blades flashing me the street at the pace of a frenetic metronome. After four blocks to the cop shop I pull into the driveway and park behind a blue and white cruiser. Inside, Hall is spooning himself a bowl of soup. Upon seeing me he smiles and sweeps his huge hand invitationally in the direction of a chair opposite him.

"That's an impressive rain," he states.

"Thank you."

"I wasn't giving credit."

"No one does any more."

He pushes the bowl away, dabs his mouth with a paper serviette. "There's no need for horseplay. I thought I already made that point."

"Not everyone agrees with you. Some think horseplay's exactly what we're lacking around here."

"Well, I hope you've done your best to convince them they're wrong."

"I suggested he apologize and Dewey said no. There's another letter in next week's paper."

"Well, son of a.... Excuse me."

"Naturally."

"Our deal involved you getting the job done, not just trying to."

"I didn't try that hard."

"You don't think I'll arrest you, Mr. Raymond?"

"You seem to have faith in community policing. I wonder why you don't work all this out with Dewey directly."

"We've spoken a little, as you no doubt know."

"We don't conspire quite that much. What's he say?"

"He's about as easy to talk to as you are. You're both a couple of . . . you both avoid straight answers."

"You've got me wrong, corporal. I'm a big fan of the truth, just like you. It's just I'm willing to believe the truth might be bigger than I am. You can't straighten someone out if they weren't straight to begin with."

"But you can certainly twist people around. Me and my two officers can't keep hold of everyone who's decided to go shoot up the river valley."

"You don't blame Dewey for these animal findings?"

"If you bother to trace the source of those tales, they'll take you to the meat counter at the Co-op store."

"There weren't even any carcasses?"

"Of course not. How come in this town the plain truth can't get two steps into daylight without getting shot up?"

"Don't complain. Your next station might have alot of inbreeding. Have the Coca May contacted you?"

"They must have. I get flagged down in the street ten times a day by people asking what I know."

"They're just amusing themselves. No one really believes there's a monster out there."

"Then why does the valley sound like a free-fire zone each night?"

"Exactly. That's what I mean about the big truth."

"Well listen here, then." He rises and addresses me in the voice of something other than a national institution. "The big truth you might like to know is that I've had more than one call from people who say they're on the school board and want me to confirm or deny a certain explosive rumour about you."

"You blew up your evidence in a gravel pit." I smile agreeably.

"I don't need evidence to do you damage. I can tell stories too. I just shine one up and roll it out into town and see what happens."

"I wish I could help you, corporal. Someone might get hurt out there, but nothing I do is going to keep the town from hunting down whatever we're afflicted with."

"Maybe not, at least until someone catches the damn thing and strings it up in public so we know it's safe here again. I guess that's what they've set out to do," he says.

9

SOMETIME IN the night I capped what was left of a twenty-six of Wild Turkey and stood and fell back into my chair and stood again and then walked through the dark and out the back door into sounds of distant gunfire and headed down to the two o'clock break in the trees. From that spot I lobbed the bottle with a painful grenade toss and lost it in mid-flight. I couldn't hear it hit the water. Clearly a river goddess had caught it on the fly. I shouted to her, "An offering. Apologies from my plundering species. Here's to the quiet life of greenness. I mean greenery." Winds were strong out of the northwest.

Now I'm riding the ferry cable across the river and expecting an afternoon of difficult climbs in a half-mile stretch I've not yet searched. I used to bring along an extra helping of home-baked goodies in my lunch to give to Jim, the ferry operator, but I don't bake much any more. I hand him a few sticks of licorice which he puts in his shirt pocket. He tells me there's a huge herd of antelope somewhere north of the sand hills though there's no way of seeing them today, if a person had that in mind, what with the dirt roads in those parts having been washed out in the storm and then dried hard again faster than is locally natural. My narrow-angled imagination comes up with a jumbled African scene, a Serengeti bounty wandering atop the Sahara, but then that's the surreal way things are going. Jim drops the gate and ties up. He taps his shirt pocket and says thanks as I drive by. I try one stick myself but it has been annealed to industrial strength, so I remove it from my mouth and polish my teeth with my tongue until I find the turnoff to the severely potholed ranch track that I follow to its clifftop end.

The hill-faces have already started to burn off on my side of the river, but here the generally north-facing drops are greener. I've diagrammed the valley on both sides of today's search area, which is mostly flat and obvious but for one long isthmus, an inverted wedge that runs east-west with steep grades on both sides meeting in a narrow, peaked crest. The sort of hill a person shouldn't climb alone, I know full well. Especially when hung over. Especially now that the holidays are here. Extra-especially for the sake of a long shot. I'm startled by the scream of a killdeer a few feet beyond the truck. It walks awkwardly, faking a broken wing. I must be very near its nest so I walk with particular care through the scrub, towards the wedge, which happens to be the killdeer's direction. When it's led me far enough it flutters up and circles far behind me into the grass beyond the truck. The joke is very much on me, more so if I fall and break myself.

When the drop is this steep it's best to start from the bottom and work up but there's no easy way down that doesn't involve a half-hour's drive and walk. At least if I can get down I can no doubt get back. Traversing will be impossible so I choose a route passing nearest the two deep ledges on the north side that are visible from the top. Assuming I make it back up I might then try the south side, though as I walk the length of the crest I see nothing worth investigating.

It's one thing to choose a point of entry and another to have confidence in it. I see a way into the first ten feet and begin, not so much stepping down as launching off. To control the slide, to keep your weight low with your legs bent, to keep your feet parallel to the grade, every so often stilling yourself with your inside hand to the wall-face like a surfer in the tube. Then the controlled jumps. In getting the best of the fall line I've taken myself too far to the side of the first ledge, so I attempt a daring 180-degree jump-turn and land on one foot and a single clump of speargrass. Two bunnyhops to the first ledge. Of course there's nothing much to find, only a few small holes in the back wall, the work of some burrowing creature, likely a gopher, and long ago abandoned to birds who have better places to be in mid-afternoon. The prospect is lovely but it's not the sort of place you'd bury someone and certainly nowhere to bring a girl. I sit and let my feet dangle. A peculiar feeling something like déjà vu presents itself but the sense is less that I've been here before than that I've seen an Imax film of this view, a great vista in which everything is in focus and not much is happening. The hills are nearing the colour of deer. The sage and grasses are already bleaching to yellow-white. Only the silver leaves of bullberries are distinct from any distance, the colour and texture of the grey felt hat that Eugene wore long ago. The smell of cap guns as a kid. We claimed the most unlikely hits, and took to carrying bean-gun pistols as side-arms for stalking close and actually shooting one another. The cap sound travelled farther but the line of fire was visible with bean guns. There was nothing to negotiate.

Not long ago, this land was in the easternmost range of grizzlies. Now even cougars and rattlesnakes are rare. What has replaced our innate and now mostly useless respect for animal menace? Like people in most parts of the continent we watch a lot of tv and every so often change our diets.

The next ledge is only a few feet below me but I'm sure there's nothing there. To go back without a look, though, would render this whole exercise a half-assed waste of time, and even time wasting should be performed with heart. I shove off and immediately see that my next foothold is a cactus, so I come down early and entirely off balance, and when my instep catches the cactus anyway I'm tossed horizontal and then nose first. The ledge is upon me before I can fully extend my left arm and I drive into the ground with my shoulder and roll into my life's first cartwheel, which disintegrates into an acutely painful confusion of rolls and bounces.

What I recognize—sucking air because the wind has been knocked from my lungs, the sharp penetrations of cactus spines along my left side and in one foot. What I don't—a pain sharper than that of a pulled hamstring in the latissimus under my left arm, and a still-rising outrage in my shoulder. On an embedded rock near my face a grasshopper sits beside the stains of petrified moss. Nothing looks pretty. My right hand is useful enough to remove most of the spines. For some reason I'm too embarrassed to moan.

The long and indirect walk back to the truck provides time to contemplate my recent tendency towards self-immolation, the very signature of the old Toss and those bad times immediately before and after the breakup. The last time I drank heavily and alone on two consecutive nights must have been during my aimless escape to the road only days after learning Alan had skipped out on Wanda and all their domestic bitterness. Because I hadn't the forethought to tell Cora I was leaving, people naturally supposed I'd left in pursuit of Alan or Marcie or both, though at least I knew they weren't together. If I'd had enough faith in the dramatic potential of my pain the idea of a chase might have occurred to me, but I didn't, and it didn't, and I aimed only for targets visible from the moon—the Rocky Mountains and the Pacific Ocean. I drank every night in the bars of motels squared to service roads and set beside gas station cafeterias with faded green canvas awnings inscribed with white suggestions like "EAT" and "GASUP," meant to work subliminally on high-speed passers-by. But I drove sober and quite by accident found that the road signs triggered memories of grim news stories from the years since I'd last gone that route. The trailer park where a family was murdered in their camper, the mountain road where a trucker lost his brakes and took eleven people with him, the town where an airline bomber lived while planning his murder. In four nights I'd made it only as far as Chilliwack. In the lounge of the inner courtyard of a Best Western, I explained to the waitress that for people like us, the name Vancouver would always bring on dangerous notions. She didn't know what I meant. The next day I started back home. I could smell the salt air and that was enough.

I hurt badly and need a doctor. There are people who truly aren't bothered by a degree of pain that would make most others faint, and then there are those people, usually men, who pretend they don't notice the pain. Here in the national birthplace of free medical attention the second kind of person exists for no good reason. We've fallen for the stupidest of mythologies. I decide to go home and have a bath. Then the ultimate masochism of grading papers while sterilizing my wounds. Meantime I drive in agony and hate myself for the inconsequential sorrows in my life of wasted pursuits, pronouncing by rote the list of all that tires me: the Canada geese on my fully personalized cheques; complaints after all these years about the metric system, though I admit buying lumber to renovate is a wasteful experience for everyone; asshole drivers everywhere; elected officials who are known wife-abusers; people who nod when listening to the lyrics of top-twenty songs but only dance at social gatherings designated for the purpose; closet malcontents like myself, who live greyly in hypocrisy.

Incoming calls. Hours added to days and years I spend alone in conversation.

"What's this I hear about your being a werewolf?"

"Fine thanks, Karen, and yourself?"

"I thought you might be here at the party."

"I don't know what party you're talking about and I can never find Earl's place anyway. Have you met his wife yet?"

"Which one is she?"

"Filipina. Exotic in the gorgeous way. A fashion genius."

"Oh, with the shoes. She's what all the fighting was about. Her husband practically killed one of those American ball players."

"How did you get there?"

"Drove myself. I know this part of the land. It's a little awkward, though. Eldon's here and he's introducing me to people I should already know. They know me. Someone said Zinvalena might show up after work. Dewey probably won't if you're not coming, and everyone would just be embarrassed if he showed 'cause it'd remind us all this monster thing might've been a hoax. There have been rumours to that effect."

"How is it you can leave your mom alone?"

"She's moved to the cabin for a couple weeks. I'm staying with her at the park tonight. You're invited to drop by any time."

"Thank you."

"No pressure."

"Thanks."

"You haven't said you will but some time or other you should meet her. Whenever you feel the time's right. No rush. Maybe check your horoscope." She pronounces her words carefully, no elision, like someone trying to sound sober.

"I don't believe in the stars. I hope you're not one of the New Age crystal-sucking types."

"But you're a birdwatcher. In ancient Rome they'd say you had the auspices. They'd make you an augur."

"Mayford has nothing in common with ancient Rome. Ask Zinvalena. Nothing."

"Except birds." The party sounds are suddenly muffled but I can hear her say "No thanks" to someone.

"What are you wearing?"

"Maybe see you at the cabin some evening. It's the little red and fuchsia one in the loop of the east court." She hangs up.

With too much to assimilate I venture again into my accrual of thought-terminal devices. Memories of a swimsuit issue provide exactly the sort of warped perspective that gives fantasy a bad name. The Brazilian-looking girl in the orange one-piece. The anonymous bounty held in fishnet. What an interesting use of contrast. Notice the lovely fringe that harks back to the stylized beachwear of the American twenties. No, don't. Time to take measures, stomp on all varieties of avoidance. It almost ruins my resolve that at the moment I must stomp while wearing the powder-blue velour slippers Marcie gave me one Christmas. While I dial the Palace, my eye catches the black badge on top of my injured right instep, the gold stitching. What I'd always thought were lions turn out to be stylized initials. Not mine but the slipper company's.

Zinvalena. "He's not accepting calls. Can I take a message?"

"Tell him it's me."

"Is this you, Mr. Ray? Have you got my grade?"

"You've nothing to worry about unless you can't get him to the phone. Certain of your exam answers require a generous reading."

"You can't threaten me, you know." I hear her calling Dewey. She tells him it's an emergency. There are cactus spines in my toes. She tells him it's me.

He tells me, "The film's running, I can't talk."

"That's not like you. Word is you started these monster stories."

"Look, I know what you're gonna say. I've taken a drop in the polls—"

"And you've taken me with you. I don't need this just now."

"Just picture this," he says. "T-shirts. Front and back is a set of fangs and inside the mouth it says, 'I've seen Blank, the Mayford Wolf.' I need a name for the wolf. We stock a big order and sell them here at the Palace. Five bucks with admission, fourteen without."

"You make another killing."

"I need you to draw me a prototype."

"Try Karen, she's the artist."

"She declined."

"Does it matter to you that some people suspect you of demented jokerism?"

"This town is way too in control of its emotions. We need our outlets, it's only healthy. Here's a departure from the usual gloom about repossessions and fixed grain markets. My work might even give you more space to blow up the homes of people you don't like."

"But you admit to starting the rumours?"

"Marty."

"What?"

"Marty the Mayford Wolf. Or Clyde."

"Fine," I say. "Clyde's fine." There's no reasoning with the spirit of windfall. I hang up.

The hedging language tells me Dewey has more invested in these stories than entrepreneurial verve. Alarm bells are sounding and, for once, they're not warning me off myself. It never occurred to me until now just how much is possible once you find the courage to behave aberrantly. Dewey has failed to understand the congruity in Mayford between how we appear to live and how we do live. The congruity is an illusion, of course, but an inviolable one.

Into my eagle-claw tub. How to lower myself without my left arm? Turn and kneel and sit and turn. Then the phone rings again from the kitchen for nine and a half counts. When Marcie and I first moved here we were still on a party line. Two long, one short. The only other party was Alan and Wanda. Even then, before Marcie knew anyone and after I'd been out of town for five years, we received twice as many calls as did the Nashes. For a while Marcie thought this was very sad, and those few times they visited she was even uncomfortable using the phone and reminding us all of our relative popularity. Maybe her earliest attraction to Alan grew from falsely based pathos. Then again, pathos never worked in my favour. The lesson of seducing kind hearts—sadly stupid works better than drunkenly stupored. But these are unprofitable thoughts—Marcie is innocent.

My wounds look bigger under water, as does my waist. When I think of all the hard work I put into quashing expansionist tendencies of the stomach. It's true that everything is political, vanity being merely an impulse to reform the system and sell it. I do my best with an undisciplined regimen—the pattern goes haywire for two months every summer and then restores itself. So there is a larger scheme, as Dewey would be quick to note. It's just that when soaping my scars I'm not a good advertisement for myself.

Two long, one short. A sound that approximates nothing when you hear it but when remembered makes me think of a bird. I'm not sure which one sounds that rhythm. Maybe it doesn't nest around here, but if I hear it again I'll take pleasure in listening and not having to respond.

10

THOSE SUMMER days very highly on the prowl we used to target two or three towns where no one knew us and Perry might make the right sort of impression on a certain sort of girl, beginning by pulling up and asking directions to a "fine restaurant," a ploy that despite its lameness actually worked once so we didn't give it up. The vicarious buzz that afternoon ended for me when the two of them dropped me at the Antelope Room in Goose Lake and disappeared for five hours, by which time I was regarded as both a regular and a local. Later, Perry said he'd seen her farmhouse and they'd had a "nice" time watching tv—turned out we'd both seen the same episodes of "Hogan's Heroes" and "Gilligan's Island," he while eating potato chips, me while railing at the bartender about cultural imperialism—and I must have looked disappointed because Perry was quick to add, "we kissed a little." I wouldn't tell him so, but I was happy nothing else had developed. It seemed important that his sexual adventures on those jaunts never moved beyond early pubescence. Little kissing, and pain control all around. Other days we'd more adventurously play a bar scam, which at least held the real danger of violence. I'd enter first and start a tab with the bartender, telling him I'd just had my car stereo ripped off by a hitch-hiker while the two of us were stopped for gas and I'd gone to the men's. After I'd had time to down a couple of beers, Perry would come in and sit somewhere behind me at a table. I'd get a glimpse of him and tell the bartender, Speak of the devil, and so on, and ask him to keep an eye on the kid while

I went outside to see who he was travelling with and find the knapsack where he'd stashed the goods. Five minutes later, after Perry had sampled the bar snacks, he'd get up with an audible profanity and run out into the street, where I'd be waiting in the getaway truck. This all for fun rather than small profit.

We took overnight trips to Swift Current, just ninety miles distant, and a day trip on a whim to Regina, five hours each way and a football game in between. Marcie complained about my "disappearances" and assumed I was up to particular and unmentionable no good. She said, "Small town women might learn to tolerate this sort of crap but I'm not from here and I don't believe in long-suffering if you can do something to stop it." My inability to defend myself is partly attributable to the very real guilt I felt at playing the role of the wild one when I'd put so much time into rehearsing the lines of upstanding characters. It was certainly no defence that Cora had mentioned Perry's aimlessness and wondered if maybe I couldn't do something to make him a more directed person. I liked to think that Perry didn't need me. He'd done well to shake off the stigma of "mild retardation" his Grade 4 teacher had tagged him with. (Though he was never diagnosed, it's obvious now that he has a learning disability that interferes with his visual language processes, and that his Grade 4 teacher was an insensate poodleturd.) That I might have needed Perry didn't occur to me until I started to come around after the breakup and read one night about the "sympathetic lockjaw" Thoreau claimed to have suffered after his brother's death of tetanus. The summer of our misbehaviours was the same one I learned that Eugene had died and around the time Marcie announced that she didn't want to have children because they would anchor her and she still had hopes that we could be a cosmopolitan and option-positive couple. She actually used the term "option-positive." In discussions of our future her language invariably sprouted the ugliest of jargon. I opted for time alone on the island, listening to the river, and in the truck with Perry, listening to ourselves sing radio songs.

After Marcie and I bottomed out, Perry stayed clear of me and the two of us put an end even to reminiscing about our rambling ways of a few years ago. When school restarted I resumed my adulthood. We haven't spent much wayward time together since those days, but Cora thinks he's developed a streak of recklessness since our glory summer and, whenever she can, lays the evidence at my feet. When I might have served as a father figure, I instead acted like a brother on shore leave. We are all of us self-tending artifacts, forever reconstructing ourselves and never getting it quite right before we're again fractured. It's painstaking work.

Three summers ago I built some winterproof boxes and wired speakers from Cora's front room out to the back patio. That same year, Perry secured his present reputation by repeatedly bombing the town with "Jumpin' Jack Flash" while his mom was at work. The speakers have been off limits to him ever since, so it's with some curiosity that I come around the house to the wailings of Bob Marley. Perry's on his haunches, working on the hose attachment of the barbecue's propane tank. Tonight we eat eye of round, my favourite cut.

"Tell me it works," I say.

He starts, turns his head and falls on his ass. "Christ! You scared me shitless. Don't sneak up like that."

"You don't talk like that around your mom, do you?"

"She's still at work. I'm trying to fix this before she comes home. Otherwise it's the hibachi."

"Don't say that."

"And it gets worse. We don't have a stand for the hibachi and I'll bet anything Mom won't let me prop it on this grill. She's always paranoid the house will catch fire."

"So we have to barbecue on the ground? Like animals?"

"Unless we make this hose attach."

"You do it. I'm the cook." I play a hunch. "Oh yeah, you said there were *three* sticks of dynamite?"

"I think so. It was Matthew's show, I was pretty drunk." Perry contradicts himself so frequently I can't believe he's lying, but his revision has suddenly revealed the possibility that Hall really does have evidence, and all that saves me from cuffing my cousin is that I'm trying to get in the habit of keeping the peace, just the way Hall wants.

"You better call Matthew and find out. Right now."

We go inside, where he makes the call and I turn down the stereo. Roving among a scattering of cassettes laid on the cabinet my eye catches something called "Tranquil Dawn," no doubt one of those nature-sound recordings, the popularity of which I've never understood, especially among non-urbanites. Marcie had an album of marsh noise. It skipped on the cricket sounds. Likely attracted snakes.

To the kitchen to check out supplies. I see someone has already loaded the chef's tray with seasonings, sauces and implements that serve no real purpose but that I like to use anyway. Behind the tray, on the counter, are bottles of vitamins and a yellow pill-sorting box of the kind people use to keep their medications straight. I've never seen it before. It's full of pills. I get a can of apple juice from the fridge, well stocked with beer for Perry and me. Something about twist-off caps makes me uneasy. I take a beer outside for Perry, who's back at work on the hose. He says that Matthew swears there was just one stick but he thinks Matthew would lie to keep him happy so Perry won't get angry and tell Matthew's dad, who'd hit Matthew pretty hard if he knew.

So nothing's resolved. I play another hunch.

"Is your mom sick?" He's got the hose on and is checking the pilot.

"Everything's negative."

"What's negative?"

He begins to turn around but stops and looks back into the grill. "Ah shit. Why did you ask?"

"What's negative? Did she have tests?"

"I didn't say anything." He drums his fingers on the hood. "Yes she did but they were negative. She had a procedure done but it turned out to be minor. It would have to be minor, right? Otherwise they wouldn't call it a 'procedure.'"

"When?"

"She had it a couple of weeks ago. We got the results Friday."

"Did she tell anyone?"

"I don't know. I guess not."

"I guess not."

He takes the beer and sits in a patio chair. "She's more or less all right. Do me a favour and don't tell her I told you."

"Will you be in trouble?"

"A good chance."

"Fine. I owe you some trouble."

"Are you really mad?"

"Hopping so, just hopping. Let's say you owe me three favours."

"I thought there'd be something like this."

The music stops. The best way to get news out of Perry is to keep moving and strike from odd directions. "What exactly is wrong with her?"

"Plumbing."

"What the hell does that mean?"

"Not so much the pipes as the faucet."

" . . . Uterus?"

"Yeah."

When Cora comes home, I'm wrapping the potatoes in foil and Perry's asking me for reasons not to dangle Dewey from the water tower "if he thinks we're so stupid." Cora moves through the house in some ritual pattern almost but not entirely stripped of inefficiency, leaving small repetitions, disappearing to change her clothes and then again to change her shoes, putting away what she's brought home and adjusting the windows to the late afternoon, all the while a part of the conversation, whether with words or with the soft vocalizations that attend each task.

"Millie Frank at the Co-op says he's a pathological liar," she says. "Some people say that about Millie, though. I wish everyone would just mind their own business."

"I guess the stories themselves aren't so bad—"

"They're warped, Perry," she says. "They're sick and unchristian."

"But people don't know whether he wants them to laugh or believe him. And everyone knows Toss is a friend of his and then Toss starts getting accused."

"What have I been accused of?"

"I don't know, that you're in on something, trying to get up people's ass."

Cora turns and glares at him.

"What's my motive?"

"Oh, that's enough. Wesley, tell your friend he'd better keep quiet for a while. Get him a girlfriend or a good book to read or something."

"I don't know if he reads. He's an idiot for movies." My hand accidentally brushes a potato and sends it rolling off the counter and onto the floor. I stoop awkwardly to pick it up, trying not to engage the muscles on the left side of my back. When I finally get hold of it I let out an audible sigh.

"What's the matter with you?" Cora asks.

"Nothing," I say. "I'd have told you if something was wrong." I regret these last words as soon as I've said them, and so does Perry, who's avoiding his mother's accusatory glance and no doubt looking for an escape from behind the kitchen table where he's unthinkingly trapped himself. "I fell off a cliff."

"What were you doing?" asks Perry to advance the conversation.

"The moon was full. I was hunting cattle."

Cora ignores this. "Have you been to a doctor?"

"Maybe he needs a vet," Perry says.

"I think I tore a muscle. I'll just let it heal."

"Did you at least find a medicine wheel or something?" Cora knows about my searches and has told me she thinks the Indian grave was Eugene's invention.

"I've found a few things lately." I take the Polaroid shot from my shirt pocket and hand it to her. "What does that look like to you?"

She holds it at arm's length and peers.

"How about Dutch elm disease?"

Perry takes it from her. "It's a cave drawing."

I tell them about the winter count and the other artifacts, and where I found them. "This is just between us, of course."

"What gave you the idea to go in there in the first place?" asks Cora.

"Curiosity. I guess you'd call it perverse curiosity." She won't nod for me. She flatly disapproves. By now she must have heard about my strangely long-delayed act of reckless jealousy. "Anyway, I'm hoping to find a way of verifying the authenticity of the stuff, and the calendar in particular, but I'm going to have to do it myself. If I can find a corresponding event for each of those symbols, maybe I can figure out the years they represent and then the tribe they belong to."

"What's this one?" asks Perry.

"That's a tally, probably of graves. Some battle took place that year."

"What's this?"

"I don't know. It looks like an 'I.'"

"Looks like an 'H,' like the Square H on your branding irons," says Perry. "Unless these triangles are part of it, in which case it would be an 'N.'"

"They aren't letters. They didn't use our letters."

"So you've broken in the house more than once," states Cora. "You keep going back."

"So obviously this is the year the Nashes stole your dad's cattle and rebranded them," says Perry. "I wonder why the Indians were so upset about it."

I tell him, "You have more in common with Dewey than you realize." Cora leaves the table and makes her way to the patio door. "Yes, I've gone back a few times, but now it's in the name of history and archaeology." Nothing can save a weak defence.

"I don't want to hear about it. I wish you'd never told me, it makes me an accomplice."

"For God's sake, I didn't murder anyone." But she's done with me. Perry and I gather the food and join her on the patio. I fire up the grill and close the hood and the three of us take our positions and wait for the gauge to climb. I say, "At least it's my policy to be open. Openness is changing the world."

"Are you speaking in the name of history now?" she asks. "And are you by any chance planning to sell that Indian stuff once you've justified stealing it?"

"This isn't my problem, Cora. I'm just curious. I haven't stolen anything. Besides, it's illegal to sell artifacts. I just happen to know that. You make me sound like some voracious imperialist."

"Are you hungry?"

"Yes."

"Then let's leave it at that."

The last line of the Maracaibo card keeps sounding like some inane jingle that won't leave my head, like a wasp that refuses to fly out the car window, like neither of these because it invites pondering—"It seems important that no one I know has ever been this far south." How does the south side look to you now, say in comparison to the unexamined if not quiet life you once lived here? But please don't answer or things will get nasty and the exchange will end with me ducking something. To escape this conversation I listen to my boots along the middle of the road. Just hear the steps and try not to count, even though every ten strides is a first down on the vacant lot I'm passing, where I sometimes played football with Perry and his friends and still would if they had time for football any more. Something crunches under my boot. I look down at a few grains of hard wheat. I pick one off the pavement and roll it between thumb and fingers as I walk. There is no market for this stuff, though it's the best there is and thousands die each day for lack of it, to revise someone's observation about poetry. Eventually it rots, or rodents get it, or livestock.

When I finally answered the phone last night, Dewey asked that I be at Honkers at 9:50 sharp. I come through the door at 10:07 by the clock above the bar, the precise moment at which the ad for "Leesa's Beauty Salon" flips over on the electric rollo-card device beside the clock-face. Leesa left town last year.

"You're late," says Roger. "He said you'd be here by ten. You better read this." He hands me a nine-by-twelve envelope, then sets a shot of bourbon on the bar.

Inside the envelope are a note and Dewey's draft of his latest letter to the *Weekly News* in response to spanking new and as yet unprinted insinuations about him—namely that he and Alvin Hall ran up against each other a few years back in the town of Pridemore, where besides so much dark fibbing Dewey added spice to the local nightlife with a legally unverifiable arson spree.

> Re the burgeoning assault of Coca May. Frankly this troubles me, this digging around my old haunts and stomps. The enemy has reconfigured the battleground in mid-exchange, and has done so carelessly, I'll add, by blindly trusting the unnamed source, who himself has it in for me. As I see it, the accusations must be countered directly, in the sort of nuts and bolts language you can fake better than me. Here's my go.
>
> It saddens me and perhaps others in the hereabouts that a useful dialogue on our beloved but sometimes ambiguous social rights and responsibilities has been lost to the sort of slophog smear tactics usually associated with the vile backroom fiends whose only talent is pulling excrement from their shirtsleeves. Now let's consider my probable accuser. Have we been

deceived by boot spurs and bilingual phone manner? No one knows better than Corporal Alvin Hall just exactly what happened in another time and town where he was stationed, where and while I myself lived. Yet we never knew one another then, so how could it be that he is able to correspond the "arson spree" he describes to the period of my residency?...

Baffled, I look to my drink and then up at Roger, who shakes his head slowly and says, "Can you fuckin' believe that guy?"

"I'm not sure yet. What do you know about this?"

"He said it was private so naturally I read it. Or I started to. When I couldn't see the point I just baled out."

"Did it make sense to you?"

"I figure he's running some scam. I heard him telling Karen about t-shirts the other night. Maybe he wants to turn the town into a theme park. You know, the home of the river werewolf. You come and buy t-shirts and dolls. Visit the House of Horrors. Take guided tours to the places the monster was sighted. We fake a picture, sell it as a postcard. Sell aerosol werewolf repellent. Silver-bullet key chains."

"You've obviously been doing some thinking about this."

"I got the time."

I take my drink and Dewey's letter to the table beneath Lenny, then call to Roger so the few others can hear, "He was just kidding about the shirts. It's his sense of humour." He nods, then shakes his head. I read on.

... residency? And then there's what I've heard called "familiar rumours of unattributable violence in the countryside." How come I've never heard of these earlier monster stories that the Coca May claims were even picked up by the Swift Current paper last summer? And where are the details of these fires and stories? Has anyone bothered to check all of this out with a simple call to the relevant Aunt Hazel or paper or hotel bar

(Pridemore Inn—ask for Willy)? I'm being made out as some fang-mouthed travelling flame, nipping at and torching the social fabric wherever I go, and all because our corporal doesn't want you to know that something other than me lurks in the night out there. Well I'm saying it does. It does. It does.

Looks like the tone needs some downshifting I guess. Go ahead and rewrite the whole of everything if you like, just don't lose the logic of the defence.

P.S. I need a woman but no bites. Is it these corduroys and do I wear them too much?

Given that my recent past lives (but twelve months distant) show me possessive of a wildly vagarious nature, I can hardly bring myself to be angry with Dewey for his, which is simply more evolved than mine. Maybe it's a sign of my good health that I wonder what he's up to in the letter. He is so far beyond my usual notions of cause as to be a singularity, and it seems his reality is not to scale with mine. Maybe, like me, he sees people resenting his imaginative dimension. But I'm speculating.

I rewrite the letter to half the length and then decide that I don't see the point of it and I'll have to redraft. Meanwhile the bar has started to fill and before I can get back to work Dewey himself shows. He waves in the general direction of everyone (and everyone fails to wave back) and takes his seat.

"These summer releases are designed to make us all stump-headed. And tonight's was a dog besides. I'll never break even with this product."

"You mean the Palace won't. You do okay."

"There's the hourly base, but I live on commission percentage, minus dips in my liquid stock. Have you read it?"

"I remember doing so."

"Did you buff it?"

"You don't really shoot straight about these slaughter stories."

"No." A casual glance around. The question of most importance is whether it's a good sign that everyone pretends to ignore him. "But it's simple. It doesn't take long for a newcomer in town to get drift of the local lore. In fact it was only when I'd heard the third or fourth version of the valley madman story that I took a notion. It lends validity to my cause to tap into a pre-existing fear of the truth. I didn't realize you'd be involved."

The "valley madman" story. Here is a best-forgotten lesson in what happens when a gale force will-to-believe meets up with people's flimsy imaginations and twists them like so much fatigued sheet metal. The widely known tale has its origins in a badly kept Nash family secret. It is said that an uncle of Alan's who used to live at the homestead, who'd gone silly during the First World War, was "sent away" after wandering off one night to be discovered the next morning, howling and naked at some farmer's door. According to Marius this uncle actually existed and was harmless, but the Nashes didn't know what to do with him and the town made matters worse by conflating the uncle's tragedy with a nasty incident around the same time between the Raymonds and Nashes involving what Marius believed to be cattle theft, or rather *cow* theft—one animal went missing from our stock and turned up neatly slaughtered in the Nash yard. Eudoras and Marius conducted the investigation and pressed charges, which resulted in a cash payment and a change of plea on the Nashes' part from innocent to guilty by accident. I don't know the evidence in the case but it surely wasn't a rebranded hide, a notion Perry lifted from some old western. The whole matter was grandly forgettable until the madman angle was applied, wherein the uncle roamed the prairie at night, hunted the animal, and killed it himself. This bad Hollywood did the Nash clan more harm than even they deserved.

"So you're just reviving an old story?'

"Roger."

"But why?"

"Don't ask why. Looking for motive misses the point. Roger!"

Roger's busy telling a story to some old couple at the bar. Without interrupting himself he sets up a shot and sends it sliding down to Walter Wall, Zinvalena's dad, who has just deposited his coins on the rail of the pool table to put dibs on the next game and does us the favour of delivering the drink.

"Walter, you know Dewey."

Without so much as a nod, Dewey takes the drink and downs half. Walter eyes him with a look that suggests he's got Dewey all figured out.

"Don't shout names," he advises. "Roger there, he's not at your . . ."

"Behest?" asks Dewey helpfully, finally looking up and smiling.

Walter leans close. "Disposal," he says. "Disposal." He straightens up, finds himself face to face with Lenny and for a moment seems willing to stare the moose down, then thinks better and walks off.

"Ominous word, 'disposal,'" says Dewey. "What do you suppose it means?"

"It means just because his daughter works for you doesn't mean he has to like you. It means if you keep up this bad form, someone will take it upon himself to permanently depart you from convention."

"Is this your way of saying you won't help with the letters any more?"

"Look, you don't have to sell me on the value of living a life open to mystery, but what you're doing, it doesn't feel to me like you're tapping into anything too deep. It's just . . . pranksterism."

"It's *inspired* pranksterism. My moves are largely intuitive. But here's a hint." He cuts his eyes both ways, leans forward and whispers and pretty much cinches me as a co-conspirator in everyone's eyes. "Those rumours I mention here," he points his chin at the letter, "that I was an arsonist in Pridemore? Alvin Hall never started them."

"Let me guess."

"You'd guess right."

"You know, it's one thing to make sport of the Coca May, but have you asked yourself why you feel this need to make an enemy of the only guy in town who wears a gun on his hip? It's all good fun until someone loses an eye. Why not just invent an understandable motive to please people like me?"

Dewey looks up to Lenny, mouths a few words I can't make out, then pauses as if listening for a reply, and bows his head.

"Let's just say there's a . . . higher reason. You see I have to use expressions like 'higher reason.' While others guess their way through all this slow dying around here, I'm certain this approach is the one I've been called upon to take. You see I have to use a phrase like 'called upon.'"

A few words with Dewey and I could swear I've been transported to the outer spheres, somewhere farther along the galactic centrifuge where extremes are greater and firm ground doesn't exist. It's a wonderful feeling, frankly, but what Dewey wouldn't guess is that, if it should come to a choice between one way of meeting the world or another, between indulgent out-of-bodiness and responsible earth-boundedness, I'll take the earth. It's just I've been taking too much of it lately.

When we finish up, he gives me a lift back to Cora's house. Along the way we stick to trivia games, a language we can share. Who avenged the dead archer? Clue number one: Fred C. Dobbs, who guesses a mountain lion. I know the answer but string the game along until he drops me off. Clue number two: He didn't mourn but he wore a black suit. The answer is Sam Spade.

"Bogart."

"Very good. The second clue gave it to you. I wasn't sure how strong you were on the black-and-white genres. We've never gone earlier than '73."

"A good guess. Next time let's do history trivia."

"It would have to be something we both know, so that could

be a problem." He pulls out the envelope and hands it to me. "You might deliver this for me," he says. "Part of this being sacred is that it's all mine." A matter-of-fact statement of his convictions. "Something is being prepared for here. I don't know what it is, exactly, but it's important that people continue to take these reports of mine seriously. It's like some cartoon element is trying to creep in. I don't mind people keeping their distance, I don't mind if they include me in nothing but their suspicions, but it's important I'm taken seriously."

I hand back the envelope. "You're still jigging the line on me, Dewey. I never asked to be part of any brotherhood with you. If this is really so sacred, just keep the secret to yourself."

He seems to want to say something, then just shakes his head. I close the door and stand there until he drives off. As I walk to the front door I notice my truck has been moved. I see Perry has left his Pittsburgh Pirates cap on the seat. He owns a cap for every team in the National League East and superstitiously wears whichever one he got the best odds on with his friends in the spring. This year he's riding the Pirates on the theory that pitching wins. Oddly, the cap makes me think of Bogart, my favourite pirate, pitching on the waves, heading back to Key Largo, the storm past and Edward G. Robinson dead on deck, and Bacall a sure bet still to be won.

11

I'M SHAKEN awake at dawn by a dream memory of past June mornings in this same bed when the whole town would be buzzed by the full-throttle takeoff of a chemical-heavy spray plane into perfectly still air. Today there's no sound, but there are more aftershocks. A single memory comes from the corner window, which seems so much smaller now than it did the night Eugene propped himself by it and let me talk him out of sneaking away for a few hours now that it was dark and everyone was asleep, even the kid who never seemed to shut up. He said he liked staying over in town, though there didn't look to be much happening out there that night. She needs new shingles, he said later, when I was almost asleep. Don't tell Marius or we'll get stuck doing it. He talked for a while about asphalt shingles, of all things, and for some reason this stays with me, yet I remember nothing of the nights and mornings I spent here in the days after Marius died, and nothing specific comes back from any of the week-long escapes I made from Marcie, because much of the time I wasn't sober. But to think I can't remember a thing, not even an emotion that may have attached to these lime walls—Cora would say it's just as well.

I take my clothes downstairs without waking anyone and make a pot of coffee, have a quick shower. Shaving, a sinkful of town water so hard even a few inches looks brown. Back in the kitchen I take my day's first coffee and check the window thermometer. Twenty-five or seventy-seven at eight a.m. Summer's heating up more than usual, for the fourth year running. It's so bad the whole country takes notice. A recent tv news dramatization showed Saskatchewan as it might be in thirty years, a vast desert of sand dunes, which seems only a little unlikely given that we already have sand dunes and they're growing noticeably each year. You live in a place all your life and then it begins to lose its mind. What excitement I felt that day two summers back, when it looked as though the season's first storm was moving in from the west. I'd spent the day helping build a new snack booth behind the grandstand, and when we finished up I took a drive out to a little rise on the first grid road west of town, where I sometimes took Cora to watch the sunset. As the blackness moved in, one of the farmers on that road pulled up behind me. He got out and we stood together, and he said, "You'd think you'd stop feeling it after a while." He could see it wasn't rain. As the filter moved over us he said that people over-react to this sort of thing. "It's just the thirties all over," he said, "'cept more." I made it to Cora's house but then stayed in my truck and watched the place fade. All that moved became shadow play. After that early dirt storm I noticed that, even on what I thought to be clear days, each night there'd be a film of dust inside on every surface.

Footsteps overhead and water running upstairs. The first favour I asked of Perry last night was that he attend his July first class reunion. He said he couldn't see a way out of it anyhow.

"With some of them, there won't be much to talk about. What am I gonna say to Hog Kelleher? He's a lawyer now. I used to like him quite a bit but how was I to know he'd end up a lawyer? Not that that's bad, but he's probably a little out of touch. I bet anything the shirt he wears will have short sleeves and a collar and some animal on the chest."

"So what?"

"He'll try and dress down but he won't want to look like he tried."

"You can tell all that by a shirt?"

"Can't you?"

After dinner, Perry watched tv while Cora and I loaded the dishwasher. She finally told me about the "procedure." I didn't have to ask her why she'd waited so long to say anything.

"It's just as well to wait," she said. "Things are more definite now. I'm having an operation but they don't expect any real troubles. The specialist actually called it a 'routine hysterectomy.' I'm booked into Saskatoon in two weeks."

"I'll drive you in and stay over however long."

"I'm tired of asking favours, Wesley, but I sure appreciate it." Then she wiped her hands and leaned over and hugged me, which was pretty unusual, and held me longer than a thank-you called for. "You're a kind man. I think you're very kind." I thought she would choke up but she didn't. I've never seen her cry and I've heard her only once, when she phoned to tell me Marius had died of a heart attack while driving to town. She hadn't been able to talk for a moment. He'd gone off the road and the truck had tipped over but, surprisingly, was only lightly damaged. The need to communicate this small point had brought her back to speech. I remember telling her I hadn't been home in weeks. We'd just returned from visiting Marcie's grandmother in the Qu'Appelle Valley. We were on our way back to Saskatoon at the time of his death. After Cora's call I stupidly tried to remember if I'd seen anything unusual on or near the highway to interpret as a sign from beyond. All I came up with was that for the first time I'd seen a potash mine at night. For a short while this fact seemed important, but I can't say what I thought it meant.

When we'd cleaned up I joined Perry in the living-room, where he slouched with the remote control, flipping between baseball games in Detroit and Atlanta. Everyone in town is hooked up to a satellite dish near the water-tower. There is no more alien viewing experience for me than watching a newscast from a large American city. And is it my imagination or is there an unusual number of fires in Atlanta?

"Did she tell you?"

"You didn't say anything about an operation."

"At least I done that much."

Now I hear Cora moving around upstairs too. I sneak a refill of coffee and drain it, then take my jacket and head out before either of them comes down.

My summer starts in three hours. Tonight I see Karen. I am bang-happy, I am pinball.

Someone once wrote that the only good that is not subject to chance is that which is outside the world, and that knowing this is beautiful because it projects the soul beyond time. Sitting alone in my home classroom, in natural lighting, it occurs to me that though the notion of eternity seems not to frighten most people in these parts, I would rather go bare knuckles with the Easter bunny than contemplate it. The paradox of eternity is that it exists in the realm of miraculous reversals, a happy-hour philosophical subtlety that is a difficult sell even at the most prosperous of times. But there is a state of collective depression wherein people are reduced to the simplest functions. They become meticulous at work and tidy the spaces they control. Yet how much worse it must have been—the figure to note on page one of the exams I return this morning is sixty thousand Canadian dead in the First World War. The historical angle I take to this number, that Canada was blackmailed by Britain and the Boer War was a dry run, is all wrong. Next year I'll dispense with any explanation that doesn't make a picture. We'll call it the lesson of mud.

In the hallway someone is coming, the feet falling evenly, judging by the sound (not at all like mine, for my left foot has a deeper resonance owing to imperfect alignment so my knee torques and over time has acquired barometric sensitivity). Basso stops in the doorway, wishes me a good summer. He provides the itinerary of the trip he's taking in July. Cypress Hills, Waterton, Banff, Kelowna. Somewhere in the interior Rockies my students begin to appear by twos and threes and I start to come around, circling ever closer to my Mr. Ray.

"How do you make sense of this wolf thing, Toss?"

"What you're asking is how a thing that doesn't exist can have so long a life. Any answer to that would require some long thought, I guess."

"You might do me a favour by verifying or dismissing certain theories about your possible involvement."

"The honest answer, Milt, is that in my opinion we are all of us complicit."

He produces an envelope from inside his unseasonal tweed jacket. "Corporal Hall says you're a hard fellow to get ahold of. I told him I'd pass this along." The moment he's out of the room I read the note: "Your truck has been spotted at the scene of a few break-and-enters. I'm about to begin investigating. Tell Beyer peace is best for everyone."

I readdress the envelope and write a response under his note: "Peace is one thing but the rest is history. Sorry, but I'm the sort of guy who holds no sway with anyone. And I'm growing tired of the lead-up so you may as well run me in. It will cause some unrest, of course, but let's be strong. We have reputations to uphold." Hall's bluffs are becoming easier to read, but I still wonder why he's relying on me as an intermediary.

The morning's news for the home-room class is generally good. They've done well in the subjects that count for them. We say our goodbyes in the spirit of deserved sendoff rather than of simple release, as can be the case for a group of lower scorers. Zinvalena outwaits a few others and I'm happy to see she's the last to leave. She gives me a hug. Then the tears start.

"Don't get too worked up. A couple of years from now you'll realize I'm a fraud."

"I'm not going to university," she says. "The family agrees I better learn something practical so I'm taking business management at the college in Medicine Hat."

"But I thought you *wanted* university?"

She checks over her shoulder to make sure no one out in the hallway has seen her.

"The family agrees," she repeats.

"Who do they agree with? Your dad?"

She nods. Then leaves, knowing before I do that there's nothing left to say.

III

SUIT OF HEARTS

12

EACH YEAR on this day I buy a new keychain, choosing from the available stock in town and discarding the old one now that I don't collect them any more. Happy to be getting rid of the small metal horseshoe that's been biting my quadriceps, I inspect the well-appointed display rack at Richard's Convenience and Video. Half the offerings are of the jokey variety, the kind meant to pass as cheery novelties: a small plastic tusk with "horny" written across it, a Ghostbusters emblem, a simulated gold bar embossed with "Fort Knox," and a not so vaguely racist depiction of a Mountie's hat lassoing a Sikh turban. Then there are the stylized vowels, the signature designs of auto and grain companies, musical instruments in miniature, a prism, a bottle opener, a chrome-spoked hubcap. I choose a pewter prairie dog that doubles as a moneyclip. As Richard rings it up I point out the turban and he shakes his head and tells me it all comes from the same load. I buy the turban too, and drop it with the horseshoe in a garbage bin outside the door. Across the road the one o'clock lunch shift of highway workers is heading into the Flyway. Good food but lentil soup each day.

The odd little keychain ritual is more than simply a way of measuring out my life with the most meaningless junk I can find. It's a test of my ability to invest meaning into *anything*. The Toss Raymond calendar year begins on the last day of work before summer, and each year is identified with whatever dangles from the keychain. The drought began in the Year of the Leather Braid. The rumours about Marcie and Alan began late in the Year of the Saskatchewan Roughrider Plastic Bubble. And last summer when Marcie left, and then Alan and then Wanda, all in different directions, it was, too ironically, the Year of the Horseshoe. In these terms, time began for me six years ago on the day I finally met up with a small part of my brother's life and learned a little of what happened to Eugene in the years after he left home.

The letter had come from Miles City, Montana. A woman named Carla expressed regret at having to tell me that her husband Gene had drowned off the coast of Cancún.

> I wasn't with him down there. We split up a few months before but that was nothing new and I suppose we both thought we'd come to our senses again before too long. Anyway, he always said he might like to see you some day and to tell the truth I'm long past worrying about whether or not he really meant what he said, about you or anyone or anything. I only just looked up where exactly he came from and it's a guess that this will ever find you but if you still live where I'm sending this then there's a place I've thought of we can meet. Gene had a road job selling and servicing pumps all over the state, mostly for irrigation setups, and he had a few favourite places he'd phone me from, and one he promised to take me to, which it turns out is straight south of you and on my way west.

She asked that I write back if I couldn't make it on the night she planned to pass through Sweet Grass County on her route to the coast and "new prospects." Otherwise we'd meet at the Clown in Barrel. I first read the letter in my truck on the way home from town, one day in the early spring of that year. I don't recall displaying any outward signs of shock or sorrow upon learning of Eugene's death. There were a few moments, I think, when I stupidly wondered for whose sake the letter was written, but more than anything I felt disbelief—a disbelief that by the time he died

Eugene could have been to me just about anyone, living anywhere, and disbelief that he in fact lived so close to home without ever returning. I decided to let Carla get on with her prospects—I wasn't going to help her close off her years with my brother by coming between the then and the now—and I didn't change my mind until five in the morning of the Saturday I was to meet her.

The strange feeling of coming upon a place he knew well, pulling into the gravel lot, seeing how small the bar was, trying to account for the depth of black beyond the light from the neon Stroh's sign in the window. The moon was a sliver of dying ice in the trees and close upon me the mountains shadowed the valley from starlight, which I never before thought provided much in the way of illumination. I walked in and the bartender, a blonde woman in her thirties, perhaps, said, "Well hello," as if maybe she knew me, then just smiled as I wandered to the back wondering who, among the dozen or so patrons, might be Carla. No one, it seemed. I took a seat and ordered chili on the waitress's advice, and when I'd almost finished she came by again and I said it was good and she said, "I made it before shift. You're eating my one talent." She was small and dark, with a finely featured, attractive face. I supposed Eugene knew these women in here. I could have asked the waitress but instead asked only if there'd been a woman here earlier waiting for someone and she said, "No one but me, honey." I waited an hour or so, and resolved to consider the long drive a hopeful act even though I hadn't met Carla.

By the time I left, the place was emptying out. I managed to get as far as my truck without noticing that there was someone in the hatchback parked beside me. When I opened my door, she opened hers and got out and stood looking over the roof at me, her face lit from below by the interior light.

"The way you walk, even." The words didn't seem directed at me, though it was me she was looking at. "I've been waiting out here for I don't know how long. When I drove up I didn't really think you'd be here, and then when I saw the plates I wasn't ready for it. I almost left but I couldn't do that either. Those sorts of reasons for not doing something never made sense to Gene." She looked towards the Clown in Barrel, then back at me. "He always said I was a coward whenever it mattered."

I went around to her side of the car. We exchanged an awkward moment in which we didn't know how to say hello and then we shook hands.

"Would you like to go inside?" I asked.

"I don't think so. Look, I really don't know why we're here. It's occurred to me I don't know why I asked to meet you. Do you have an idea why?"

"I'm glad you took the trouble to write and to show up here. It isn't that I'm expecting any explanations. And I don't have a lot of questions," I said, though, depending on what she might have said, of course, I might have had a thousand.

"It's even your voice," she said. "Not the way you speak so much as the sound." She shook her head. "This isn't getting too easy. Why don't we get inside my car and we can keep talking."

Inside, she kept her eyes front when I twisted around to look at her. She reached under the seat and got out a cigarette pack, opened it and took one out. Without looking my way she offered the pack, and when I declined she tucked it closed and put it back under the seat. She found her pack of matches on the dash and lit up.

I said, "I'll say thank you right—"

"No. I can't do this just yet. I'm sorry." She rolled down her window and tapped her cigarette outside, though there weren't any ashes yet. "It turns out I don't exactly want to make friends even. I thought I did but I don't."

"Well, I'm sorry to have to put it this way, Carla, but now that I'm sitting here talking to you I'm not going to just let it go." What I wanted by then was only a single perfect moment of knowing by which I could remember my brother. From even a short distance such a wish is obviously naive, but I didn't have any distance then.

She surprised me with a quick smile. "You really do sound like him, you know."

"That's a start right there. I'm happy to know that for some reason."

"I don't know that you should be."

"Did he ever say why he never came home, I mean home to Saskatchewan?"

"There's a whole history there before I got to know him, and frankly I didn't pay much attention. He was in Mexico for a long time. He worked on a bull ranch or something, but I think that's just what he said. He made a lot of the wrong kind of friends down there, other Americans, and they'd still call him up out of the blue and get him to burn off a weekend somewhere. After Mexico he did some small-time rodeo, which he was no good at, and he hurt his back. I don't know the sequence of what all happened. I met him eight years ago next month at a pancake house in Great Falls. It was my fault. I asked if I could use his syrup. One thing led to another."

"You said in the letter that he mentioned me. What did he say? Why did my name come up?"

She said he'd come home talkative from his road trips and tell her about his past sometimes, and that was when my name came up. He thought his dad was likely dead but he wondered about me.

"I don't remember he had a lot of stories about you or anything. He said you were just a kid when he left. He thought you'd be too smart to stick around home all your life. Maybe he didn't think there'd be anyone for him to go back to."

"You don't have to make excuses for him, or for my sake."

"I wouldn't ever see the point in doing that." She was looking at me then, and had been for a while, though I couldn't say when she'd turned to me. Despite the uncertain light she looked wan and tired, a long-day's-end sort of look. "When you go through his life it doesn't seem to add up to much." I thought that at least something of him would come back to her, that it takes time to get high enough above a person's life so you can see the whole thing instead of the details. "I just realized I should have something to give you but I didn't think to bring anything along, not even any pictures of him. All my stuff's been shipped ahead." She turned on the interior light and started looking around the car, bending over into the back seat, then reaching across me into the glove compartment. Her breasts brushed my leg. "There's not going to be anything," she said. "You can tell I didn't think you'd really show."

She sat straight again and rested a hand on the wheel and stared at the cindertip of her cigarette.

"Just tell me one thing," she said. "I see your wedding ring. Do you screw around on your wife?"

I looked at the burning tip now and imagined riding the smoke as it trailed up and out the window.

"I feel like I'm taking another man's heat here."

"Won't you pay a debt for your family?"

"I guess so."

"Then just tell me if you screw around."

"I've been married two years and I haven't yet."

"Well, there's still every night of your life to get through."

Then she got out and opened the trunk. The outside air was very cold and I noticed I'd begun to shiver. I got out too and watched her.

"I don't know why I should worry about this," she said. "He never left me anything. Never once and never in the end. You might as well know that about him." She'd opened a suitcase and seemed to be looking for something specific. "Maybe I can give you something of mine, or of ours, I mean. Unless you want his emergency snow shovel here." She stopped leafing through her things and began pulling out handfuls of clothes and shaking them out over the bag. "You can't see in this light. What I'm looking for is a key to the hotel room in Reno where we spent the last two Christmases. Our lucky key. Gene won a bundle in keno the first night we checked in. We almost broke even on both trips." She stopped and held up a pair of slacks, examining them. "You can't even make out the colours in this light. All this stuff looks strange to me." Then she went through the rest of her clothes. "It's in a pocket of something. It's a sort of charm. Or it was."

After a minute she dropped a jacket she'd been holding and turned and looked me up and down.

"You could come back with me to my room and we could go through the stuff together."

"I don't need anything, Carla."

She resumed her search through the clothes and said evenly, "Well, I don't really care about you, it's not you I'm asking for." Then she slammed the trunk shut. It was very dark again.

I walked to my truck and climbed in. There was nothing to be done for her.

She came to my window and handed over a room key, and I took it rather than ask which room it opened, theirs or hers.

She looked over at the Clown in Barrel and said, "This place looks just like I thought it would. I never want to see inside." Then she walked around behind the truck to her car, and got in and left me there with her offering. The key and tag both had been stamped with the number 211. There was nothing else on it, no address or hotel name. I keep it with my other family mementoes, at home in a cardboard apple box, in my closet. If I ever go to Reno, there's one door I'll never open, and one number I'll never play.

Like every other car and truck here, mine smells of grasshopper death, so it's into the coin-wash to gun them away and leave in the original lapis and silver. I make a quarter-mile before the bug-crust starts to form again. Bear east at the ten-mile turnoff and before long you can't help but notice the insidious geometry of satellite dishes visible through every farmyard windbreak. No one here makes decisions on aesthetic grounds. For a short stretch the fields change direction, abutting the road in narrow strips. A dried slough provides such peripheral evenness that if you fix on the horizon it seems you aren't moving at all, merely observing a still phrase. Somewhere ahead is that unlocatable border between what I know for certain and what I'm unwilling to trust. So many wheat towns that at some point I'll have to think a minute before remembering a name, and then the land gets a little worse, the soil harder and the grades steeper, and a short space up ahead where no elevators are visible, a phenomenon I once thought was impossible. I turn south and leave the gravel for asphalt, the new surface ending one long inflection and beginning another. A sign wags in the ditch, promising Mayford Riverside Regional Park in three miles. Sudden loss of altitude, porcupine roadkill, long view of the east-side cabins and the deepest ground-level green, denoting the newly irrigated golf course, which attracts both finely tuned amateurs and hackers like myself, who onomatopoeically call the game "whack-fuck." Some families spend all summer here in recreational retreat.

A half-hour ahead of Karen and two or three days out front of the holiday crowd, I have time to kill but no one to flush it my way. What I really need is food. The snack booth isn't open, as I should have known, but as I park the truck by the swimming-pool I see Eldon's little brother, Blair, inside the fence, painting a lifeguard perch, and I bet he'll have a snack for his old teacher, or at least something I can raid. If it comes down to it I'll bait him with insider news about Zinvalena, whom he's been sniffing the wind for since she broke off with her last buck on New Year's Eve.

"You know anything about martins?" he calls as I approach.

"Patty and Phil?"

"Purple ones. I took an order for a martin house but nobody's got the plans." The chair is dripping from two corners.

"I'll ask around. You should stir that paint a bit more, though. If a fly won't stick to the surface then it's not thick enough. Hell, there's a lot I could tell you about painting. Why don't we have something to eat and discuss a little theory."

"My jean jacket's on the bench at the shallow end. Keys are in the right pocket. One of the little gold ones will get you in the booth."

"Thanks."

"Just shut up about painting. I know how to paint."

"As is evident, my son. It's just the fine points need attention."

There are forty or fifty keys on the nylon string in Blair's jacket, and I count no fewer than eleven "little gold ones" as I navigate the sprinkler fire across the lawn to the booth. All of them fit the lock but only on the third try does number seven open the Mastercraft. Inside is mostly webdust except where the new stock has been unloaded. I pull two packets of beef jerky off the wall, disturbing the accurate bodies of daddy-long-legs, and till the deep-freeze for a pack of wieners and a Popsicle. I poke a few boxes in the corner hoping to find licorice but come up empty. A five-dollar bill clips neatly under the freezer lid, a cold bluc thank-you. Back outside I see Blair disappearing into the workshed across the road. As I pass by my truck I lay the dogs on the hood to thaw, then deliver Blair his jacket and almost prop myself against a table matted with years of grime, before I remember I'm wearing my semiformals.

"Ancient grease."

"Eh?" He reseals the paint can. "I can take a propane torch to those dogs."

"No need. Have some jerky. Who's the martin house for?"

"Mrs. Shaulter. She moved down on the weekend. Karen asked me to check on her every day around noon, so I drop by to see if she needs a refill from the waterpump or anything. Today she asked about a martin house. She says she's seen one in town but can't remember whose it is. If you see Karen before me, ask her if she knows."

"I'll see her tonight."

"I sort of thought so, but Eldon says you two are on the rocks so I wasn't sure. He says you told him yourself."

"I did. I can't remember if it was at the ball diamond or outside the theatre when I was waiting for Dewey and Zinvalena."

Blair stalls a moment. "That Dewey's got people on the run. Eldon phoned at lunch. He told me what was in today's *News*. I guess you've seen it."

"No."

"He wrote another letter, said we should consider whether or not this Coca May group really exists. And he said we might ask if the local police aren't maybe behind those letters that set all this off. He didn't mention the werewolf, but Eldon says if you ask him he'll stick by what he's said all along about the animal parts. He claims Hall is covering up something very scary. The best is, there's six or seven other letters taking up his side, people saying they've seen something running around their farmyards at night scaring the animals. You'd think there'd be someone who could come forward and straighten all this out."

"I used to think that too. Actually, for a while I thought I was making some headway myself." Now I can only wonder how many different ways Dewey can play his hand.

"My dad thinks he should be gut-shot. He doesn't say stuff like that much."

"I wouldn't take it as an order, Blair."

Blair starts up the grindstone. He puts on his work gloves and begins sharpening a thirty-inch mower blade. Sparks stream onto the floor and out to the step. Inside the door is a can with "gas" painted on the side. Every so often a spark bounces off it. I say nothing, imagining my life as one dangerously on the edge. He takes the blade off the stone, removes from his mouth the jerky that hangs like an overlong cigarillo, and purses his lips to let drop a well-rounded and cleanly cut ball of spit. It hits the bevel and sizzles like raw meat on a pit grill. He dips the blade into a pail of water, where it hisses. Then he removes it and holds it in the door light. It steams dry in seconds. This is all a display but he'd perform it whether or not I was present. I see that he's smiling now, though only to himself, in a vague way that suggests how much he enjoys this sort of manual work, the weight and smell of it. He again submerges the blade, then takes up the next one.

"How's the farm holding out?"

"It's no hell. Look, there's something you might give me some advice about, Mr. Ray." He hasn't called me Mr. Ray in five years. Trying to tickle my helper instinct.

"Something more than birdhouses, Mr. Kay?" I tell him the rumours about Zinvalena are in his favour and he should act fast.

"Strike quickly," he says.

"Act fast."

"I will," he says. "This is real. I don't mind telling people either. I've had girls before but this is dead serious. The past few weeks it's turned into something beyond control."

"I'm happy for you, Blair, but you should really approach her in some way."

"I've been waiting 'cause I'm superstitious," he says, absently removing his gloves. "But today everything's come up right so far. Everything's a little strange today."

I turn to look out the small window behind me but the top half is boarded and the bottom too dirty to see through, so my eyes settle on the mass of dead flies along the windowsill. Why do they like dying on windowsills? A child's question.

"Do those showers in the pool work yet?"

"Do you know anything about handling chlorine?"

"No."

"Me neither. Yeah, they work okay. Go ahead."

"Good luck with Zinvalena. You can't very well ask her to a movie but whatever you decide, if she agrees to go out with you, then stick to the basics. Don't try to mate the first night."

"Hit the shower."

"No, that won't work either." He pulls the blade out and

throws the bucket of water at me but I'm already through the door and out of range. "You probably wish you had my experience, kid, but don't hold it against me. There's a method to most things."

When I'm showered I climb gingerly over the pool fence and take the back route to the east court, following a series of well-obscured footpaths overgrown with ivy and grass that never fail to stain a pant-leg. From somewhere comes the sound of screen doors slamming and children's voices, the first carloads already spilled out and mother cleaning away the winter to make room for her season of anodyne routine. Through the trees I see the river side of several cottages and am reminded again how indifferent I am to cabin life. Veranda or gazebo, tough choices I'd rather avoid. Years ago Marcie and I would drive north through five hours of dusk to the A-frame her parents owned at Turtle Lake. Something about all the birch and blackflies set off in her a sort of sexual eagerness that often sent us canoeing to some untamed island where we'd lie on rock and commune lustily to the sounds of distant motorboats or loons. Yet when we moved here she wouldn't come with me to the river island in our own back yard for a little sport, offering the curious accusation that I was "perverse." Naturally, I thought, craving the onion taste of her skin, much the same taste as that accompanying the onset of general anaesthetic. What clung to her was a trace of going under.

I emerge onto the east loop. Here the poplars tower above cabins of deep blue or green, though some have faded to a shade liable to induce instant anaemia in a certain sort of person. Fuchsia has a more inviting effect, especially with Karen's car parked out front. She calls my name as I approach but I don't see her until I'm close enough to look into the back yard that slopes sharply and then levels off only a few feet from the water. She's sitting in a lawn chair, drinking something brown and wearing cut-off jeans over bare feet. She smiles, beckons almost imperceptibly with her head. I'm mindful of my back, which apprehends stress completely apart from the rest of me, so I take the slope at an angle judicious even for a person twice my weight.

"I'm usually more agile than this. I had an unfortunate accident." I lean over to kiss her on the head but bale out at the last minute and give her an awkward one-armed hug around the neck, remembering that Marcie hated to be kissed on top of the head and considered it an act of condescension.

"It's probably okay to kiss me. They're all unfortunate."

"Are not. By accident is how you and I came together."

"And here I thought it was destiny. I should've known. Lulls in conversation. The freaky way you dress sometimes. Want a Pepsi?"

"I wouldn't send you up to get it."

"You'd get it yourself, except I want to introduce you to Mother. She can see us now. She's up in the veranda. I don't think she can hear. Can you hear us, Mother?... She can't hear us."

I sit on the grass beside her chair, looking out as if the river were particularly interesting.

"I hope you didn't dress up for her sake. We're all a bit old for that sort of thing."

"I haven't been home since I left the school."

"I thought maybe you wanted to make a good impression."

"Don't think so much—"

"I'm just making fun. You don't be so tense always." She tugs the hair on the back of my head.

"You're sure she can't hear us?"

"Sure."

"It's just that I want to bite your thigh and I can't even lick your shin. This is absolute honesty you're getting from me today."

"And this makes you tense. You ought to find a way of channelling your energies."

"Don't use that word. Channel is a river word, or maybe a tv word. It's not energies and spirits. Besides, I know a way of relieving my tension. What we're in need of here is a large bush."

I hear the ice in her glass and again feel her hand, now tugging on my collar. She drops the ice down my back, causing me simultaneously to spring up and pull out my shirt-tail. The cubes are already melting in the grass, she's rocking in her chair with laughter, I'm breathless with a degree of pain well beyond conveyance.

"Don't swear," she manages to say between hoots. "Mother will hear if you swear."

When she finally gains some understanding of my condition, Karen becomes so earnestly apologetic that I have to calm her with a "s'okay." She had no idea and have I seen Doctor Earl and where does it hurt exactly? But I've already delivered the only response I can muster at the moment and all I have to counteract the dorsal hatchet-dance is a mind's-eye picture of a Cuervo Especial bottle seen from the back, the magpie (or is it a raven?—how can I quibble?) on the inside of the label visible through the tequila gold. Why this should come to me I don't know, given that the bottle I imagine lasted four years and didn't tempt me even during the worst of my drinking days. But there it is, holding twenty-four shots of Mexico. It says, I can hurt you in better ways. And no one to tell me, Beware the firewater.

By now Karen is leading me to the slope with her arm around my waist. She obviously hasn't pinpointed where I hurt because she's paying too much heed to my feet, as if I might limp. When she nudges a little too close I let out a groan and she detaches herself.

"You're in what they call serious difficulty. I'm taking you to town."

I shake my head. "I'll be all right in a minute. Takes a minute." I turn and face the river again so Mrs. Shaulter can't see my grimace. Now it's Karen's turn to sit on the grass.

"I'm such an idiot sometimes. You just finished saying you were hurt. You should sue me. If someone did that to me I think I'd sue them. You've got a solid case."

"I'm sorry."

"Not your fault. Don't be stupid. I'm the one who's stupid. I do stuff like this all the time."

"No, I mean I'm sorry about last time. Sorry what I said."

She looks up. "Oh that." Then she hugs my knee, gets to her feet, and starts up the slope without even asking if I'm ready yet.

"Guess she wasn't watching after all." Mrs. Shaulter isn't in the veranda. She's napping in the bedroom. In what serves as the living-room I lie on a rock-hard pull-out couch that smells of its considerable age while Karen fetches a glass of wine from the kitchen. The walls are done in a pleasant wood panelling, but the bookshelf is fake mahogany on particle-board and the table beside me is lost in green Mactac. Hanging on the wall opposite is a gold-framed reproduction of Dali's *The Crucifixion of St. John of the Cross.* Karen comes in and explains that when she was little she used to think it was a picture of Tarzan, "Which shows how stupid I was even then. Mother brings it down from the house every summer. Sort of a totem for her." I close my eyes to a long silence and begin to nod off while trying to remember the name of Tarzan's chimp. It seems terribly important that I recall it. In fact it will remove the pain in my back. This is a relationship only I can see, but I'll try to explain it to Karen when I come to full consciousness. It's a name with ice-blue spots. A name of an animal not itself, a name with a shape the animal doesn't seem to have, a name larger than the animal as we think of it.

A car radio wakens me. A DJ says that today is the birthday of these celebrities. The only one I recognize is Helen Keller (whom I've never thought of as a celebrity), the rest probably being recent American tv stars. Feeling only a little better, I sit up and start on the wine while listening to the car turn out of the courtyard and lay rubber. Karen is leaning against the bedroom doorway saying something to her mother. She laughs softly, as I've never heard her before, then turns and walks towards the kitchen, smiling. One more sip as she glances my way and has a spasm of shock to see me awake. For some reason I think of Mary Shelley's monster—maybe I look a wretch and should spring from the cabin window.

"They got you too. That wasn't much of a nap. You didn't even have time to drool."

"Kind of you to keep an eye out."

"Mother will be ready in a minute."

"She's ready now, dear." A woman appears in the kitchen, and on seeing her I realize I didn't get a very good look at her the morning of the church-going fiasco. She's a silver, squarish woman, wearing slacks and a man's dress shirt that hangs to mid-thigh. Even in thongs she looks taller than Karen. I've seldom been damned by a woman so physically imposing.

"Hello, Wesley."

"Hello, Mrs. Shaulter."

"No such person," she says. "I'm Kate. You wouldn't remember when we met before." She is for all the world delighted. Her smile dominates the room. "It was on Main Street and your mom had your brother by the hand and you in a stroller. You were sleeping, I know."

"Sounds like me."

"You were sleeping and your brother was very concerned that I keep my voice down so I wouldn't wake you, so he and I had a little whisper about something or other. You never stirred an inch. Though in those days cars didn't drive by with their radios blaring." She takes a glass of water and the three of us move into the veranda. "It was time for me to get up anyway. I always have a little nap from four-thirty to five-thirty. How was your day, honey?"

"Not exactly busy. I read a three-hundred-page junk novel," says Karen, who had known we were alone when she said otherwise. I could have bitten her thigh after all.

"I would've guessed Eugene was a loudmouth kid," I say.

"That's his name!" Kate exclaims. "I was trying to remember his name just now. I thought he was a darling. No one was going to wake up his little brother. He wasn't impolite, he just explained the matter as if I were the child in that conversation. Naturally he would. That's how it was explained to him. Will you get me an ashtray, dear?" As she leaves again, Karen flashes me what seems intended as an apologetic look.

"Now you teach up at the school."

"That's right. School's out as of today. Sounds like a lot of people are moving down here already."

"Karen says you've been there a few years. You live in your dad's house now, by the river. I always thought that was the prettiest setting for a place you could imagine." And not at all the spot to blow up buildings, I imagine her thinking.

"Pretty doesn't take you very far in the winter, not that we get much snow any more." I can't believe I've brought up the weather. Karen returns with the ashtray and Kate lights up a Craven A.

"Does Wendy have a picture of the river, Karen?" she asks.

"No. Why should she have one?"

"You should show off the nicest places to out-of-towners. People think this province is boring to look at, but there are a lot of nice spots."

"She likes it here, Mother, but she's lived all her life in Vancouver. It's hard to impress people out there with a few trees and a river."

"But she likes the quiet here. She told me that."

"Why not tell her to hop a bus and get out here?" I ask. The question is grossly unfair to Karen but I want her to consider the possibility and, besides, I want to see how Kate will react. She reacts by ignoring the question.

"When Karen moved to Vancouver she forgot how lovely it can be here at home, and the sound of it, how quiet it is. This is the longest she's ever stayed."

"Enough, Mother." Karen explains, "We don't get much chance to quarrel with each other for an audience."

"Oh, we're not quarrelling. Do you think we're quarrelling, Wesley?" asks Kate. They both look my way for an answer and when I come up empty they laugh together. What fun. Feeling unnecessarily tamed, I keep quiet while the two of them debate a few small points. Kate insists we are having "noodles" with the chicken. Karen calls it "paw-sta." Kate wonders why Karen bought red wine. Karen says it's old-fashioned to colour-code your food. Their exchanges are practised in the natural way of small talk delivered in a lifelong context. Given my question about Wendy I'm sure they intend to keep me ill at ease, so it seems natural that the conversation will turn back to me soon enough. One of them will ask the sort of question I purposely never ask myself.

Karen says it's "very progressive" of me to offer to help with the food—I didn't—but everything is following its simple course and I will only "screw things in every direction." Kate doesn't seem to mind this sort of language. Eventually they disappear into the kitchen and leave me in a side-tilting armchair and an undetermined mood. Through the screen window I watch a Dalmatian trotting along the lane, reading the ground with his nose. I have an immediate affection for all varieties of dog no smaller than a large terrier. Most dogs are smart enough to know they are dumb, and dumb enough to aspire to greater things, if only they knew how to go about attaining them. Our family was something of an anomaly among farm and ranch clans in that we owned only one dog and for just five years. Romeo died the summer before Marius did. He was a blue heeler we picked up in the Swift Current pound, and though he attached himself to us, for some reason he never identified our home as his and consequently measured strangers with a pathetic, cowering scrutiny. He had no sense of duty other than self-preservation—a dog in tune with his decade. He was flatulent.

The Dalmatian makes a line for the veranda and presses his nose against the screen door. He sniffs. I say hello and his tail wags absently but when I move over and open the door he's taken by surprise and hightails it for the next yard, where he stops and looks back. I squat to my haunches and sucker him with the old cupped-palm trick. When he's close enough to see I have nothing for him to eat, I scratch behind his ears. He accepts this without particular enthusiasm, which only strengthens my quick appraisal that he is block-headed and overweight. He follows me up to the lane, where I root around for a manageably sized piece of wood among some small branch trimmings. He already knows there's no food where I'm digging, so he focuses somewhere in the distance, perhaps hoping a rabbit will appear. I get his attention with a "Here, boy" and toss the branch in a smooth underhand motion so that it lands fifteen feet down the road. The dog just looks at me, then goes over to a nearby poplar and scratches and snuffles. He pisses on it, staking his claim while ignoring me. I tell him he's lucky he wasn't born in China where dogs are routinely killed for being loyal to the individual rather than the state.

"Hey, Missy." On hearing Karen's voice the dog begins convulsing with joy and is barely able to keep her feet while running towards her.

"I thought it was a he."

"It is. What do *you* think those tanks are for? This is Nancy Edmund's dog. She named him Missy after her horse, if you can believe that." Nancy Edmund is a farm wife of prurient looks and champion promiscuity. Her son Bill, in my Grade 10 class, has made a name for himself locally as the most violent hockey player in town. He is an irretrievable dullard. "The chicken burned in the pan so we skinned it already. There's not much for seasoning either. Anyway, food's ready." We pat Missy until he calms a bit. Naturally he is disillusioned as we go back in and leave him. Even in the kitchen I can hear him sniffing at the door.

"Karen says you're very political," Kate begins when we're all seated at the small dining-table, "so I promise to steer clear of the usual issues. No free-trade talk. I won't mention grain subsidies."

"Thanks, but that's a short list of the bad waters around here."

"Why would you bring those up?" asks Karen. "You've never in your life had a thing to say on either topic."

"Well dear, it may come as a surprise but even when I'm not in your company I think and talk, just like most people. I even have opinions."

"I'd never claim you had a shortage of those. I'd never claim that. But I'd say you rely on some pretty warped information sometimes." She smiles in the general direction of the noodles/pasta. She is on the verge of recalling something.

"Please don't misrepresent me to Wesley. Imagine getting bad press from your own daughter."

"Bad press is an eastern occupation," says Karen. "Some Toronto reporter did a story from Yorkton on tv last week and he called it 'an isolated community.' It'd never occurred to me. I still don't know what he meant. Isolated from what?"

From some place the spice route reaches, I'm tempted to reply. The fettucini is sticky and bland, the chicken a tasteless obligation. I take a sip of wine after each bite—Kate might think I'm a drinker but she won't think I'm wasteful. Missy himself seems to have given up on this meal, his sniffing no longer audible. He probably got a good whiff.

After I've pretended to consider a second helping and the three of us seem to have finished, I insist on doing the dishes. A surprising lack of resistance lands me at the sink with a half-bucket of stove-warmed water and a plastic cup's worth of congealed soap. While alone with my chore I have time to reflect that I'm sadly ingenuous in understanding interfemale communications. It's one thing to recognize a false conception but another to form an accurate one. Begin with the premise that no one is typical but most of us are exposed to the same consensual reality, are subject to the same poisons. Then consider historical evidence, the social positions, the common struggles. The sexual equation usually plays out with the men in red and the women in black. But then I'm not such a bad guy, I note, and hence the danger of generalizations. Ask any imperialist. A little reflexive psychoanalysis suggests that my anxiety bespeaks a tenuous character. Simply put, I don't always know who to be when I'm around women. This is no real revelation because I've struck on it before, and dismissed it as too obvious and logical to be true. But moments of self-knowledge come tagged with stagy exempla. The day Marcie told me her idea to use my room at Cora's house two or three nights a week while working in town at some or other part-time job. What I shouldn't have said, and did—"What if I want to use it?"—an indefensible question considering we both knew a queen-size mattress was no limitation in itself. Should I have supported her? Yes. Were there not already signs that she was going a bit stir-crazy in the valley? Could my behaviour be termed insensitive? In fact, given that I left her each day with no means of transport, and beyond walking distance to any other house but one . . . but I'm exaggerating here, because she did scout around and secure an old Impala, and in our last months reacted to her freedom by farm-hopping like an Avon cowgirl, stirring up a patch of dormant feminism, introducing the notion of a support group for abused wives. She called a meeting at our house and was surprised when no one came, not even those she knew needed help. She said, "They would've come if they knew me better, if I was *from* here." Though she might have been right I suggested for the first time that she give up trying to organize. Then she nailed me, dead on: "Some people must think this is pretty funny. And you just want a little quiet." As often happened I came around to her view of me as a sometimes ass.

The talking in the veranda has stopped. I enter from the kitchen just as Kate comes in through the screen door. She pauses and meets me eye to eye for a moment, as if not recognizing me, then says, "Karen just went over to give Nancy Edmund back her card table. She left it here last summer."

"I'll carry it. Is she out there?"

"That's fine. You just sit and digest, which is what I should be doing instead of finding dandelions to poke at." She takes a seat overlooking the yard and river, and I pull up a folding chair and sit beside her. "Do you play cards?" she asks.

"Not much. I know a few games but I don't play them much."

"Vernon used to do nothing but play cards before we were married. It seemed there was a poker game every few nights. After our marriage he quit that bunch but he made me play a two-handed game every so often, which isn't much fun. I took no interest, anyway. I like to play solitaire when Karen's not here. She thinks it's sad to watch a widow play solitaire but that's just her notion. I've been playing it since I was a girl. I've got my favourite games—I don't remember what they're called, if I ever knew, but I know how to cheat in each one. Though there are some things I'd never do." The woman knows how to set up her punches.

"I think Marius played poker when he was young. Maybe he was in the same game as Vernon." Someone has turned on a blue-light bug zapper. It's nowhere near dark but the current sounds to be getting a greater share than any early bird might hope to.

Kate says, "I hate that thing. Not only the noise, but it's wasteful. A part of the natural cycle is just cut off. I've asked a young man to build me a martin house. Bugs are for birds and other bugs, not for hardware items."

"Did you know Marius, my dad?"

"Of course I knew him, but I didn't see him much after your mother died. She was in my grade at school. But she was a year older than me. Her sister was four or five grades under us. She was in that old photo Karen found. And her name's Cora?"

"Cora. That's right."

"I know she's still in town but I never kept in touch except to see her at the hospital now and then. Your mother and I and Joan Lester were all good friends when we were girls."

"I don't remember her at all." No less true because of a life's worth of impressions, even images, all of them belonging to other people and each new one revising my view of the rest. But still she is real. She exists beyond what has been imparted to me by witnesses who know with the first hand but pass to me with the second.

"I'd say you don't look very much like her, even in a general way. You probably know she had black hair. It was very thick and I think she was quite proud of it, not that we talked about hair all the time, but she put some effort into looking after it, maybe because she didn't think of herself as pretty. She had a small birthmark on her back that she was embarrassed about. Shaped like Hudson Bay, she always thought, but I saw a jack rabbit, an upside-down rabbit. And that led to Joan calling her Bugs for a time when we were just out of school, until your mom got upset about it one day because the name had caught on with some man in town—not Marius, I don't think—but whoever it was had actually called her Bugsy."

At some time during Kate's reverie I sensed we were both of us only vaguely perceiving one another, and now that she's silent I feel no urge whatsoever to speak. Something has been forced upon me like medicine for a child. When I hear movement in the grass outside I'm suddenly aware that I've unconsciously assumed an attitude of lumpen dejection, elbows propped on knees and face in hands. I look up to see Karen standing outside the screen door with her arms crossed and tucked firmly under her breasts, looking down to the river. When she's resolved whatever has occupied her, she comes in.

"Nancy says hi to everyone." She sits beside me. "How are you doing?"

I assume she's wondering about my back. "To tell you the truth, it hurts not unlike hell."

"Nancy says we should all get to bed early tonight because it's a full moon. Maybe that's what you need."

"A full moon?" Karen's giving me a chance to exit, though I don't really want to, at least not alone, and I'm not sure Kate is listening anyway. She's lit another cigarette but hasn't yet turned to look at either of us.

"How about a walk? A short one?" asks Karen.

"Sure. Unless Kate has something in mind."

"Would you like to go for a walk with Toss and me, Mother?"

"No thank you, dear." She finally turns in her chair. "I'll just sit for a time."

"We could take a drive if you like." But she doesn't answer me. Karen leans and whispers, "We better just stay a bit," to which Kate insists, "You two go on with your walk. I'll be all right." Karen nods. I thank Kate for dinner.

She says, "Karen thinks I'm going senile. She thinks I talk to Vernon. But I know he's dead. I know Vernon's dead. Now you leave, but Wesley, be sure to come back again. We'll play cards sometime. We need to have a private chat, anyway."

"I'd be happy to, Kate. But I won't play for money if you know all the tricks—" Karen tugs at me. It's time to leave.

We're well beyond the east court before Karen asks me what Kate and I talked about.

"Am I right in guessing she did most of the talking?"

"She didn't mention any of what she's heard about me. I guess she knows you told me all that."

"No she doesn't. Maybe she's just sympathetic to the vilified."

"She was telling me about my mother. Did you know they were friends?"

"She mentioned it but I didn't know she was going to say much about it. It wouldn't occur to her you might rather talk about something else."

"I don't mind. Actually I was a little worried about her. At first she seemed so energetic and then she just ran down."

"There's less for her to do down here, nothing she can really take to. She hardly ever leaves the cabin. Maybe it wasn't such a good idea to come down. But anyway what did you think of her?" Before I can answer she says, "Don't answer. I take the question back. Discussing my family's how we got in trouble last time."

"I think she's great and you're too hard on her."

She flashes me a smile that implies she doesn't care what I think after all.

"You shouldn't trust her memory, you know. Whatever she told you about your mother, she may have been thinking of someone else."

Ahead of us kids shout accusations of "Liar!" at one another on the grass outside the pool, and behind is the sound of something closing fast. Missy shoots by us to the end of the path, where he skids and pounces around, waiting for us to come and play. Despite my back and all the other distractions attending dinner, I'm unreformed of lust for Karen, but the prospects are nowhere to be found in the lie of the well-tamed land before us. An orange frisbee curves lazily around the reach of a poplar. Below, a young girl waits for the descent, while around her the kids take a break to watch the reception.

This is when it begins, a great opening up. The branches give perspective to the late-day blue, a clear and penumbral sky redolent of childhood early bedtimes. Everything is wonderful and nothing adheres to the idea of time-place, of Tuesday at the park, but rather these moments are of an eighth weekday we've all been blind to, like a distant planet hiding from us in the gravitational shadow of another. I stop and watch. The girl catches and throws the frisbee in one motion. The kids run up to the pool fence. Karen and Missy begin a circle-chase.

As we walk on I recognize the girls as graduates from the junior wing who will be in one of my classes next year. I seem to make them nervous. The game deteriorates—easy catches are dropped, the frisbee hits the tree. Missy springs up to intercept but gets thwacked in the head and hits the ground with a whimper. He takes cover beside Karen.

"He loves me," she says with the delight of a little girl. "They say animals are good judges of character."

"Then you better be careful he doesn't get any ideas about your leg."

"Did you hear that, Missy? Kill! Sic'im! Sic!" But Missy is absorbed by a wound he can't lick. When the kids run along the outside of the fence and past the pool enclosure, he turns and instinctively considers joining their romp, but seems to decide he is beyond such puppy-play and ducks into Karen's stride, almost tripping her.

"What does she want to chat to me about?" I ask.

"She just wants her own opinion of you. Whether you're solid or not, whether you're a provider."

"What if I convince her I am those things?"

"Then you'll never know what she thinks because the town's opinion matters to her even more. If everyone else thinks you're bad news then it reflects on me, as far as she's concerned."

"So there's no winning her over?"

"I don't know, Toss. I've never been through this before."

I look back over the ground we've covered. I'd like to spend a less complicated afternoon here some day.

"Dogs on your hood," she says. My truck is no longer alone in the parking area but it does stand out. "What a curious life you lead. Do you suppose someone is trying to tell you something? I mean, couldn't they just leave a note?"

"Maybe they were illiterate. One in every four and a half adult Canadians couldn't leave me a note if they wanted to."

"But what's it mean?"

"Missy knows." Luckily the packet hasn't melted on my truck. I pull it open and feed a wiener to Missy. This is how you make friends and win over the unwashed.

Karen says, "You better give those to me or he'll get shot up in the hills somewhere trying to follow you home."

"No need to follow, I'll take you both along. We can pick up Kate and make an extended family of it. All of us living happily in the prettiest place around."

"You're a dreamer," she says with a laugh. She takes the pack from me and tosses it onto the grass, where Missy attacks it. Then she puts both arms around my neck and pulls me into the deepest kiss I've ever had in public. "A living and breathing hopeless romantic," she says.

IV

DOMINION

13

JULY: WE are all on the lip of a yawning debt. I spent last night on the pull-out bed at Karen's cabin and came home in the late afternoon to a phone call from Harrison Lee, whose land is just north of the hills. From his kitchen window he'd just seen two elk heading south through his fields and naturally I'd want to be on the lookout for them. Elk don't belong here—even the worst forest-fire season on record shouldn't drive them this far from home. For a week the sun has been swollen by the smoke from those fires and dulled to a comfortable pastel for two hours before dark. On the riverbank I sat and waited for the animals to appear, the river to the west a Venetian orange that didn't belong either. Apocalyptics everywhere are pointing out that this time the end really is near and anyone who doubts it should heed the heavens in August, a time of fire (meteor showers) and wonder (full lunar eclipse) just four days apart. But if the end is visible in portents, I doubt they will be so dramatic. More likely that hue of orange, those rumours of elk.

Something took shape in the glare from farthest upriver. At first I assumed it was an animal, though from a distance it was only a darkness reminding me of the spot on the sun that Marcie and I found so peculiar while sitting on our hotel balcony in San Miguel de Cozumel—the next morning we flew home through a solar radiation storm, the kind said to cause cancer in airline crews and frequent flyers and so strong it knocked out the power in Quebec. As the form grew nearer what eventually emerged could not have seemed stranger to me had it been a sea monster spouting campfire tunes. This stretch of the river has for years been the zone of inboard Evinrudes and pull-start skiffs, and around here watersport is a loud undertaking, so whoever was paddling the canoe was apparently from elsewhere. I was spotted and waved to. The boat finally rode into darker water. There was another wave and this time I waved back. He was now headed my way in the channel of slow water north of the island. Wire-rimmed glasses and a beard over orange flotation device on grey t-shirt.

"You must be Wesley Raymond," he called. So much for spotting elk. "Were you waiting for me?"

"I didn't think so."

"I've been asking around for you. I stopped by on my way upriver but you weren't in." He nosed into some reeds beneath me and pulled himself steady with a sapling that angled out from the bank. Then he almost capsized by reaching over and offering me a hand to shake. I nodded instead.

"Christopher Mulwray," he said. "It's appropriate we should meet like this."

"Possibly. You didn't happen to see any elk along the riverbank, did you?"

"You won't see elk in this region. I thought I might come across some deer but they tend to be quite timid."

"Really? You must be a zoologist or something."

"Not exactly. Though I've done my homework on animal life. One of my hobbies is evolutionary biology, so I guess I know the wrens from the starlings. I have something I'd like to show you. Maybe I could drive by in an hour or so, if you'll be in."

"Not unless you give me a clue."

"It concerns the artifacts you described in your letter to Dr. Lucas. He phoned me about them because I'm an archaeologist myself, actually a post-doc student, and I have an interest in your collection. I'm at the U of S."

"Is that your canoe?"

"Do you like it?"

"It seems to want to buck you."

"As they are wont to do."

"It's very quiet. Come on by tonight." I left the bank before he did and returned when he'd reached open water. Within minutes two deer stood at the river, somewhere near the Nashes' back yard.

Even shepherds, even peasants, are begrudged our simple ways. Whenever we found ourselves in Saskatoon I'd coax Marcie to the university rep theatre for a much-needed dose of non-American cinema. The last movie we saw together was *Jean de Florette*, with Depardieu as the hunchbacked city tax officer who changes his life and dies trying to succeed in a rural existence. Before the final credits rolled we both teared up and seemed about to share one of those moods some movies induce even in unlike-minded people, but as we made our way down the ramp to the first floor and out the door of the Arts Building we were subjected to a loud post-viewing analysis from a couple walking just ahead of us. She wanted to discuss the Jewish holocaust allegory in the film but he was intent on ridiculing the subtitles, which contained so many erroneous translations that the whole intellectual exercise had been ruined for him. She added the unrelated observation that in the States they never showed foreign-language movies like this in small cities. The two of them spoiled my mood so thoroughly that I kicked a small stone in frustration, and it skipped by the man at such speed that he glanced over his shoulder at me, more or less at the same moment Marcie gave me a glare. I told her it was an accident but when we got in the car she called me on my habit of wishing people ill fates. She said, "You get mad for the stupidest reasons. You go around cursing people under your breath. You should never curse anyone." Her point was that resistance takes many forms and that things sometimes connect whether or not we see them. Christopher Mulwray reminds me of my tendency to make snap judgements, mostly because anyone so self-fascinated invites them and I can picture him leaving the same theatre in loud complaint about the unrealistic animal demographics in Fellini ("There couldn't possibly be milkweed butterflies at that latitude. They are not wont to so wander.") But he isn't wholly unexpected, and now that he's here I realize I've been waiting for him, despite recent distractions.

Every evening for two weeks I've gussied up and gone a-courtin'. My back has sufficiently healed to allow me the role of tour guide of the valley for Karen, and we've been rewarded for our exertions with countless sightings of white-tailed and mule deer, including an eight-point buck.

Last weekend we took Kate to Saskatoon for some shopping. Karen left Kate and me alone in the Holiday Inn restaurant so we could have our chat. We were seated near a multi-generational assembly with three screaming infants, and next to a dessert trolley wheeled away every few minutes and then parked again minus another section of strawberry mousse. I would rather we had been almost anywhere else.

"You couldn't know how much Karen has been through," she began. We were done eating and she'd declined coffee refills for both of us. Her hands were on the table and mine ended up there too, finding nothing to gesture or distract us with.

"I have some idea, Kate."

"I want Mayford to be more of a real home for her than it has been. Now that Vernon's gone, it can be."

My focus wandered to a streak of chocolate icing smeared unappetizingly inside one of the glass cake-covers.

"I'd like her to feel comfortable there too."

"It can be a difficult place at times, especially for some people."

"I think I know what you mean."

"Yes, I suppose I don't have to tell you. And given...what you know about Mayford, do you think—"

"You know, I think we'd do better if you just laid out all your concerns so I could respond to them."

"All right. Do you think it's . . . acceptable for her to be seeing a married man?"

Just then a waiter swept in behind the trolley, spotted the offending cover and gave it a twist so that the smear was on the back side of the cake, safely hidden from the angle of presentation.

"That's her decision."

"You don't intend to take advantage of her, I know, but she's naturally lonely."

"Kate, I seem to spawn stories. Most of them are inaccurate. Which isn't to say there's not a true story with some unfavourable moments for me, but I'm really a pretty decent fellow."

"I don't know," she said, leaning back in her chair and looking off finally at something behind me. "My concern isn't that you're . . . not a good, honest man. But I have to keep watch. I just don't want her to . . . dispense with her standing in Mayford."

"Now that sounds like a pretty old line. I don't think your heart's into this chat. You've done the right thing to be concerned for her, but I sense you don't believe what you're saying."

"What don't I believe?"

"You don't think I can really damage Karen's standing, and you don't think her standing matters as much as her happiness."

She lowered her eyes to her hands for a few seconds, then closed them.

"Are you okay, Kate?"

Then she locked into me, dead on.

"I won't just give her up, Toss. You'll have to prove you're worthy."

"Of course I will. But I have to prove it to her, not to the whole town, and not even to you."

She stood.

"I'm going to the Ladies'. Right now I won't venture an opinion to her, but if I ever sense she's making a mistake with you I'll tell her so. And if you think I have no influence with her then you're mistaken. I'm her mother, after all, and part of what she's been through, we've been through together. Now put your money away, it's my treat."

And that was the end of our chat. I'd completely underestimated her resolve, and by the end she'd convinced me that I did have a potential rival in her.

Imagine my predisposition to read too much into Kate's suggestion to Karen that they go together to buy me another pair of boots. I came away from the trip quite unsure of my position and had trouble regaining my balance, especially in the boots, a deep brown cowhide with ropers' heels and pinto stitching. Though I didn't need them and they've taken a while to get broken in, and my feet hurt, I've worn them on my visits to the cabin as a matter of courtesy. I've also chauffeured Kate and Karen to a few ball games, which we watch from Kate's Chrysler LeBaron, angled with dozens more cars into the home-run side of the outfield fence.

About the only pleasure Karen and I have not shared is a movie. Dewey has continued his assault on Corporal Hall in the *News.* Meanwhile I'm still a card that Hall hasn't played, but I don't find myself waiting for the jingle-jangle of his spurs in my yard (not that I brood around home much any more). Dewey's been angry with me since Karen saw him in the Co-op last week and let it slip that I'm thinking of buying a VCR. He told her to tell me he would consider this an act of hostility, though in fact he simply resents me for spending my time elsewhere. I phoned him and told him I could no longer be bothered with his capricious silliness and would accept only a large cash payment as apology. All of a day later Perry told me Dewey had reserved my seat at our table in Honkers for John Murphy, the Navajo shortstop, who, word has it, is lovesick for his Arizona girl. Meanwhile Roger tells Perry (who tells me) that watching and listening to them is downright painful. To complicate things, the town is now blaming Dewey for the poor performance of a depressed infielder and even for the five-game losing streak with which the Bucks have opened the season, ignoring the real problem—the fact that the final American still has not arrived, and likely never will.

It hasn't rained for sixteen days.

At seven p.m. a blue Chevy van with a canoe strapped to the roof pulled into my yard. As I stood in the doorway Mulwray smiled at me and then just sat looking at the house and yard for about thirty seconds. He rolled down the window and asked if I had a dog that might like to bark at him for a while before he got out. "They have to be allowed to make their point," he said, "and I don't wish to surprise a biting animal." Rather than tell him I had no dog I went back in the house and waited for him to screw up his courage and come in. When he finally peeked his head in and scanned the floor I invited him to join me for a coffee at the kitchen table, where we conducted a somewhat one-sided getting-to-know-you chat.

"You're a schoolteacher," he told me. "Unless the gas station attendant was misinforming me. His directions certainly got me lost."

"He probably didn't know you were coming by canoe."

"I eventually pulled into a farmyard and took coffee and cookies with a couple named Ned and Alice. They said I might find you at the regional park, though they forgot to mention the seven dollars it would cost me at the gate. I got directions from someone there and then decided I'd paddle up when I learned you lived on the river. It's certainly quite a setting."

"I guess I don't think of it in those terms."

"But I'm sure not the only one lost around here this weekend. There were convoys of campers and motor homes on every road."

"Tourist haven."

"Ned said you're having your local sports day. I'd only planned to see you and do some canoeing but maybe I'll stay two nights, see the parade in the morning, take in the attractions."

"Sounds like I'm the only thing that isn't gonna cost you money. Now I don't mean to rush you, but given all the goings-on around here this weekend you can imagine how excited a local fella like me might get. I've been having trouble sleeping for a week. It always happens. And I'm about ready to begin the celebrations, so unless you're up to questioning a drunk, we should get down to business. You said you had something to show me."

"I do. But first I should ask you not to be so suspicious of me."

"It's just you're a cityboy."

"Please don't play the yokel. If you have something you intend to hide, I'd appreciate it if you'd tell me now and I'll go about my business another way." I wasn't up to this conversation so I stood and removed both coffee cups from the table. When my back was turned I heard him getting up, presumably to leave, so I told him to sit down and then reached for an American fifth of George Dickel from the cupboard. I hated to waste it on him but if you pull a detective stunt your best chance is to seem to play straight.

"Apologies," I said as I fetched the ice tray and twisted loose a few cubes. "If you've asked around, then you know I'm subject to dangerous mood swings. This is the nicest thing I've done for a stranger in years, so I'm hoping you'll answer a few questions yourself."

"I've never considered archaeology a business but I'll make you a deal. You show me the artifacts you described in your letter and I'll answer any questions you have about burial grounds. Naturally, I'd also be happy to accompany you to any sites you might want an opinion on."

"Dr. Lucas seems to have spent more time telling you about my letters than he did answering them."

He took his first sips with no complaint and followed them soon after, a good sign. We backed up the conversation a little and he told me the uninteresting history of his association with Dr. Lucas, whom he'd studied under and who'd supervised a thesis on "Economic Systems in Early Plains Settlements." Then he told me about the thesis. A long time later I got him onto more colourful topics.

"There haven't been enough burials excavated to identify many patterns or practices. Some human remains are found in rock cairns, some underground, but after hundreds or thousands of years it becomes difficult to assess the physical or cultural landscape of these burials."

"Are artifacts ever found alongside the remains?"

"In some cases. Usually ornaments, sometimes stone tools."

"I was wondering if what I found, the items I mentioned in the letter, if they might have been near a grave."

"I see." He waited for me but I wouldn't say more. "I would've guessed you didn't find those items in the field."

"I didn't say where I found them, but why would you guess one way or the other?"

"It concerns the special interest of mine I'd like to show you. The problem is that I can't show you until such time as we're both sober and can discuss a few matters at length, should we need to."

"Where exactly is this special interest?"

"It's under a sheet on my mattress."

"You hid it in a hotel room?"

"I sleep in the van. I'm sure that doesn't surprise you."

"You can always tell if something surprises me because my eyes get big and my mouth drops open. Where do you plan to park your van? It'll cost you twenty bucks for a camping space at the park."

"Twenty-three. I'll park under a tree or behind someone's granary."

"You're welcome to keep it in the yard."

"I hate to impose."

"No you don't. But seeing as how I'll be in and out all weekend maybe this is the best place to catch me. How are you on early mornings?"

"Tomorrow would be fine. I really would like to see the parade, though."

"At six you come in and give me a shout. I'll probably be in no shape to make breakfast."

"I'll take care of that. As for tonight, can you provide me directions to a fine restaurant?"

Now some high jester was casting my lines back at me.

"Best to head back to the park and snap up a few burgers. And stay out of the bar in town. It's pretty rough. Outsiders usually leave on their heads," I lie.

"Don't worry. I'm done asking around." We finished our drinks while discussing our respective university days. It turned out I once lived in the apartment building where he now had a one-bedroom. Remarkably, the place had the same super, a man I'd gone to the downs with once or twice, and he was a friend of Mulwray, who found the coincidence particularly amusing. By the time he drove out of the yard I had a vague feeling I'd been swindled, though I didn't know what I'd lost.

An hour later I was still drinking, trying to ward off a concern that certain laws had been broken and I had broken them, and that if Mulwray were to state his business to anyone in town I'd be forced to devise some tangled evasion or risk offering Corporal Hall yet another chance to nail me with a career-ending embarrassment. An insight into the nature of guilt in the criminal mind and the comfort that so far I'd played as well as possible were just enough to keep me from spilling my guts to the house. At least I'd arranged to keep Mulwray out of town at night so he couldn't sniff around and dig up long-buried troubles. With any luck he might not attract attention even during the day, given all the strange faces in town for the holiday weekend. I retrieved from the front seat of the truck all the notes Karen and I had made and the Polaroid shot of the skin, and clipped them together inside *The History of the Classical World* on my front-room bookshelf. When I'd shown Karen the photo she'd guessed it was an underwater rock painting, likely from Greece, or Crete to be exact, because the triangles drawn above a four-legged animal and on both sides of an "I" shape were common symbols of Minoan sacrifice. It turned out that her university specialties had made her a big fan of the Minoans. I stopped her just short of lugging out Kate's oversized art book of frescos from Knossos by asking her more about the "I" shape. She explained that it usually represented a two-headed axe, though it sometimes appeared as a tree or within the horns of a bull. The impaled triangle was the mark of sacrifice. So if nothing else, Karen's educated wrong guess provided a new perspective on the "I" or "H," which might well represent the shape of a tool. "Or might not," she said somewhat angrily after I let her in on the details of my finding. The other ideographs were less ambiguous, but even after supplementing our meagre knowledge of Plains Indian history Karen and I couldn't attach dates to the figures. What we needed was an expert more interested in answering questions than asking them. What we didn't need was Christopher Mulwray.

Tomorrow is Canada Day. I cap the bottle, decide on one more swig, then recap it and lay me down.

14

EARLY MORNING, slightly hung over. Mulwray is whistling "The Early Morning Rain" in my kitchen and seems very much to have the jump on me. I look out my bedroom window. No rain.

"Good morning," he says.

"Please shut up."

"Certainly. Here's some coffee. I couldn't find the filters so I used a paper towel. I hope you're not in the habit of using these. The wood fibres will damage bodily systems." He sets down the mug with a baleful smile that brings on its own ill effects.

"Forgive us. I'm not always myself, especially in the morning."

"I slept out on the ground last night," he says. "I've never seen a blacker sky—"

"It's never seen your kind either."

"Perhaps not. The starlight was practically enough to—"

"I should've warned you, you're taking your life in your hands by sleeping unsheltered out there. Some monster is running around killing cattle, ripping them to their components. Maybe you'd better keep inside tonight." He gives me an assessing look and apparently decides he's missing a big joke and coughs up a short laugh. Then he looks at me again and shakes his head.

"I'm such a cutup, aren't I?"

"I'll say," he says. "We've got about two and a half hours to get to town for the parade, so why don't I fix us some food while you tell me about your collection."

"Fine. Let's cook something up. I don't know much about their origins, but as I told Dr. Lucas there are several flint blades and arrowheads, three trade axes, a crooked knife, a firesteel, three catlinite pendants."

"Is that all?" He beats the eggs and slides the mess into the skillet.

"Sure."

"That's a nice collection, though small, of course. How did you come by the stuff?"

"I stole it from a dead man."

"You're telling me this is all from a burial ground? I'd like to see the area."

"You don't believe there is a burial ground, at least not one with all that in it."

"You're right. I don't even believe it's likely the artifacts are all from the same tribe. Will you show me the ground?"

"Not just now I won't."

"The artifacts?"

"After breakfast maybe. Till then let's not talk any more."

Breakfast is quiet except for what I think is unusually loud chewing on Mulwray's part. He's done something strange to the eggs but they taste good. Though I try to placate my headache with pleasant childhood emotions about parade mornings, I can't seem to retrieve any because the idea of floats unfortunately associates with coke floats, which I once got sick on, a particularly vivid technicolor memory. I steady myself by staring into my mug of Columbian dark. A biology teacher once told me the wonderful coffee scent that wafts up when you open the vacuum pack is in fact produced by ground-up insect bodies sprinkled on the top layer. I think of these things only when they can hurt me.

When I have the confidence, I go to my room for a paper and pen, then return to the table. Mulwray watches me write.

I am going to be in public today and it's important that I get some things straight. First, when speaking of Wesley Raymond in the third person I will refer to him as Wesley Raymond, using both names. When the two of us are together with others I'll try not to say his name at all. Second, should anyone ask me why I'm in town, I'll say I'm a baseball fan from Saskatoon. I am in housewares and advise against aluminum products. My visit was prearranged. Third, I'll say nothing to anyone about our conversations. Whatever Wesley Raymond reveals to me is between the two of us. I'll neither speak nor write to anyone regarding anything I learn while in and around Mayford. This condition can be overridden only with the agreement of Wesley Raymond. Fourth, I will not make casual observations about the behaviour of local people or wildlife because I am consistently wrong in my understanding of the world and often miss even the largest of ironies.

"Read this. Sign it," I say.

He reads. "This isn't legal, of course."

"There's legality and then there's what's right in this instance. If you sign this I'll trust you to live by it. Otherwise you can go to town and stir up all sorts of shit for everyone and still never find out why I made this small request."

"I pose no threat to you."

"Yes you do or I wouldn't offer you this much."

He signs with a serious hand. I examine the signature. Then we shake on it.

"You do the dishes, I'll get something for you," I say. The contract clips with the other papers in the classical history book. The catlinite pendants are in my box of cassettes. I remove one and unwrap it from the newspaper. When I show it to Mulwray he dries his hands on a dish towel, then dries them again and examines it.

"You found this with everything else?" he asks.

"Not this one. When I was ten years old my brother gave me that. He said he'd found an Indian grave. He didn't say exactly where it was, but that's where he got the pendant. I've never been able to find the grave and he's not around to find it for me."

"And the other material?"

"There are three pendants here in the house very much like that one. I lifted them from the rest of the stuff, which is still where I found it. Now you might tell me about your special interest. Then I'll trade some more secrets."

Karen phones, says she and Kate will see me at the parade. She says she missed me last night, which for a moment makes me feel like a minion of luck and I tell her so. "What was that?" she asks. "I said I feel like a million bucks." She wishes me a happy Canada Day and says Kate passes on a happy *Dominion* Day. Just before Karen hangs up I hear Kate protesting in the background, "It is *not* the same thing."

I step outside to see what's become of Mulwray. The van's back doors are open. Inside, he roots. The hills to the south and west are lightly hazed with whatever moisture was around to collect overnight. The day will be hot again. A year ago today it was 44 Celsius or 111 Fahrenheit, and people with air conditioners lent out their homes until sundown. I had a holiday dinner with Cora and Perry in the basement of their house. Perry pointed out the cracks in the concrete walls and we considered the inevitable failure of backfill strategies. That night in the front yard the three of us watched an other-worldly display of lightning. The bolts curled on themselves and scrawled pigtails, alphas and omegas, and it went on for hours, so distant there was no thunder, and though the wind was strong and blowing into us, the storm never moved. Marcie left three days later. The television showed fireworks over New York harbour. When you first take hold of something you know you will carry a great distance, there is the question of weight, of whether or not you can keep a grip.

Now that breakfast is put away I feel an incipience that gathers itself in the season. I've been unduly nasty to Mulwray. Though bad manners provide me a useful strategy, Marcie would attest to a less calculated origin, a history of seasonal if subtle mistreatment. That Mulwray is full of purpose and seems not to care about my rough edges is just slightly beside the point. Something about speaking to him leaves me with an unpleasant aftertaste, but this is likely the fault of my tongue. He emerges from the van at the very moment I spit into the crushed rock around my front step. This time I smile first.

We get comfortable there, out on the step. He holds up a few sheets of paper and waves them around to punctuate his speech.

"These are photocopied pages of a letter written in the summer of 1910 to the American Museum of Natural History in New York by a Richard Wallace. Wallace introduces himself as an educated American from the northern states. He probably planned to homestead in Saskatchewan, though I've never found record of his having filed on any land. The only other facts I really know about him are that he wrote two letters to the museum asking if they'd be interested in employing him to collect Indian material. He baited them with descriptions of the collection he'd already found, belonging to an unnamed local collector Wallace described as a former North-West Mounted Police constable who later became an Indian agent among a few tribes. This contact was Wallace's sole selling-point, and the fact that he wouldn't name him suggests he was aware of this. What he may not have known was that there wasn't any great demand for most of what he'd come across. The item that most interested the museum is described here"—Mulwray tweaks the pages—"and Wallace's letter was in fact filed in the museum's archives as field correspondence, which likely means they wrote back to him. There's no record of their letter, but I can guess what they were after."

He hands me the paper. The handwriting displays the sort of disciplined flourish I associate with old people and early times; that is, the words are lovely but unreadable. Mulwray runs his pointed finger along some lines in mid-page and reads aloud, "It is to be noted that my contact is in possession of a Blood calendar in the form of a school notebook and covering the years 1810 to 1883 as recorded by Bad Head and passed on to Weasel Horse. Weasel Horse and Chief Owl recited the calendar to White Bull's brother, who recorded it in the notebook. This book is, of course, of great historical value in itself. I have the assurance of my contact that an older version of this calendar, in the form of a buffalo skin, exists, and can be obtained with the necessary means. Acquiring these items will entail a great cost, yet the sum I request is surely a mere pittance to your institution—"

"I can see you're excited, Mulwray, but why are you telling all this to me?"

"Wallace collected his mail at a delivery post twenty miles north of here, so he must have been somewhere in this area. I've made enquiries to every amateur archaeologist or branch of the society in this part of the province, but no one's come across this collection. Then out of the blue you describe almost the same list of items Wallace had, and you live right in the heart of his country."

"But what you're really interested in is the notebook, which I didn't find."

"No. The notebook turned up on its own a few years after Wallace first described it. There's no pedigree but somehow it landed in the Glenbow Archives in Calgary, among several other calendars—they're called winter counts. It's the older calendar I'm interested in, the buffalo skin. I think Wallace was wrong, it's not Blood but Sioux. Anyway, I'd like to know what became of it, whether Wallace and his agent came up with 'the necessary means.'"

"Don't you think the museum would have covered all the angles?"

"Not if they didn't believe him. By 1919 the museum's big guns had been through the region, collecting and recording their observations of Indian culture. Pliny Earle Goddard. Alanson

Skinner. Simms from the Chicago Field Museum. The skin wasn't found."

"This would be some kind of feather in your cap, wouldn't it? There's just a hint of Klondike fever in your voice. What would you do with this thing if you found it?"

"That depends a great deal on where I find it. The question of ownership is sometimes pretty murky. I might make a pitch on behalf of one or another institution."

I get up and go into the house and just keep walking straight into the bathroom. I lock the door for some reason, the first time in months. Before long I'm standing in the shower remembering the day Perry told me he was allergic to cholera so he couldn't help anyone with the harvest. It was bad enough on the tractor four months a year, he said. I didn't respond except to note to myself that he had a never-depleting stock of oddball, lying excuses for not doing things. Then one day I was in Cora's kitchen while she was telling someone on the phone about Perry's allergy to his work in the summer, "everything from speargrass to chlorella." It could be that I misheard him, and now, whenever I'm tempted by one of the many flavours of deceit, it seems important that I know which one of us made the mistake. Cholera or chlorella? A mud cloud.

I find Mulwray standing in the kitchen, fingering the pendant and tilting it into the window-grid of sunlight. I wear a grey towel.

"I've decided you're an acquired taste. We'd be better off taking one another seriously. I wasn't exactly up front about the stuff. It belongs to my ex-neighbour and he left it in his house when he left his wife. She told me about it and asked what she should do with it. She let me take a look at what I assumed was the whole collection, but then she brought it to me. I don't know what else there might be or where in the house they've got it stashed. She gave me the pendants. I never investigated further until I wrote to Lucas. Meanwhile Wanda, the wife, she left town and locked up the house without instructions to anyone about what she wants done with the house or its contents. So what I'm saying is, if you want to look at the collection you'll have to be willing to pull a little harmless break-and-enter. I'll go along if you like."

Mulwray assumes a sincere but cartoon version of a crestfallen man. His head actually droops. "What should we do?" He is helpless.

"Not my decision. You mull it over. I'm going to town."

"It's not the trespassing itself that bothers me as much as the legal complications for my acquiring the material. Let's not decide just now."

"I'm not deciding anything. You are. Now let's get ready. You don't want to miss the parade."

He hands me the stone, nods his head at the floor. "Wesley Raymond," he says. "I'll remember, but maybe you should tell me something about baseball."

We come upon Main Street from the east on Fourth, park and walk to the intersection, into the annual day of crowds. The strange aspect of these mornings is that for once not all the faces in town are familiar, and the ones that might be are hidden by sunglasses and hats. Bodies are tucked into lawn chairs. All bare limbs look the same. Mid-point of the parade, the marching band has started up a few blocks away. Two underlings of Corporal Hall ride ever closer on their blinkered mounts. Moving right to left, the procession is upon us.

In time I leave Mulwray agape at the majorettes and move against the flow of the pageant. Karen is nowhere. The band halts in uniform two-tone blue. They begin a near synchronous dance step, a boxer's shuffle, a pitch and sway. Somewhere in the deep a cornetist reaches to catch his hat and loses touch with the sequence. He generates a wave of hesitation in the players around him. For a moment the music itself is on the edge, and by now, though no one in the crowd could name the tune, we all recognize it as a tv theme from the seventies and could hum a few bars ourselves, so the band has certain expectations to meet. Trained for the threat of interior breakdowns, the outside players keep the line together and effect a sort of domino recovery. Thank God we've avoided the terror of ceremony gone wrong. We smile dumbly and applaud as the drums take over and the feature act leaves on the double. These are local kids but I never recognize them with their faces strapped and billowed and stuck with wood or metal. When I begin to move through the crowd again, someone beans me with a wrapped candy. I turn to see a clown trailing the band, pointing at me and laughing. Faces on both sides of the street smile and silently implore me to take my lumps with good humour. I pick up the candy and hand it to a little girl, then bend over and peer at the clown as if I don't know who it is, as if it could be anyone.

"Wesley!" Cora waves from the other side of the street. She calls something else but I can't make it out. A few feet away from her, Perry emerges from a knot of his friends and crosses the street just in front of the Royal Bank float.

"Morning," he says. "She wants to know if you're going to the noon ball game. The Bucks against Calgary."

"You haven't seen Karen around, have you?"

"No. Unless she was that clown."

"Maybe." Convertibles, trailer beds hitched to half-tons, plastic carnations, metacarpal flutter.

"Here comes the babe-mobile," Perry says. With the approach of Wally McGregor's El Camino, loaded with the Gopher Queen and her four runners-up, Perry's friends fall into a chorus of low hoots like so many ventilating gorillas. The girls ignore them and look instead at their teacher, who smiles and blows them a kiss. Having restrained himself for my sake, Perry can only blush.

"Tell Cora I'll see her at the game. Does she need me for anything?"

"I don't think so." He is very much distracted by the receding queen. "Do you suppose any of those girls knows where to find a fine restaurant?"

"Could be, but you'll never find out unless you separate from that pack over there."

"How about you and me teaming up again?"

"That wasn't such a good idea the first time. Better to work alone in that sort of thing."

"Easy for you to say."

"That's just the reality of it." He leaves without a word more and crosses over to Cora and passes on my message, then rejoins his friends. Cora nods and beams at me. I look back to Perry. He's disappeared.

When the parade is over, the spectacle floats on. We remove to the fairgrounds. Mulwray has the nerve to barter over the admission price so I try turning it all into a great joke for Billy, the volunteer ticket-seller, who manages to look both puzzled and askance every time Mulwray opens his mouth. "He's just putting you on, Billy. This guy's loaded. He's here to lay some money against the Bucks, thinks a lot of people will take him up." By the time we move on, Mulwray and Billy have twenty dollars on the noon game.

"You're a piss-ass, Mulwray." He keeps quiet as I tour the grounds and play my advantage a little more. "This is little league.... This is fastball, women's.... This is the chariot track.... This is the horse ring.... This is, of course, the main diamond and grandstand, behind which you'll find games of chance and hot dogs. Those there, are baseball teams." My cover of baseball fan would be risky if I thought anyone was likely to start a conversation with a stranger in a t-shirt that read "Sceptic for Nature." He knew baseball to see it, he assured me as we drove to town, but the terms I tested him on weren't familiar and he was unduly interested in their etymology. Where did the notion of "bullpen" come from, he wondered. Did I think there might be a Spanish connection, "the place where are kept the dangerous beasts that will meet the hero slash-hitter"? I warned him to use sentences of no more than three words and to hold no thought for more than five seconds else a foul ball might strike him dead. We found a parking space in an improvised motor-home court and agreed to split up for a while so I could visit my many friends and enjoy my yearly day of "festive communality," as he put it.

The view of the grandstand from my side of the right-field fence: a dominance of white in a pointillism of shirt colours massed in a failing circle with a shaded centre covering the aisle steps. The backstop screen masks the crowd as a single face, like that of the moon—if the moon had ears that dissolved and reformed. It occurs to me that I'm looking at the man in the street, though he's not a man and this isn't the street. The public no longer exists—there is only audience, a dynamics of reaction. Why do pollsters see the need to calculate an ever-growing "ignorance factor"? And why do we have pollsters?

"Toss?" It's Karen, close up and detailed. "Didn't you hear me the first time?"

"I guess not. I think I'm becoming agoraphobic or something."

"What's that? A fear of farmers?"

"Something like that. Where have you been?"

"Mother wasn't feeling well. We almost didn't come to town." She's watching the game so I do too. Murphy fumbles a routine ground ball to short and Calgary scores. "Aren't these guys terrible? Anyway, she's better now. We looked around for a place to park and watch the Bucks from the car but all the spaces were gone. It's too hot for her to sit outside. She doesn't think so, but I do. I left her in the car with Patty Stewart, watching fastball." The next batter hits the first pitch to the second baseman, who takes the ball to the bag and relays to first for a double play. "That Lacousiere's pretty smooth."

"You know him?" I ask.

"I met him at the party I phoned you from a few weeks ago."

"How well do you know him?"

"Is there any one thing you can point to that makes you such a jerk?"

"That's enough. That explains everything just fine. It isn't that I was too worried or that I have good reason to be superstitious about this particular weekend, especially as it affects my so-called personal life."

With no warning she gives me a kiss, right there in front of a thousand people, most of whom know I'm still married but aren't looking. I say, "You know, your lips move when you remember to keep a secret."

She shows no sign of having listened to me. "I'm going back to Mother but we'd appreciate a visit sometime." As she moves off I get my first full view of what she's wearing, which isn't much. The especially wide stripes on her shorts naturally call attention to themselves. Are women's knees flatter in the back than men's knees or do I just pay more attention to female joints?

"Glad she's gone. It was getting hard to concentrate out here," calls Two-Four, the right fielder. He watches her a few seconds more, then flashes me a grin.

"How many outs?" I ask.

He turns and checks the scoreboard. "Two outs." Then he notices his infield glaring at him and says, "Can't talk right now, Toss. It might hurt my game." I know the feeling. Cora once confronted me with "Wesley, are you what they'd call depressed?" I told her my emotional state was more accurately a *com*pression—"I'm compressed"—a term to describe the sort of short-breathed control I maintained over the black months. Cora was simply asking if I didn't maybe have something I'd like to get off my chest but, because the struggle to free myself would have been perilous, I stayed narrow-eyed and reticent. Of course, I also indulged myself by sleeping through entire weekends but on those days it was particularly easy to keep my mouth shut. Sometimes long explanations constrict us, even when they're truly enlightening—though it doesn't necessarily follow that aspiring to yolkheadedness can bring us through extreme circumstances.

Anyone who's ever driven with a hitch knows that the usual laws of wheel direction are reversed when you're backing up. That is, you turn right to move left and vice versa. Long before Perry got his tractor-driving job I passed on to him this law of opposite reversal, but here in the grandstand, as I watch him and his friends cruise the grounds in a Cherokee jeep, I'm hard-pressed to remember what other useful knowledge I've imparted. There's the secret of where to bury beer in the river sand so it will stay cold but not be stolen away by the current. There's not to drink and drive, granted, but there's also where to cut into the carpet of a car trunk for the purpose of concealing an open bottle of liquor. There's fly casting. How to find arrowheads. How to fire a rifle. How to correct a slice, how to draw a cue ball. There's how to throw a punch and the dirty tricks you can get away with when fighting a stranger in your town that you won't get away with in his. There's don't trust hunches about inside straights and there's two queens likely win in a four-handed game, and I don't know what else. All of which leaves a less than innocent record of direction. Then again, despite his wild streak Perry is a model of kindness when it matters, though I didn't teach him that, and people are glad to look out for him. Others of us form the habit of looking over our shoulders.

Dewey's been confiding the dope on Murphy, or rather Murphy's girlfriend. The story seems to be winding down and is important only in that it allows us to forget our differences, so there's not much I can recount about the girlfriend except that she runs track at some university and Murphy will probably jump the team to see her after this weekend's tournament (this strictly hush hush).

"It's sort of romantic," he concludes. "Did you buy your machine yet?"

"I'm not buying one till the Palace goes under. I can't see why it should bother you."

"What bothered me was the gesture of betrayal. Outright disregard for friendship."

"You have something under your ear. At first I thought it was shaving cream."

He takes a Kleenex from his pocket and wipes his face clean. "It was a good time. I've never been in a parade before. The basement of the town hall has a whole closetful of costumes. Apparently there used to be a group that put on a play each year at the school."

"That was a long time ago. I saw *The Mikado* when I was a kid."

"I'm thinking revival. We could put on a show."

"That's very Mickey Rooney of you, but people have other things on their minds." Dewey's still selling his police-coverup-of-brutal-animal-killings angle and chooses to ignore a loss of momentum. The nightly patrols have devolved into weekly movable drunkfests, and a few of the more persistent letter-writers are setting heads a-nodding by pointing out a lack of evidence. Cora believes Corporal Hall has come to be thought of as hard done by.

The game, of course, continues. There are loudspeaker announcements, the truncated ping of aluminum bats meeting balls. Four-zip in the top of the fourth. I'm squinting. I don't remember the runs. I don't know how we got here.

Dewey says, "I know the half of it. Last night at the Palace I struck up a chat with this farmer from down south who's keeping afloat by working for the government as an assessor. Spends his afternoons sitting at kitchen tables with some other farmer and his sons, going over the balances and having to tell them he can't help. The banks don't make many mistakes. People think he's a last-ditch and then they go under despite him."

"Who's he visiting in this area?"

"You kidding? It could be anyone." The up-side is the short-term growth in auctions, though bargain hunters aren't entirely comfortable benefiting from suicides and hard leavings. The lucky ones arrange to cash-rent from the bank the land they've been working all their lives, but the fade accelerates, the population now less than a million in a province the size of France. A lot of very hard-working people unable to forget the rote of strictures they've lived by and trusted, carried to a point in life when they realize they've been cheated by their sense of honest work, which is something other than a sense of entitlement. Here is your hard luck and here is some more. Here is orphanhood. I live among a soon-to-be-rare breed, going the way of eight-tracks and eight-cylinders and the rich Corinthian soil.

"It makes people want to do violence on something," I say. From his shirt pocket Dewey pulls out a pair of shades and slides into them. "Doesn't it?"

"There were ancient ceremonies for that kind of feeling."

"Yes there were. Human sacrifice, in fact. You seem to be moving people in that direction. People are wishing you ill, you know."

"Maybe soon they'll stop avoiding me. I wonder who'll break first?"

"What kind of confrontation are you shooting for?" I look around for signs of restiveness in the crowd.

"Just someone to snap and right out state the truth. Someone to show some conviction that some things might *not* have a reason for being."

Before I have time to ponder this new light on Dewey I see Mulwray waving at me from the walkway in front of the grandstand. He won't stop waving. Finally I signal him to come join us and he bounds up the steps with a paper cup of Coke held ridiculously high, giving him the look of an Olympic torch bearer who's given in to commercial pressures. He slides into our row and takes my open flank.

"Dewey Beyer, Christopher Mulwray."

"How do you do, Mr. Beyer. I'm here to watch baseball."

"Did anyone ever tell you you look like Hooper in *Jaws*?"

Mulwray is unprepared. "I can assure you I'm not."

Dewey lifts his shades and looks at me blankly. He says to me,

"I have his assurance and that's good enough for me." There follow a few moments of silence during which Eldon strikes out looking on four pitches.

"Signs of advanced stages," I say. "They don't seem to be having much fun out there."

"You make it sound like a game," says Dewey.

"Perhaps they should employ the bullpen," says Mulwray.

Dewey leans across me. "What did you say your name was?"

"I was introduced as Christopher Mulwray. I'm an acquaintance.... " He nods at me. "We're acquaintances."

"Toss, I hope you haven't neglected to mention to Mr. Mulwray the investigation. Mr. Mulwray, you should know that Toss here is under investigation for the crazed murders of... well, we believe the victims were likely cattle."

"There was some mention of a monster." Mulwray laughs and then breaches contract. "People here seem to like the diversion of spook stories."

"You mean spooky stories. I wouldn't call it diversion."

I say, "Me neither. Diversion is a water word."

"Well, whatever. I don't believe in monsters."

"Then you haven't lived," says Dewey. "Then you don't know anything."

By the time Dewey begins to ask him about his t-shirt, Mulwray is uncomfortable enough to excuse himself. A measure of our perceptiveness is how quickly we recognize even the entry-level misfit, and Dewey pegged Mulwray before he sat down. The act of exclusion such powerful fun we never worry where the impulse originates.

"Mulwray, Mulwray, what does that name trigger?" asks Dewey. "I take it you don't know him real well."

"Acquaintances, a mutual friend. He's staying in my yard."

"It's something Japanese."

Between innings Eldon walks back to the screen and calls up to me while strapping on his catcher's gear. He asks if I wouldn't like to see some action myself, maybe pinch-hit for him next time around, then grins at the very thought. His cheekbones are smeared with eye black. The conversation is very much directed at me, Eldon being among those who blame Dewey for Murphy's slump. "We're still the best show in town," he says. He pulls his mask down and finally acknowledges Dewey with a menacing stare, which he breaks off by popping the mask up again to spit one last stream of tobacco juice.

"Gumshoe!" says Dewey as Eldon moves in behind the plate. "That's it! *Chinatown*, 1974, Jack Nicholson on the trail of a hydro-dam builder whose wife thinks he's cheating on her. The guy's name is Hollis Mulwray, and he's worried a dam his partner wants him to build won't hold because of shifting earth—"

"Shale."

"Yeah, shale. This is a bad sign, Toss. Maybe you should stay away from that guy."

"What's Japanese about *Chinatown*?"

"It's gumshoe. I've always thought it sounds Japanese. The Jap word for a north wind or something."

Unquestionably time to leave. Talking to Dewey reminds me how susceptible I am to subliminal directives received on extreme frequencies I don't consciously detect though the dogs and mice within me run for cover. I set out for the swimming-pool on the edge of the fairgrounds, and the nearest telephone, to call Cora's house and see if she's on her way yet. Pass behind the grandstand and the wheel of fortune, cork-pistol duck shoot, ball and milk-bottle booths, quiet testaments to the low ceiling on disposable income in these parts, on past the kiddies' Ferris wheel, run by a small and suitably grubby troupe of travelling midway vets, one of whom blasts the small gathering of families with Z.Z. Top and "Tush," doing aerial battle with the pool's loudspeaker radio fleet, Springsteen's "Born in the U.S.A." The pool building is an ugly cinderblock thing but features a staff of young girls in bikini bottoms and damp t-shirts, though admittedly their feet always look dirty. It's a warm feeling not to be beyond the age when weathered toes can send me into glandular swoon. Polly ("Wanna") Huehmann, the going-on-senior volleyball captain and hot date queen, pulls tight the cord of the staff phone and stands in the office, dialling the number I tell her and asking me not to tie up the line for too long, this being a favour on her part. "Of course," I assure her, looking anywhere but at her itsy-bitsy yellow Speedo, "I'll be brief." The view is of the overcrowded deck and water and the noise seems to mitigate the primacy of basic elements, more concrete than earth and as much light glistening off coconut-scented PABA as off water. There's no answer. I hand Polly the receiver and say, "Not there," and smile. She smiles back and holds my stupid gaze for a moment before turning to hang up, the cord going limp in a lazy twist, brushing her thigh and swinging into the wall.

She turns back to me.

"I support you, Mr. Ray," she says. "I mean, I'm on your side. Most of the lifeguards are, except Melissa isn't sure but that's because of her mom—she's on the school board and probably that dumb Coca May—and she thinks the whole town's being punished by God because of one or two bad apples, and you're one of them. She thinks it's all connected."

"And you don't?"

"Melissa's mom is so stupid. Anyway, nobody else here blames you for the drought, really."

An hour later, having planned a rendezvous with the Shaulters at their cabin later in the day, I climb out of Kate's car just in time to flag down Perry's crew. Perry jumps out and tells his friends he'll see them at the races. As we walk along towards the main diamond he informs me that Cora's noontime stop was slotted to be a visit to the crafts in the rink. But I'll *never believe*, he insists, never believe what just happened.

"What's it-send-dairy?" he asks.

"Incendiary?"

"I guess so." Averted pupils, jaw twitching out of alignment.

"Anything you want to tell me?"

Not fifteen minutes ago, Perry and his friends spotted Dewey walking out towards the show ring. They came up behind him in the truck and when he moved over to let them pass, the driver, Matthew Short, moved over himself and trailed him for a few feet until Dewey stopped and came back to the driver's window.

"Then I realize we don't really know what we're doing, just playing around. None of us really know him to talk to, but he seems to know us. He says he heard Corporal Hall's given us guys details about making a ... device and that we're sending it his way. He says, 'You just make damn sure Toss Raymond's name doesn't come up.' Then he walks off." At this point I veer away and take a seat on someone's open tailgate. He follows. "I swear I don't know anything about it, Toss. I don't even know what it is. Matthew and them didn't know what he was talking about."

"Dewey's just strumming you boys. You tried to intimidate him and just that fast he's set you up to be implicated in a criminal act."

"That doesn't sound fair, we were just playing around.... And I don't think I get it."

"Well, how many different ways can he run this one? Let's say, I don't know, Dewey's take at the theatre's getting pretty small, so Jasper would sell it to him for nothing just to be free of the property taxes. Then suppose Dewey torches the place to collect the insurance. It'd be too obvious unless we'd all been waiting for someone else to torch it for him."

"So we get blamed."

"Blamed but not charged, which would make it look all the more like Hall's idea to persuade him to leave Mayford."

"And Beyer'd collect the money."

"Yeah, in theory. But it won't happen. Dewey doesn't do things for money."

"Then *what—*"

"He wants an audience. He's starting to try too hard, but I think we're just supposed to admire how easily he set you up."

"But I wouldn't have seen his angles."

"But he knew it'd get back to me, and he knew I'd see one. That's why he dropped my name."

Neither of us speaks for a time. I actually doubt whether Dewey had any such reasons for saying what he said, but like us all, Perry isn't comfortable with effects that don't have obvious causes.

"Why don't you guys talk in person more?" Perry asks. "The rest of us don't want to be messengers."

"I'll tell him that, but don't you try to. Just stay the hell away from him, and tell your friends to do the same."

I hit the ground walking. Perry trails me silently. He's angry at me for being Dewey's friend, but he won't say so. I try to give him something else to focus on.

"You might call home from the pool phone. Tell Polly she let me use it and you'd appreciate the same favour."

"You don't listen to me. I told you Cora's not home, she's at the craft show."

"I know that, but Polly doesn't. You've got to learn to see daylight and run to it. *Make advances.*"

Late-breaking news. You can never know the exact dimensions of your confinement any more than you can know how far the ground goes down or comes up inside you. Moments when everything is worthy of time-accelerated newspaper headlines. *Running Board Rusting. Napkin Escapes on Noon Wind. Overhead Line Dips. Fastball Rides High. Folks Chatter. Wright's Dog Randy Sniffs Child in Stroller—Lifelong Trauma Predicted. Wind Shifts but Serviette Makes Getaway. Sharp Curveball Nabs Catcher. Bicycles Fill Day's Empty Spaces. Spokes Clatter.*

After the watercolours and the price of a ten-by-twelve listing-

and-abandoned-farm-building-against-stormclouds for Cora's spare room, after I've separated her from the ladies-of-volunteer-family-updates, we find space to sit in on the feature game's ninth inning. The Bucks are down only one going in, and tie it up on a sacrifice fly. Two out and no one on, on a one-and-two pitch, and Murphy takes a hanging curve over the left-field fence. And we win. Fans in cars and campers ringing the field lean on their horns and there is suddenly a lot of milling about the home dugout. Cora observes that the town is very obviously starved for success. Eldon breaks away from the crowd and comes to the backstop. Maybe because his face is still blackened, his expression is unfamiliar, peaceful and epiphanous, something to be later debased and hardened into words like younevercantell. He sees me, grins. I return a thumbs-up. Cora and I wait out the slow dispersal from the stands.

"I'll stay over tomorrow night. We'll get an early start, be in before noon."

"That's fine," Cora says. "Aren't you coming to the game tomorrow?"

"I might see you, but just in case. I could end up tending a few rapid boils tonight, and maybe tomorrow."

"I hope this doesn't have to do with Perry."

"So does he. Don't worry. He doesn't make trouble, just meets up with it too much. My theory is it's just a stage."

"Stages don't last ten or twelve years."

"Sure they do. You're thinking of phases. Anyway, he calls his own shots now, and he'll muddle through better than most."

"Through what?"

"Anything. Through anything." I give her a quick, one-armed hug. "I've got to find someone." She says I look good, no doubt thinking I'm going to meet Karen, and suggests I gun down a kewpie doll. When I leave she's peeking into the bag at her purchase.

I find Walter Wall leaning on a railing, watching parents lead their kids around the petting zoo.

"Walter."
"Toss." We're both staring at short animals here. "Not much other use for a pony like that."
"You're right there."
"I bet that old goat wonders where he's ended up."
"He never saw this coming."
"I bet not."
"Nope."
He sets a foot on the lower rail.
"You think Zinvalena'd do okay at Saskatoon, do you?"
"I'm sure of it, Walter."
"You're the same guy hangs out with that Beyer fellow."
"I see your point, but you can trust me on Zinvalena's chances. I mean, if she wants to go."
"Uh-huh." He glances my way without actually looking at me. "Your goat is a strange animal, ain't he?"
"It's probably just we don't get many around here."
"Uh-huh."
"Guess I'll be off now, Walter."
"All right then. Thanks for the opinion."
"You bet."
In a half-hour's walk and a ten-minute stationary chat with Walt Sandor about the growing unworkability of automotive metals, I cross paths with Mulwray twice, Perry once, and Dewey not at all. Mulwray has accepted his mission and reasoned away his criminal turn with a bit of Latin that sounds like "Ow-dah-kays fawr-too-nah yoo-waht," which he says translates as nothing ventured and so on. Perry found Matthew and the gang and told them he'd be running alone for a while but his fighting days weren't yet past should anyone get his cousin in more trouble and they knew what he meant. He was on his way back to the pool because Polly wasn't behind the desk when he first went in. He has, it seems, taken a notion. She'll already have a date for the next several months, he assured me, and if she doesn't she'll say she

does. And you'll be happy for her, I told him. Just don't mention the weather. "Stick to concretes. If you can't touch it, don't talk about it," was my advice, which for some reason embarrassed him. But this is how he needs to think, at his age. Perry hadn't seen Dewey for a half-hour and when I asked Mulwray he just shook his head and said, "Most people here are quite friendly." As we leave the grounds I take one last cruise by the venues but come up empty. At the gate I pull over and get out to fetch Billy from the ticket hut while Mulwray waits in the truck. Billy bounds up to the passenger door and begins laughing as the two of us lean on either side of the window, watching Mulwray flop around trying to dig deep-stuffed bills from his pockets. He comes up with a crinkled sum of eleven eighty-five, which he hands over without the wit to apologize. Billy says, "You must've found a lot of action to be cleaned out before you're paid off. Hope you didn't lose the farm or anything." Then I tell Mulwray we'll make an exception though he's from out of town and accept a cheque for the balance. Besides being cheap, Mulwray seems reluctant to leave traces of himself, given his felonious intent, and he gives me a glance as if I should know better and help him out, so I say, "Never top off another man's mistake," and moments later Billy has his cheque. As we head for the river road I consider telling Mulwray he should know better than to bet on a game when he can't speak the language, otherwise you might spend a very long time riding the wake of a bad guess.

15

KAKATOSEN OTSITSENISIPI. Stars, when they fell.

"This is 1833. This is then." On November 12 the Bloods were camped on the Highwood River under a meteor shower, the same one recorded in winter counts of other Plains tribes. "This is fantastic. I *know* this calendar, its written form, I mean spoken, I know its spoken form as written down. This is what Wallace was after. I can't believe no one knew about this." Mulwray was full of solemn purpose during the break-in, but since finding the calendar he's been on the verge of wetting himself.

I point to the markings, feigning wonderment. "Well I'll be go to hell. And these look like graves, the Bloods lost some battle that year. And the next year too."

"1836, children died of diphtheria. 1837, *Apixosin*, a plague of smallpox kills two-thirds of the entire Blackfoot nation. It came on a Missouri River steamboat, and came again on a steamboat in 1869." He points out 1869. He actually licks his lips. "I never expected this, not this particular count." According to him what we are looking at is the only known instance where a Blackfoot winter count was painted on a skin, and it belonged to a Blood chief named *Pakap-otokan*, which means Bad Head, or alternately *Manistokos*, Father of Many Children. He signed the 1855 treaty with the American government and was still influential in 1877 when the Bloods signed the Blackfoot Treaty with the Canadian government. "You have no idea how important this document is in historical terms."

"What's this one?" I draw him to the "I" over animal on the outer tail of the spiral. He counts the years from '69 and arrives at 1879.

"In the spoken count that's the year the buffalo disappeared from the Canadian side of the border. You have to understand no one's ever seen Bad Head's actual depictions, if that's the word, so some of these may take some lateral interpretation."

"So what's your guess?"

"I don't know. Actually it looks classical, more Minoan than anything"—news to please Karen. "The animal is probably buffalo. The triangles might be warrior lodges, tipis made from tripods set within the H-shaped burial platform. Warriors were often buried with their possessions in their lodges, and others were buried on tree platforms, as you know. Maybe it was a year of starvation because the herds were gone, though if these are graves they aren't consistent with the tally markings of the smallpox years. This will be a marvel to play interpretations on."

"Not that anyone will get the chance."

He manages to look away from the skin long enough to glance at me.

"They certainly as hell will get the chance. This isn't the sort of thing to be kept private. You have no reason to oppose my acquiring the skin."

"Acquiring how?"

"Contact the owner—"

"The owner and his wife have disappeared, and in different directions. We've been trying to track Wanda for months just to warn her this house isn't going to look after itself, but she's gone off somewhere with her daughter. And no one's ever tried to find Alan. Besides, if he wanted this stuff to go public, why wouldn't he have let people know long ago that he had it?"

"It hardly helps to speculate. I'm sure the right contacts will put me in touch."

"How do you propose to explain what you know and how you came to know it?"

"I don't know anything. I just have some questions, prompted by my discussions with Dr. Lucas and you. In fact your part in this could bring you some credit, assuming we're on the same side."

"And if we're not?"

"Then we're probably both in a little trouble, though I'm willing to take the risk." He bites his lower lip and claps his hands once, hard.

"Just don't want you bothering my neighbours. Besides, we have a contract."

His laughter is outright derisive, but at least he ends it with a pat on my shoulder. "Please don't suggest my motives are strictly personal. You're the one acting guilty." Presumably in time I'll see the foolishness of my objections, look back and see the funny side. Before we leave I take a Polaroid shot of the skin and one of the table. Mulwray wants his own shots but I tell him I'm out of film so the photos I have will carry some bargaining weight.

In the truck he wants to fill me in about his "contacts," ask about Wanda, about my concerns and motives, but I fend him off by opening the vent and blasting the cab with a chokeload of dust and with questions of my own. Did you know that Saskatchewan is the second-dustiest place on the continent behind Texas? We lose 161 million tons of dust a year, more on a year like this, the water table being fifty-seven inches below normal. At the same time we use more energy per capita than anywhere else in the world, the climate being so extreme and the distances so great. You understand that self-knowledge is without numerical terms, though in any instance it can be partially systematized into appropriate grammars and other convincing misrepresentations. It helps to walk through backwards. At the most elemental level Mulwray is something to be resisted. I've known this from the time he first appeared. He doesn't understand the complexities involved, to use an old political out, and I can't explain them because they can't be reduced. They are processes, maybe. That sounds right. They are occurrences, near-perfect repetitions, correspondences between my lineage and everything represented by the Nash family secret and the form of that secret. There are certain angles to be covered and I need time to cover them.

When I drop Mulwray off at his van I tell him to keep his mouth shut and stay out of trouble and just maybe I can be of some help to him, though not until tomorrow. I suppose he's broke.

"I've got some cash in the bed. Look, I'd like to talk about this now if we could."

"I'm all ears," my last words as I spin him some more dust and he scrambles outside the frame of my rearview mirror. After a few minutes I see the van trailing me. Miles later I pull up in front of a barbed-wire cattle fence and wait for him to come alongside. Then I crawl through the fence.

"Come on." He manages to get through without ripping himself open. We walk into a rather dramatic view of the valley and the river and stand within a stride of a sheer drop once used as a buffalo jump.

"You came to be here because of letters and phone calls—that's one hand. On the other, my great-grandfather Bonurges (Nurge) Raymond left Kentucky when it became clear he'd have to declare his allegiance to either the North or the South. He had no vested interest in the plantations or in free trade with England, and apparently wasn't one to hold grudges. He took off for Mississippi and then Arkansas, where he became a bushwhacker—I've always liked that word—so the Confederates wouldn't think he was a Northern spy. When it looked like Little Rock would soon be taken, he went AWOL and found a regiment of Union soldiers camped by the White River, so he joined them and worked as a teamster until the war ended. Then he settled in Broadus, Montana with his brother, Flavius Josephus (Bub), who'd fought for the South but was caught stealing horses and sentenced to hang. The story goes that Bub broke free from his guards and jumped off a bridge into a river, with his hands tied behind him, and despite a badly injured shoulder managed some form of locomotion and escaped. Then he found an untended campfire, burned off the ropes, and stole another horse. Bub's family stayed in Montana, Nurge's son came north to Saskatchewan. To tell you the truth, the story bores me and I don't feel I owe anything to those men, in that no one should take credit for the contingencies that bring us into the world. But I'm still glad I know the story."

"Why tell me this?"

"For the sake of perspective," a sweeping gesture with my hand.

"You can be a very difficult man to talk to, if you don't mind my saying."

"So I've been told," I said. Then he asked if I'd led him to the area of the burial ground and I told him again that I'd never found it, Eugene had. He said it was his opinion that the pendant Eugene had given me came from the same place as the other three because all four had been described carefully by Wallace. He thought it likely that Eugene had taken or been given the pendant from the Nash collection. I told him he'd made a mistake to intimate my brother was a liar and a thief but I was right to tag him, Mulwray, as a piss-ass. Then I got back through the fence considerably faster than he did and more or less escaped. "He'll probably be lost for days."

The story is meant to be funny but Karen takes no visible interest whatsoever. Instead she pours me a midnight-size dose of the horrible scotch she's drinking though it's only late afternoon and there's very likely some road time ahead, and though she knows I'm doing my best this weekend to regain the purest form of the chemical me. I accept the drink in the name of national celebration but I can tell this isn't a happy time in the old cabin. For one thing, Dali no longer hangs on the wall and Kate's back home in town.

She says, "There's a chance the pendant could be from a grave. If this Wallace bought them from the agent, maybe he still had them when he died."

"Except why would Wallace be buried in some inaccessible spot of the river valley, short of an unhappy end?"

"I don't know. Maybe it was an unhappy end." In clumsy segue she continues, "I don't mean to make light of possible murder, but there's something I'm going to tell you." Lagging somewhat, I mistakenly think she's still discussing the burial ground. "Nothing's been decided." She manages to focus on the middle distance between us, and that's where she's aiming her words. "But more or less out of the blue last night, Mother said she's been thinking about a drive to the coast this summer. Naturally I'd be the one to drive."

"What about the museum?"

"That's one thing. I'd maybe have to let it go. Quit."

I mentally cross my fingers and keep them crossed as I grip the drink. "That wouldn't leave you much to come back to."

"This was her reasoning. She said before long she might not be able to look after herself, and she knew I wouldn't leave her alone in that state, living a thousand miles away. She said it made more sense for her to move close to me than for me to move home, not that she's looking forward to a city where she doesn't know anyone, but there's Wendy to be considered too." She's looking down at her feet now, toes turned slightly inward, inclining towards each other.

"What you're saying isn't what I thought you meant when you said a drive to the coast. Why didn't you mention this at the ball game?"

"That wasn't the right place." She looks to the moon in her thumbnail. "But listen, nothing's been decided for sure."

Of course it has, I feel like saying. We wouldn't be here otherwise. "And I thought Kate was coming round to me. And I thought you were, too."

"This isn't only about you, Toss."

"That's pretty evident. Karen, this might've been Kate's suggestion but it's not her decision. It's yours."

Finally she looks up at me. "That's right, Toss. And if you can tell me how to include everyone I want in my life, I'm open to your suggestions, too." This is not a point of argument. Her voice falters enough that I know she's being honest, and she wishes for all the world that I could make a case for her staying with no career prospects in a dying town, with a man of failing reputation.

"Well, I guess I'll know what it means when I stop seeing you around." She begins to speak but I tell her, "Please don't say another fucking thing," and she doesn't, and I'm left suspended there feeling exactly like someone sitting in a chair with his eyes closed and suddenly hating himself for what he's just said, though far too angry and confused to apologize. She waits me out.

"You ever notice how life's taller in person?" I say. Then I get up and leave. She doesn't follow or even say anything, and soon I'm too far gone to turn around.

16

HOW DO you remember at this latitude of the mind? By way of escaping my current life I find my furthest thought somewhere under a flat winter sky, an interior landscape, we keep inside, there's something out there that wouldn't think twice about killing us. It's Halloween night in Churchill and in the dark just past the edge of town polar bears move in the infra-red tracking needed to keep them at a safe distance when they get curious about the taste of small ghosts. I saw this scene on tv a few springs back when the tube was all mine because Marcie had decided to remove from her life all the low-frequency emissions she could. She'd come across some scary scientific claims. Thus no VCR machine, no home computer, no repair for the microwave, not even any visits to the Warren clan, who live near a giant transformer but chalked up a strange series of calving deaths to statistical coincidence. But now I'm back to the colourful seasons that show up past behaviour, mine, Marcie's, as a little unbelievable. As actualities recede they often seem less plausible. Example—Marius once explained that some trees explode in the winter, and that a hard snow could leave cattle hanging from tree branches, and that grain harvested too early and mounded had been known to spontaneously combust. I've never seen these particular marvels, but know them to be true. Marius himself is the mystery, more of one each year, a sad condition with no antidote which sometimes leads me to futile and excessive attempts to erase myself, usually to my public humiliation.

Last night I remember describing a certain movie poster, my favourite of all time, picked up in a nostalgia store in Edmonton. Dewey kept coming and going and I felt I had to start over a few times so he could follow my line of thought. He was setting up early so he could open, this being a potentially bumper-crop night what with the holiday and a sure-fire summer blockbuster. He said I was drinking too fast and I said something witty like Look who's talking. The poster's title, in giant but crumbling blocks, was *The Valley of the Maya*, below which were elephants and lions and some brand of overgrown housebird and kids out of Disney's *Jungle Book*, and then in smaller blocks "From the Jungles of Amazonia," starring a few Anglo names, and finally, at the bottom, "Shot on Location in India." A big budgie release, quite obviously. You don't seem to understand (I might have told him, forgetting my malicious suppositions about Mulwray and the milkweed butterfly), this is a geographic impossibility and Hollywood thought no one would notice. His response semi-audible as he vacuumed the foyer, Noticing is one thing but caring is another, it isn't really inaccurate because it's so common, these unpopped kernels don't pick up, the studios call it time-neutral. Then I finally spoke my sorrows—first about Karen, which didn't surprise Dewey in the least, given the unwelcome portents of my visitor, and then about last Thursday's card from Marcie, now in Costa Rica. I've been reluctant to think about it too directly but it's always there, rattling around in my brain pan—her resolve to stay put for a good while in such a natural paradise, her providing me a return address, of all things, to extend a measure of kindness and cinch my long-divided attention.

Dewey said I could talk all I wanted about my marriage but not to suppose he'd value my version above any other he'd heard, and he then ran the others by me, maybe to keep his cold distance from my own understanding. Certain matters were agreed upon, namely that I was the last remaining member of my family, resentful of my neighbours because they'd made a go of ranching at my family's expense, and so with clear motive I had taken revenge upon the Nash clan by ruining the marriage of Alan and Wanda by means of (only here the variants begin) seducing *or* attempting to seduce the said Mrs. Nash *and/or* her daughter Eileen, *or rather* I myself was a victim of my neighbour's adultery and retaliated with a counter-coupling and the recent attempted demolition of Alan's house. I had had no idea of the variations.

I commented how the women in these accounts were remarkably compliant with the machinations of the menfolk—for which, Dewey added, they had been sent into exile while (some have heard tell) with child.

"And the reason I know there's not a grain of truth in any of it"— Dewey unlocking the door—"is that it's all reckoned on the basis of obvious motives, which, as I've already told you, are usually a too simple fish, and unoriginal besides."

"Have you told this to Karen?"

"We haven't discussed you in those terms. For reasons I can't guess she seems to be attached to you, so I don't suppose she'd fall for anything so farfetched as a story of sex, murder and revenge. Though it's true stranger things happen from time to time."

The arrivals began. I stashed myself out of the way behind a curtain on the stairwell to the projection booth, pathetically cuddling Dewey's bottle of rye, which wouldn't have been my first choice, and worrying about—of all possible concerns—Zinvalena showing up any minute and finding me so far gone so early in the night. There was a long time of drifting between states of consciousness, bodiless voices prompting mini-dreams, exotic scaly animals that never blink staring me down on the steps of some ancient pyramid or observatory or ball court, each structure a mathematically designed calendar based on the positions of some planet or other, tourists in floppy shorts milling about in awe of the sheer *concentration* that must've gone into all this and yet in other respects this noble race was primitive, sacrificing their own, and small.

"Small it is," said Zinvalena, scooping a bag of popcorn.

"And with not quite so much butter please, dear." The voice of another Marleyfoot, Eunice's daughter-in-law, the woman known as "Mrs. Donald, The Backbencher's Wife." She once complained to Basso that she'd examined her sister-in-law Altha's notebook and discovered our revered national history reduced to cartoons.

"It's not exactly butter," Zinvalena ventured.

"Surely you don't mean." I'd called her up and said, Don't think of them as cartoons—think of them as doodlings. She said, It's no difference what you call them, there's nothing to be learned from them. I said, Even now, I'm doodling on a pad by the phone here, and you know what I'm drawing so I'll remember your concerns? I thought she'd hang up but, stupidly, she hung on and asked, What? Our provincial coat-of-arms, I said, the one your husband sits beneath over in Regina. You must know it. She said she'd seen it but couldn't quite recall. I said, With the three wheat sheafs and the yawning red dragon. In my version here, the dragon gets a fiery little voice, and you know what the dragon says? She says, "Please come home, Donald. I'm sorry I burned your ass."

Of course, there was no fallout. Who could she bring herself to tell?

"But it's perfectly safe. And more yellow than butter," said Zinvalena with not a trace of impatience.

"Well that's fine, dear. Maybe I'll just have a package of these."

"The strawberry licorice is fresher."

"Oh, but I'm allergic to certain fruits."

The word I called out was "hagglehag!" The voices fell silent for a few seconds, presumably wondering where the word had come from and what it meant. There was, as I remember, no real commotion, and it was with some disappointment that I eventually nodded off and lapsed into a rerun of the tornado-delivers-riverboat-to-1930s-China dream I'd told Cora about, which now seemed very obviously a reference to Norman Bethune, he of the world's most serious face, who looked nothing like Donald

Sutherland. I'd seen one of Bethune's medical bags once and read some of his letters from Madrid and Sung-yen K'ou, and resolved to reinstate the term "hero" as part of my earnest vocabulary. Mobile blood banks and medicine shortages. I diagnose traumatic bursitis below the left patella. Where are my anti-inflammatories?

"Will you shut up?" Dewey, climbing over me on his way down from the booth.

"What was I saying?"

"Zinvalena's trying to sell candy and you won't stop mumbling 'Norman.'"

"Is she out there?"

"She's gone off to the Riverside bash."

"Did she see me?"

"No"

"Did she know it was me?"

"Of course."

"Ahh. . . . "

"I told her you were distraught."

I realized I was on my feet and he had his arm around me, helping me across the lobby. Briefly I glimpsed my face in the window of the popcorn machine and noted I looked like some freakish thing just hatched in an incubator.

Outside, we buddied over to my truck. Dewey propped me up and told me to give him my keys. I fished around for them and looked back at the Palace and was flooded with a swill of memories.

"Are you gonna torch this place?"

"Of course not."

"Then why did you tell Perry—"

"It loses its effect if I have to explain."

I gave him the keys. He opened the door and shoved me in.

"I'll look in on you later."

"Karen's leaving me, Dewey."

"Yeah, you said."

"I don't know what to do."

"It doesn't show. Another prairie stoic."

The rest of the night has even less continuity. Impressions suggest a lot of people transporting me from place to place. Presumably by Dewey's agency I appeared at Perry's reunion dance, or rather outside the dance, propped on a bench in front of a fire pit. People kept poking the flames with sticks, pretending to roast marshmallows and wieners, and the flames kept asking me to make them stop. It's difficult to recapture the degree of misunderstanding that ensued. There was some one-sided wrestling involved, which could also explain my fat lip, though I'm not sure who or how many I lunged at and can only hope they were my size. But making an ass of oneself in any memorable way requires more labour than I first realized, it turned out, because someone thought it safe to let me inside the dance hall. The band on stage looked very early seventies and featured long guitar and organ solos that set everyone into conversation about the stupidity of reviving a decade of wing collars. Or at least that's what we should have been talking about. The people at my table, whoever they were, didn't seem to say much of anything, at least not to me. At some point I hit upon a strategy of exercising control over a dance partner. I wandered lonely from table to table and recognized a good many former students, though not all of them recognized me, until finally Perry laid an arm over my shoulders and led me to dark virgin air. We passed by the fire and when it called to me one last time I knew I was sobering up because I said, perhaps aloud, The real world is a place where fires don't ask favours. What a great surprise to be guided to my own truck. Perry even had the keys. He listened for what was perhaps a very long time as I tried to explain that I was at that very moment trapped in a country-and-western song and my heart was a-twangin', my stomach providing slide-guitar accompaniment. He asked did that mean I was going to puke. I said I hadn't had a drink in a few hours and wasn't as drunk as I pretended to be, though I wished I were.

"I do this in full knowledge of the consequences," I thought or said, popping open the glove box and removing the stack of postcards. I went back to the fire and spoke in loving terms about wounds and balms, nothing very eloquent, maybe I even used a brand name or two, Polysporin seems likely, but the assembled listened politely. Then I offered the cards to the flames and watched them disappear until the fire had the nerve to spit an ember at my pant-leg.

Now my head rests on what I've always thought of as the foot end of my couch. The glass doors of the stereo cabinet reflect 11:4 from the digital clock on the tv behind me. Perry must have put me down this way. When I sit up and look out the window I'm surprised to see in the yard the dark forms of both Mulwray's van and my truck in its spot next to the house, which means Perry didn't go back to the park and is likely asleep in my room. Caught up in my stupor I forgot to ask if he'd had any luck charming Polly to the dance. Obviously not. To make matters worse, the very cousin who set him up for rejection and for the reunion horrors then caps off the night by launching drunken assaults at innocent wienie-roasters and generally haranguing the would-be celebrants. Some people in my position would hate themselves but I know better. Mine are ordinary failings. My only regret of the past day is that I was angry with Karen and behaved like a cornered rat when she told me Kate's plan. The night's events were just the harmless consequence of telling myself to get lost, the one thing I do well. As for the postcards and the Costa Rican address, I can't honestly say I feel lightened, but whatever she intended by them, Marcie's reports were setting back my efforts at home improvement. Though I'm very close, I'm not quite yet willing to readmit certain universals to myself, at least not in the usual terms like love and loss. They are both absolutely beyond the reductive powers of language, even if love is not beyond sensual understanding, not just sex but loving someone as a movement in the background, sounds from another room, or, as with Karen, the sour smell of blue jeans left hanging on the arm of a chair. But then maybe language isn't always reductive. Who's to say and what difference does it make? I'm back home, my head hurts, my best judgement lags severely. I have furthered my local fame.

I make my way to the kitchen to turn on the stove light and put on the kettle to fix a medicinal dose of peppermint tea, then laboriously take off my clothes and the distinctive odour of firesmoke. Sitting at the table I notice I have my morning shape—a slight expansion around the middle I attribute to the pooling of blood in the vital organs while horizontal, a little bodily principle I once learned by way of a coroner's testimony at some murder trial, either in the paper or on tv. The boyfriend claimed that the girl had fallen from the balcony while stoned, and landed hung up vertically in some power lines or tree branches, and yet the blood was collected around her stomach, meaning she had died lying down and had then been tossed off the balcony. Or something. Everyone was satisfied the boyfriend was guilty, given that it's tough to argue with the circulatory system and he was a known trafficker of mind-altering substances. As the water begins to boil I can feel my viscera start up. I stupidly look to my bullet-hole navel, as if it could tell me anything about what's going on beneath.

Finally, you fear blood more and more. Blood and time, wrote some French poet, blood and time meaning something different to me now than when I first committed the lines to memory. The terms are now precise and I don't bring to them the adjectives of limited perspective—flowing, coursing—because even these are approximations. Instead there is just blood, stupid and untrustworthy, no more measurable than fear, and fear like memory a visitation. There are no distances between me and the remembrances or imaginings made palpable by whatever is around me to prompt them. In the sound of a kettle boil are undertones of wind or thunder, buffalo herds, not just their weight but the animals themselves, their cries as audible as the human cries of the hunters. And when the tea is poured and the kettle grows quiet the sounds are still with me, the roar and squall of abandonment so clear, so very clear, so clear at the moment, in fact, that I begin to worry whether this is the onset of delusional psychosis. Now follow inhuman screeches. A glance to the living-room verifies that the tv and radio are off, and yet the shouts grow more urgent, several voices calling above the screams and howls, so that, much as I'd like to deny it, the general impression is that someone, perhaps myself, needs help. As I turn off the light and run to the front-room window I consider a half-formed explanation involving some troupe of monster hunters moving in for a kill (or have the antelope appeared? the elk? do such animals screech?), a notion so implausible that what I see through the window is by comparison almost believable.

The daily-news heroes, people who run into burning buildings to save children, are forever telling us their actions were not courageous but instinctive, often adding that if they'd had time to think they wouldn't have had the mettle to act. The instant I leave the house I realize these people are liars. What I run towards does not make sense in any conventional way, not the shadowy commotion or the shouts and hellish howls, but even in the dark the assault on Mulwray's van is clearly delivered with vicious intent, and the beast rocking the vehicle cuts a feral line. I stop just outside my door and consider my likely fate. The creature is obviously other than human or benign and looks to be about seven feet tall on its hind legs, about the size of a well-nourished werewolf, I suppose. There is hair, snout, no doubt the sharp particulars. Its forelegs are bashing the side windows. In all the noise I can distinguish Mulwray inside the van, screaming.

I wave my arms and shout a "Hey hey you!" in half-hearted hopes of drawing a charge from which I might run into the house to think of something else, maybe locking myself in the bathroom. But the monster can't hear in the clatter and hasn't yet scented me. As my luck would have it, Perry didn't put the elevation lights on and the yard is lit only by the moon.

I run to my truck and jerk open the door. When I pull the rifle out from under the seat a box falls over and spills shells onto the floor. In the interior light I load up, my hands suddenly all quivers and tics, but through the back window the light glares and I can no longer see the monster, and am confronted instead by my own reflection in the glass, the outside showing through only where my lips should be. I back out and close the door and fall to one knee as riflemen do in the old westerns. For three or four seconds nothing is clear but then I see it again, now on the other side of the van, thrusting its bulk at the door. The animal screeching has almost subsided and Mulwray is clearer than ever, and now I hear somewhere to the east an animated conversation about stupid risks and useless weaponry. A man and a woman, and the woman's voice is vaguely familiar.

The beast is in my sights now. I'm surprised to find that my hand tremors have subsided. Marius said everything rides on the first shot.

Just as I squeeze it off, something hits me from behind and drives my bad shoulder into the ground. The shot takes out one of the van's headlights and the .22 is thrown from my grasp. I bellycrawl to get it back but someone beats me to it.

"Jesus Christ, it's me!"

"Over there," I say weakly, then look up at Perry. "A wolf." But the wolf isn't there. Perry points to the yard entrance where I see the monster in bipedal sprint to a pickup truck.

"My guess is Beyer," he says. Without losing any time the intruder sheds his outfit on the road and gets into his truck. A second later the voices stop. "You could've fuckin' killed him." The truck and Mulwray's van start up at the same instant. Mulwray is first out of the yard and up into the hills.

Perry explains, "It was *Aliens.* I recognized Sigourney Weaver right off. She's what woke me up. He's spliced the audio from the big encounter scenes and piped them through roof-mounted speakers on his truck. I could see the truck from the upstairs window." Then he runs off to collect the disguise, which figures to be the lion from an old school production of *The Wizard of Oz*, stored with the clown suit in the town-hall basement.

"Everything's changing to wilderness around here." He unbundles the suit and holds up the head. It's a bear suit, the giant brown grizzly named Grady, former team mascot of the Bucks back when they were known as the Bears. "Better get some clothes on before the Mounties show up. Things like this don't stay quiet for very long." I get to my feet and we start towards the house. "Let's face it, Toss. The guy's cracking up."

Perry goes inside but I turn around and look for a few seconds at the rifle, left leaning against my truck, then walk back and pick it up. I take it down to the river and confirm that the chamber is empty. I spin once in a shortened hammer-throw motion and release it out over the river and into the first signs of day.

17

"HE SHOULD'VE said 'housewares.'" Late morning, I drive Perry to town. It looks like rain.

"He said 'dishes.' Said, 'I sell dishes.' It was more the way he said it that made you take notice, like he was ashamed to sell dishes."

"And Dewey was there."

"It was at the horse ring when I went to tell Matthew and them I was cutting away. I thought it was a bad sign they were crowded so near Beyer, but they weren't bothering him. Anyway, that's it. Beyer thought the guy sold satellite dishes and he wanted to scare him off."

"No, he just wanted an honestly scared witness to this monster he's invented. He wanted the story carried out of town. He won't let go of the monster thing."

"Toss, the guy's nuts."

"He's just overcreative."

"L double-O N."

The cloud over us stays dry but it's the outrider of a natural system stalled over town a few miles ahead, stalactites of rain dark and heavy enough to wash out the last day of the tournament, though the sheer irony of such hard luck seems likely to prevent it. From somewhere a new pain has surfaced below my left kneecap, and my right elbow is tucked close and hides a small bloodstain which has seeped through some bandages on my ribs. I intend to crash at Cora's. Then I'm going to save my life.

"Bet you get a visit from Hall."

"You just keep quiet and that'll be the end of it. Mulwray won't want too much digging around into his part in this."

"It has to do with the Indian stuff?"

"It has for Mulwray."

Perry reconstructs for me the reunion dance. At the pool Polly had said that she'd already agreed to go with someone else but she'd try to get out of it, at which point Perry realized he'd never liked her much to begin with and he could trust his own judgement at least as well as mine. She showed up with Wendel Irwin, another high-schooler, but she winked at Perry five times in the first hour. His rescue of me is somewhat as I'd imagined it. He corralled me just as I made a loud and open offer to sell my land for a dollar to the first woman who'd dance with me. With his help I now mostly recall that before he got me out the door I said something to a skinny cowboy standing alone in the entranceway, holding a full cup of beer and in full formal attire—many-galloned hat, flowered acrylic shirt, narrow and baggy-assed "dress" jeans, rider boots with what southern cowpokes call "roach-killer" toes. I addressed him as "Slim" and asked if he was lost, there being no movie sets in this part of the province and the nearest cow at least ten miles away.

"How did I get away with that?"

"He was ready to plant one of those boots in your lonesome parts when I offered him the rest of my drink tickets. He took them, and predicted you wouldn't live much longer, but he let us go."

"Long as he wasn't a doctor. Or weatherman." Seconds later I'm laughing aloud at the thought of Slim explaining pressure systems. Perry asks if maybe he shouldn't be the one driving. He leans over and checks the speedometer, glances down at my right hand, the one on the steering wheel. A thumb and two fingers at six o'clock and the same grip I use to hold a pencil.

"Since when did you get so nervous?" I ask.

"Sometimes it sounds like you're talking to yourself instead of me."

"Sometimes I am."

Perry has no idea how I hurt my knee unless it was during the fire-pit wrestling or when he tackled me. I tell him that he must live the rest of his life in the knowledge that he's a hero, though so local only the two of us know it, and that all his debts to me are naturally forgiven.

I gear up to sing a few lines from an old song by The Band. I can't remember the title. Then I can't remember the lines.

Irony being a part of life, we hit town inside a ten-ton rain that would have made more sense in the late afternoon. There's little traffic. The fairgrounds are empty and impassable with mud. Rain never seems to set in any more, it just beats the hell out of the small patch of earth that least needs it and then gives up to higher skies that burn for weeks, not an inaccurate description of the general state of mind around here. Needing recovery time, I'm simply unable to contemplate particular concerns or the people who warrant them, their names unevocative, only the same dull yellow sound.

At the house Cora is waiting with chicken soup and saltines. After downing three spoonfuls I apologize and announce my intention to sleep for the rest of the day. I tell Cora that Perry looked after me last night and has set an example I hope to live by all my life, however little of it remains given my condition. Then I promise to be in serviceable shape for our journey to Saskatoon in the morning.

"Perry's got some time off so he's coming along, but maybe that's not such a good idea if you two can't stay out of trouble."

"Who said anything about trouble?"

She says, "Your fat lip didn't have to say anything."

"Slipped in the mud. Looks like a washout."

"Yeah," comes Perry again to the rescue. "It's sort of a crying shame. It's hardly raining at all in the country."

"Hey, it's no tragedy." I start up the stairs. "At least the garden's happy. Think of all those petunias and impatiens and vegetables.

Happy tomatoes in every yard, rhubarb, carrots, corn.... " I keep talking until I'm safely in my room and in bed, where I close my eyes and think about all that water seeping into the earth.

Though I feel horrible the sudden security of Cora's home brings on an appreciative amazement at all that's befallen me in the past few hours. The kicker was after sunrise, when I decided to take on a more direct role in the winter count-Mulwray question. The idea was to put the skin under my own keeps until I found a Blood tribe who might want it and then let them have the upper hand on the various Mulwrays, which seemed a fair enough solution all around. But when I arrived at the Nash house I found the basement window broken and bloodstained. The jagged opening required a sober negotiation that I was incapable of. Though I gashed my ribs at least I managed not to bleed on the floor, unlike Mulwray, whose blood led straight to the downstairs room.

The skin had been removed from the wall and laid across the table. On the wall where it had hung, another smaller skin had been revealed. It looked to be a winter count also, except that there were fewer figures and, though some were almost identical to those on the larger calendar, they had been drawn in a linear pattern rather than a spiral. I counted thirty-one years. Then I noticed on the skin's border the left half of a Lazy N, the Nash family brand. What I was looking at was the first draft of a false story.

18

GOD, BUT I fear the rollaway background. In mid-song we're made fools of by some japing stagehand.

Dreams of copious pissing wake me into dead light. I get out of bed with a slight ache behind the eyes and what I know will be a short-term reprieve from my interrogatory throbbings. In the bathroom I relieve myself and fight off some old dream anxiety about pissing into the Amazon while exotic bugfish swim upstream and eat my vitals. I take in and spit out a shooter of mouthwash but avoid the mirror rather than begin on my appearance. Without any firm notion of the time of day, I go downstairs and find that Cora has gone to bed for the evening and Perry is in a video daze before the tv. He says the skies have cleared. Having made a round of the streets in my truck he is of the opinion that none of his friends is to be found and so the town will not burn tonight. "And by the way," he adds, "your reputation is finally dead and buried."

A drive to the Shaulter house, I park across the street and sit there with the engine running. I wait for the right moment but it doesn't come so I turn off the truck anyway, but continue sitting. A while later I give the key a quarter-turn and hear the Eagles taking it to the limit, whatever that means. Then I start up the truck again. Throwing my legs on the seat I hang my head out the window and watch the stars. The Milky Way effect seems to have been achieved with an atomizer and at the moment stands as an accurate visual statement of my less than coagulate resolve. In sitting up again I accidentally brush the horn and then curse aloud.

Finally the curtains in the picture window flurry and out comes Karen, barefoot in nightgown. She takes the passenger seat.

"Do you know what time it is?"

"No. Were you asleep?"

"Dewey only just left. He told me what happened. We actually had an argument over whether or not you were a stupid ass. He took your side."

"I didn't realize how much time you two spent together. Another man might be suspicious."

"You tried to kill him out of jealousy?"

"I thought he was a werewolf."

"I see. Looks like he's finally got you."

"I was drunk—"

"I think it's *you* this is all about. I think he's decided you're the one person around here who can appreciate him and rescue him from this course he's on. But you don't see it. I'm the only one who knows what I'm looking at. He wants you to save him from this extreme . . . this need he has to fill up all the empty space around him. He needs you to contain him."

"It's just plain flat here, Karen. No one can change that. People see him as having an unrequited circus aspiration, but that's just the face of it. With clownish features."

"So where does that leave him?"

"Who knows? I expect now he's had a near-death experience he'll go off in some other direction. He takes cues that way." She squirms on the seat, again her trouble with furniture, broadly defined. "Since you told me you were leaving I've made a spectacular fool of myself and saying so now doesn't save me anything. Just please, will you tell me that tonight you like me not considerably less than you once did? Or do I flatter myself in assuming you ever took a shine?"

"It was taken, but..."

"Look, I know we've got a problem here but for now that's all it is."

"Meaning?"

"Meaning it hasn't yet reached greater proportions, say those of a dilemma."

"My Lord." She gets out and walks around to my side, leans in, kisses me somewhat perfunctorily.

"I'm going to Saskatoon for a few days with Cora. I'll call."

"You might catch me." She hugs herself against the cold.

"What does Kate think would happen to you and me if you left?"

"She says smart men know when to follow a woman, and idiot men go their own way." Kate would not have used the word "idiot."

"Another rule to live by?"

"Just something more to think about."

Though I'm tired I must drive home to collect my five-day bag for the trip to the city. I pick up the town line and head south. A small bank of dry cloud has moved in and buried the moon. It leaves me only blackland. I don't know if I'm a night-time person, but I am a different person at night, especially here in the driver's seat, the peripheries unavailable, the dash lights and road lines drawing me out like a supplicant to the dark. Nothing can surprise me here. Even this far from water and sunset you must be ready for deer. You look for their eyes, daytime black or yellow at night. When a deer looks, she looks not at you but into your light. Very simply, she waits to know if it is her time. And before I'm past she must know, one way or another, an instance of sharp certainty.

It's strange how we surprise ourselves, how the dead serious can sometimes not seem that way, how in considering bleak prospects and the lessons of history we might yet find ourselves believing things are not as they seem.

V

THE RETURNS

19

IN SASKATOON on the day before Cora's surgery I called Mulwray and suggested we meet. He said his office would be best unless I was armed. It was understood this was a statement of some humour.

The name on the door read:

Dr. C.C.Y. Mulwray
By Appointment Only.

"What's the 'Y' for?"

"Pardon me?"

"Gash wounds healing well, I take it?"

"I'm sorry about the window. I would have left payment but I didn't have the money, as you know. And if you know about the window then you also know what I found under the skin."

"But I don't know what to make of it."

"It's fraud, Wesley. I've never come across artifact replicas being sold as originals, but it happens. Apparently it happened even seventy years ago. To be honest, I had a hunch before I saw the other count, but it was worth all the time I spent."

"My own hunch is that you weren't entirely up front with me, which makes us even that way, but I don't see a reason for you not to fess up." We sat facing one another across a desk with nothing on it, not even a pencil or paperclip. The desk angled to Mulwray's left held a computer keyboard and screen. He gestured to the walls. Books, posters.

"Do you like my office?"

"Impressed to the soles of my feet."

"It's not mine. It belongs to a sabbaticand. I'm only a locum tenens, here for nine months. By then my post-doc is up and I may be out of a job."

"That'll put you in the spring. Catch something tourist-related."

"I just want you to know there has been a little desperation in some of my actions over the last year and a half."

"I only want to know about the last couple of weeks."

"Well, that's what I'm saying. Your letters to Dr. Lucas were not, in fact, my first break in this case. They merely reopened it." Mulwray explained that he had lied when he said the notebook winter count, the one in the Calgary museum, had no pedigree. In fact the book was traceable to Cole Nash. Mulwray wrote the Nash family asking for information about Cole and the collection, and what he got in return was a phone call from Alan, who confessed that he didn't know what Mulwray's angle was but his Uncle Cole was long dead and none of his ancestors was willing to take the rap for him.

"He said his uncle lived his own life, no one else was responsible for it, and he couldn't care less who his uncle's enemies were or what happened to them, and he said I could tell this to the man who put me onto whatever I was after. I managed to get your name and take it down as a point of reference, then by coincidence you yourself gave me a pretence."

"Alan always assumed people knew more than they did."

"Are you suggesting you don't know more? I was hoping you'd fill in the rest."

My grandfather might have known the story, I explained, but my father didn't, and I was just piecing it together for reasons having nothing to do with the events themselves.

"Suppose Cole was setting Wallace up for a big purchase, or suppose they were both setting up a third-party buyer. Then a falling through or a falling out, maybe one of them was a card cheat, there's no point speculating. Suppose Cole kills Wallace and buries him in the hills somewhere, along with enough artifacts to disguise the grave. Years later my brother discovers it and takes a pendant, which he gives to me. Meanwhile Cole has long ago been sent away to an asylum, to safe ground." And Alan must have assumed that Eugene and I knew something I still don't know.

As I made my conjectures I was suddenly aware that two changes had come upon me. First, the ground I'd been looking for no longer connected me with my brother—there was too much in the way. Second, if Alan thought I was spreading rumours about his family, then his dumb jokes and the whole breakup with Marcie had yet another lamina of complexity.

I couldn't leave Mulwray without asking if his visit had changed his views on the existence of monsters. He said history is full of them, as everyone knows, but most people can't spot one. They cry out at the wrong thing. Even he had.

She wants to come home by way of the dam, a place I thought I'd never return to. Perry caught a ride home yesterday with friends who'd been in Saskatoon on a cd binge, and I was happy for his sake to see him go. His first taste of severe family illness had come at high voltage. He was more visibly shaken each time he walked into the ward and saw his mother doped up in a hospital bed and plugged into an IV. Almost immediately he lost his appreciable appetite and I had to insist he leave the last few sets of thrice-daily visits to me. The night after the surgery I actually caught him crying in the hotel room, a discovery which did neither of us any good and sent me into the hallway for ice to complement the old No. 7 I'd thought to bring along for just such an awkward or plain difficult moment. It had been a long while since we'd gotten drunk together, I noted to myself, as if the dry spell justified its end. Perry launched the first sip with "I know she's okay now but it isn't now I'm seeing when I look at her," and I responded, "But it never really was and it never will be." We had enough sense to shorten up after a few minutes and so went to bed feeling both sober and very real.

Gardiner Dam. On our last night out together, mid-June it must have been, Marcie and I went there in deference to old habit and better times, with the unstated intention of working out exactly what had happened to us. As usual we arrived after dark and sat on the embankment to listen to the water and watch for satellites and shooting stars. She was never content that I was romantic enough about the whole thing but, company or no, I could never look at the night sky without falling into my river-island solemnity. On that last visit she was no doubt waiting for questions from her suspicious husband, but all I could think was that the air was cold and the water unusually still. I was thinking that someone had finally caught the fugitive river, the one that changes names at the border. And then I inevitably thought about Eugene, who I'd always assumed had left home for Wyoming, about which he had had only vague notions beyond the understanding that it was a place with big-spread ranching. The name intrigued me even when I was young. Wyoming—it suggested a place you could do things—riding, ranching, and there were other words in that name too. No wonder, then, that at a time when I believed there was no understanding or influencing my sad world, I should avoid asking for the truth by imagining an escape.

"You know, one thing we've never done is a road trip south," I said. "We could drive through the States, see how it matches up with the tv version."

"What are you talking about? We've reached the end and you can't even *be* here for it."

"It's just, there's a chance to know something first hand. Everything's so second-hand here lately."

"You actually need me to *say* I never had an affair with Alan?"

My fingers found a pebble. I threw it out over the water.

"I think I know that."

"But you.... You hit him. With a boat. In public."

"A *toy* boat. There was a playful aspect."

"Oh Jesus, Toss." Her voice sounded as if it was directed up into the night rather than at me. "What's happened to us?"

"The town has happened to us. It happens to most people who live there. Okay, that's an excuse, but you admit there's nothing for you in Mayford."

"There's nothing, but I tried to make things work." Her trying had stopped short of having a child. Even then I didn't blame her for not wanting one, but I did blame her for not telling me as much a long time ago. "Do you believe me?"

Something in her voice surprised me. The question sounded important to her.

"Just now I do," I said.

After some time she got up and walked away and waited by the truck. For the first time since the confusion had started I felt physically sick, and didn't stop feeling that way until a few days after she left.

So Cora and I make the route home one of those outings of ours, usually an evening every few weeks spent on a long trip to some generally uninteresting place affording us new angles on the sublime—sand hills, badlands, lakes, anywhere playing along with the steep fall of light. Cora allows no one but me to drive her fourth and newest Delta 88, a fact that Perry has only sullenly accepted, while for me any nontruck drives are a low-slung joy. In fact setting out with Cora on one of our loops is the easiest thing in the world. We can be quiet together. What I do say behind the wheel I've learned to pay attention to. My words are unpractised and unmeasured, as close to my subconscious as sleep talk, though not at all obscure. I value the chance to be honest and accurate, even about so small a matter as a grade of hard wheat.

But Cora has things on her mind. The lap belt presses a small pillow into her incision, allowing her enough comfort to afford an occasional laugh, even on the sobering matter of the latest school board meeting. She normally pays no heed to rumour but she's had a lot of time to consider this report and she's decided I should know at least as much as she's heard. To wit, my roundly acknowledged behaviourial instability and my association with Dewey have won renewed calls from certain quarters for my dismissal, and the grounds have been prepared to make such a move look like a budget decision, overriding considerations of seniority. If I'm not seeking justifiable cause for an escape, and if I'm told to cross over and teach both social studies and English, she advises, I'd better surprise the board and sound happy to do so. This news isn't really unexpected but I'm surprised Cora's the one delivering it. If anyone is my confidante it is Cora, but I still deflect a few questions about Marcie and Karen, except to say I didn't visit Marcie's folks while in Saskatoon but did buy Karen a sterling compass which I had engraved with the words "For cloudy nights in the lead, Toss." Cora finds this amusing but when I add that if I gave the same gift to Marcie she'd think I was telling her to get lost, Cora wastes no time in warning me not to take unfair swipes at the woman who is still legally my wife.

We move on. A brief afternoon shower has cleaned the air and everything around us has a hard line to it. Cora wants her money's worth out of the climate control but I roll down my window to the unfiltered wind and the parallax mystery of stunted fields that should now be passing the far side of canola yellow, flax blue, and gold. This used to be the postcard time of year, though the fall was much prettier, when the grain dust swelled the moon by night and bled the horizon by day. Into the Coteau Hills and the sight of several hundred Angus and Charolais, and before long we pass by Lucky Lake and turn south towards the Riverhurst ferry. The crop yields here have been gradually washing away because of irrigation projects that roll lines of pipe in pinwheel circles around great pivots. We catch the ferry perfectly and cross the lake with two flatbeds.

A sign tells us, "You Are Now Entering The South Saskatchewan River Project. Please. . . ," but we're past it and I can't imagine what might have been asked of us. Since the dam was built and the river's flow regulated, the banks seldom flood and spring breakup has none of the violence it had when I was young, when blocks of ice would ride up and crush trees at the sharpest bends and glaciate under pressure, and I've never been entirely happy at such imposed control. We follow the jug-eared road pinched up from the grand design and pull into the parking lot of the Info Booth/Snack Bar/Museum/Restrooms. As always, the lawn around the building is being watered and if it yellows a little more it won't look so out of place against the sand and rock and concrete. The row of poplars near the beach is no less ridiculous this year than it has ever been, and it seems not to have grown any, out of spite.

"Would you like to go down to the beach?" she asks.

"Never thought of it as a beach. I'll help you down there if you like but I don't mind waiting here."

"That's fine then." We look out at the sprinklers throwing water in spirals that break apart just before hitting the grass. She says, "You know, when they built this dam the foundation started to move on them, more than it should, and they had to redesign it. But it still creeps. Way down in the shale, three hundred feet. It creeps. No one can stop it. Only a few inches a year, but a little thing like that, maybe it should worry a person."

"Cora, I hope we didn't come all this way just so you could use that as a lead-in to the day's prime concern."

"And what would that be?" She unhitches the seatbelt and removes the pillow.

"You want to talk about Perry."

"Why am I worried about him any more than usual?"

"Because you think there'll come a time when he no longer *has* anyone to worry about him, particularly if I do what you think is the sensible thing and leave town after all these years and find a rewarding life in some distant city, maybe the one where you've heard Karen is moving back to."

"What if I do think that's the sensible thing? I don't want you staying here for his sake or for mine."

"You two can take care of yourselves but if I moved away who'd take care of me? Karen might try but then she'd find out what she'd got herself into. Besides, Perry and I have already discussed these eventualities and we've decided to make an investment and go together to buy the Nash land, which is worthless to anyone who doesn't adjoin, and acquiring such a large parcel of worthless land is so great an act of optimism that it's bound to bring about a large payoff."

She's silent a moment. "But good Lord, even I know it's not a good spot for a ranch. There's not enough pasture."

"We're thinking of acceptable forms of economic survival. We're thinking of market considerations." I sound like Dewey. A half-formed proposal of unknown saleability requires eye contact, which I establish, but even on painkillers she is the alpha leader and I do well not to look away. "I've investigated this. Who knows, maybe an artist colony and private game preserve, though we wouldn't have to stock anything, the animals would figure it out for themselves. We put up some money and get government grants to help build, then the word goes out and we hire someone to set up programs and land a couple of instructors. Even if it's only seasonal, it'll sell. There's only a few places like it in the country and we can undercut them all, given there's no disadvantage for transportation costs and there's a lot of potential customers here and in Alberta, and maybe the northern states."

"You mean painting?"

"That's right. And not just landscapes or nature stuff, but whatever stranger things they might do." She glances out her window at the only other car in the lot, sitting despondently in the farthest corner.

"I'm one of the few people who has a real choice about leaving or not," I say, "and I'm a fool either way, and besides, getting back all of Marius's land and more—this scheme whets my interest."

"You sound enthusiastic, but you can't really expect something like that to go."

"The way I see it, eight or nine months a year." Within minutes I seem to have convinced us both that I'm serious, never mind that the notion, however long it's been forming, only reached consciousness about fifty miles back, when a sexual musing concerning Karen and a sable brush was somehow interrupted by a flash doubt as to why Perry and I ever thought buying so much remote river valley would be shrewd business. At the moment it is less difficult to plausibly evoke an artist colony than it is to imagine Perry having any association with a wildlife preserve, for, as Cora points out, "He doesn't usually take to things that don't involve a trigger of some sort." I've lost this discussion before in defence of my sportsmen friends. Though I myself am a fish-clubber and have lived most of my life beneath the rich vein of a Canada goose flyway, I'm not a hunter, a few partridges aside. The aftermath of a shoot brings the blood a little too close for me. I don't look good in green or in eight a.m. photos of "the catch," and my hands aren't those of the men who can hold a braid of goose necks with the same thick-wristed delicacy they'd use to hold a sledge. Perry is somewhat on the other hand.

"Then you see the towering up-side," I say by way of a resolution. A deeper sky has moved in behind us.

"Does Karen know about this?"

"Not just yet."

"How do you expect she'll respond?"

"I have no one expectation, Cora. All I know is, Karen and I need another variable in our little equation. I'm hoping this one will spin the numbers back into the black for us."

Cora says nothing, unless it's a prayer for me. We watch the lake fade white to gold to dying blue. The horizon holds orange for a minute after the sun is gone. We pull away and work back to prairie before full dark sets in.

Perry's home to help unload while I lead Cora straight to bed so she can resume following doctor's orders and not ask Perry about the colony. Intercepting him on the front lawn, I take him near the mountain ash and reassure him that she's even better than she looks. I ask how his workday was, and note the unfortunate hydraulic fluid stain on his shirt. Then I explain my plan.

"A what colony?"

"Artist."

"What the fuck is a artist colony?"

My approximate answer includes mention of "natural isolation" and "creative environment" and "technical instruction." I triangulate and try again, find myself spewing "indigenous culture" in the face of "American pop imperialism." His gaze is blank and pitiless. Finally I settle for reminding him that I'm putting up the large majority of the land purchase money and have full control over how it's used, a simple case of whoever drops the loon calls the tune.

"And by the way, we had this discussion three days ago and after some initial doubts you've decided to trust my judgement," I say. "Which you should do anyway. The more I think about this, the better I like it myself." For the first time since my walk at Riverside Park with Karen I feel a puppyish welling of joy, and it surprises me, and when I shake Perry's hand it is all I can do not to give him a brotherly cuff on the shoulder.

Certain happy returns come to us strangely backlit on occasion. Years ago one of my many long-gone childhood friends phoned me from B.C. to say he'd made firm plans to change his life. It had become clear to him after three years as a minor-league pro that he'd never stick in the NHL, so he and a friend had gone in together to build yet another English-style pub in Victoria. The Something Arms or The Duke of Somewhere. There had been extensive planning, he said. "We're running the heating ducts under the cedar patio benches so we're open to the sun year round.

Otherwise there's haemorrhoid danger for the customers, where this way the most you've got to worry about are chilblains." He intoned this in a most sensitive, caring register, adding that such detailed planning would make up for his never having been to England. It had been important to tell me, he explained, because, frankly, he was going through a difficult adjustment, feeling full of self-doubt, and I had always struck him as the most level-headed of his friends, the one most likely to be straight with him. "Have I thrown everything away?" he asked. "Is this all a pipe dream?" I gave him my assurance that it certainly sounded like one, but that if he sustained it long enough it would come to seem like a viable reality substitute. He swore at me and hung up and I had to dial back and mouth a retraction. Today he owns two Arms or Dukes, at both of which I have a standing offer of six free pints, and a half-price membership and starter's kit for a label-collecting club.

I don't remember the last time I played a long shot.

In the morning I call Karen with my idea and she lends some advice about where my enquiries should go and what I might ask. The doubtful tone in her voice could be interpreted as an opening. She admits it isn't so much the idea of a colony that troubles her as the thought that I'd be the one running it.

"That's been nagging me too, to tell the truth. In fact a proposal of sorts has suggested itself."

"I wondered if it hadn't."

"Darling, will you be my Finder/Keeper?"

"Toss—"

"I could offer employment from the fall until whenever you felt you'd want out. You'd plan and administer and Perry and I would have to find the goods and hire out any work we couldn't do ourselves, maybe studio construction, self-contained cabins, water systems. Yours would be the only guaranteed salary."

"I don't . . . this is kind of late in the day."

"All the more reason, and what did you have on for the year that's so much better? Hell, you're *trained* for this sort of venture."

"Look, I'll help however I can till we take off next week, but I *am* going to Vancouver."

"And bring Wendy back with you."

"That's enough. No more pressuring or you're on your own."

"Exactly the phone manner I'm looking for. And Karen?"

"Yes?"

"I'm serious about this."

"Will you do it whether I'm on board or not?"

"Subject to the results of enquiries and appraisals and a keen gauge of the actual visuals, I will."

Above all else Dewey values the choice of ignoring the difference between what is likely and what is unlikely, and though his is not yet the dominant mode of thought, I can sense it gaining favour, at least my favour. Not that saying so will make it work for me when I'm sounding out a loan at the Credit Union. In his office Pinch Martin explains the conditions of sale as Alan has laid them out, namely that the non-negotiable price is only three times the assessment rather than the usual twelve, and includes all buildings and land along the river and north to a continuous band of government pasture, and does not include the few far-flung quarter-sections Alan snatched over the years from hard-luck farmers to whom he rented them back, taking a percentage of the seasonal net but none of the overhead. It is understood that the contents of the buildings will be removed before the takeover date. The livestock was sold off long ago to a true rancher in the true ranchland about a hundred miles southwest, but at such a price that an agreement was struck that anyone foolish enough to start another herd on the Nash land would get a more than fair shake from the first buyer, as specified in terms relative to the going rate and documented in an addendum to the papers of sale, which, Pinch reminds me, are being handled by Darrel Main's law office and not the Credit Union. "So I'm only guessing," he says with a smile. Pinch has been loan manager here since the early fifties, and through the wildly prosperous seventies, when his cautionary advice was roundly ignored by dollar-silly farmers, many of whom now must rent their land from his institution and so blame him personally for ever having let them go so many hundreds of thousands in debt. Yet he's kept his humour, partly for everyone else's sake, and that's why I like him. "Now, given your profile, we'd be happy to make a modest loan. But if it's a loan on the purchase, then I advise you you're not going to get any return out of the land."

"I can carry the purchase. I might need a cushion to set things up, is all."

"Set what up?"

"The one outlet we lack around here."

"Hardware's closed down. Liquor board's set to move out. I'm not sure which outlet you mean."

"Creative. Creative outlet. Not the usual crafts, but actual art done by artists from around the country, the kind the museum puts on display in the basement every so often."

"I wasn't aware."

"Pinch, I need a respected citizen, a pillar-of-the-community type to quietly voice his approval against anyone who might question my motives. People are suspicious of me by habit now, and they're suspicious of something new coming at them. I'm not asking for a public declaration, just a nod in my direction whenever you can."

He nods. "Are we talking business or something else?"

"I won't need a loan for a while yet, but till then what I'd like is your freely stated approval." It takes all of a minute and a half to explain every detail I've yet considered, the few hand gestures meant to suggest there's plenty more I won't bore him with now.

"Just how long have you been wanting to do this? I mean, I know about your education and that, but when did this particular interest take hold?" This is not an innocent question.

"Remember those island drawings I made?"

"Never saw them." Now he looks doubtful. "You don't expect me to support obscenity?"

"That's probably what some people are going to think. Which is why I need you to say this is otherwise."

"And is it otherwise?"

"It's the real thing, Pinch. Not that I won't be seen as harbouring a colony of eccentrics, but who's to complain if they do their shopping and drinking in town?"

For several long moments he simply stares at me. I smile. He keeps staring. Then finally: "I can hardly come out against the entrepreneurial spirit, I guess."

"To be honest, I don't see this as a profit operation."

"Then you're not leaving the school?" A hopeful expression waits me out.

"A year from now people will say I've rededicated myself."

My sudden buoyancy lasts only the few seconds between saying so long to Pinch and making eye contact with the next in line to see him. Stew Gates and I smile at one another as if I don't know he's about to be repossessed, being the odd man out among four brothers, the others older and having families, though the lot of them are failing to live off the four sections their grandfather was granted through the Veterans' Land Act after the war. And to make it all the more lamentable, Stew's the best farmer of the four and the least likely ever to get used to life away from home. He tells me he's got a fishing trip up north planned for the end of the month and asks if I'd like to go along. He even pulls out his wallet and extracts a fly he's just made: "General Practitioner from Golden Pheasant." I admire. "I'm real good at matching the hatch," he assures me. It hurts more than it should to turn him down.

The actual purchase goes off without a hitch, though there is some awkwardness when Darrel mentions that Alan didn't put any restrictions on just who could buy the land, and that Darrel is happy about this point and happy for me that I'm getting my father's land back, especially at this price, due he supposes to both the market and the extenuating circumstances. His unwillingness or inability to say exactly what he means leads me to respond only that if he doesn't mind I'll use my own pen to sign the documents. He says he understands. We read everything over together, I draw the fine-point, and it's done. Possession in twenty-one days.

20

A COLD southeasterly reminds me there are just five or six weeks of good outdoor work weather until the seasonal freezing begins to take effect. Then the numbness. For those who haven't been through it, grasping this requires a degree of suspended disbelief that seems to them unwarranted—the lesson of the German car engineer Marcie and I met on the Salema beach in the Portuguese Algarve who wanted to know about American Indians and Arctic Cold. We didn't do a very good job of informing him, apparently, because he looked at me with utter blankness when I told him we had to cover our houseplants with garbage bags before opening the window to get some fresh air in January. Marcie fielded the Indian question with an observation about the frequently disastrous results of urban pull. The German looked out at the waves and noted that they came ashore like randomly generated computer numbers. Later, Marcie wondered aloud if perhaps he hadn't found our understanding of his upper-case interests to be inauthentic.

Marcie—I'm unable to rid my life of contrivances—speak of the devil in the day's mail. This time it's a letter rather than a card. The stamps are Guatemalan. She's moving north. I open it up and spread it out on the hood of my truck. It's dated ten days ago. I'm still "Dear Toss." There is heat like I wouldn't believe. She's sitting in a café-disco called Doña Luisa's in Antigua, arguing with a new friend over whether or not the American at the bar is CIA. The friend is clearly female and not incidental to the picture. Only minutes ago the American made first contact by chatting them up. When the friend asked him why he was in Guatemala, he said he had business interests. When he asked them the same thing the friend told him they were both active supporters of socialist revolution, which Marcie laughed at, though maybe laughing could be viewed as ambiguous. After the American left, the friend said, That's what they always say, business. Now she informs me she's taking a language course. She announces she's going back to school in Canada too, though likely not in Saskatoon, and she'll finish her sociology degree and become a social worker. Her friend's name is Leslie and Leslie says Marcie shouldn't dress so much like a tourist but more like a traveller. What's the difference? Marcie says she'll call in October when she gets back in the province. She hopes I didn't write to the last return address because it turned out she didn't stick around as long as she'd planned and now she'll never get the letter. Leslie says hello and wonders if I'm good-looking. I should take care.

Far away and under the influence of possible political intrigue she's told me she's found the terms by which to change her life, yet in the end they prove her to be unchanged, practical as always, intending to do exactly as she always wanted and confirming that the differences between us are more real than I liked to think after the arrival of each missive from the overgrown beyond. Though I don't fly well I'm still more the traveller, she more the tourist, and though she didn't take well to isolation she's still patient and big-hearted and tough. Whatever the circumstances, she was right to leave here and acknowledge the prehensile ambitions she first came with. And though it doesn't follow that I was wrong to stay, I was dead wrong to ignore those ambitions, even to the point of willing a marital disaster. Moreover, I'm in the wrong not to tell her so. There is a clarity in imagining her, the same Marcie in a different world, imagining me. An expanded sense of life as we know it.

Both Pinch and Darrel mentioned in passing that Tommy Bolt was looking for me and had called them. Tommy has run the *Weekly News* since I was in high school and yet, despite those years and the nature of his work, we really don't know one another very well. So why am I not surprised he wants to see me? Why, after I've said hello to him in the one-room news office and he's handed me a letter for this week's issue (appearing tomorrow), why do I guess I know what he's thinking? After I've read it he unburdens himself by revealing that Hall has been pressuring him for a few weeks now to stop publishing the letter exchange and though Tommy's refused so far he now wonders if he hasn't been grandly duped. He doesn't know whether to print it as always or to show it to Hall first or to keep it under his hat. For some reason he thought of me as a compromise solution.

> ANNOUNCING: Public Meeting at The Palace to Resolve Ongoing Rancorous Debate. 7:30 Tonight (Tuesday). Adults Only Please.
>
> We, The Concerned Citizens Alliance of Mayford, have recently uncovered sound and disturbing evidence which we think will thoroughly smother the flames of our local discontent. Our decision to release this evidence in a public meeting should remove any doubt about the role of our maligned and much-questioned police authorities in this matter, and will provide little time for ponderance for those who might wish to fabricate a counter-accusation.
>
> All are welcome, so please attend this act of public remedy.

"Do I print it?"
"Your choice. Does Dewey have a letter for you this week?"
"That depends how you guess."
"Does the Coca May have someone deliver the letters?"

"They're all mailed and signed with a code word."

"What is it?"

"You don't happen to know?" He smiles broadly.

"I'm not Coca May."

"I don't believe you."

"I'm not! Where did you come up with that idea?"

"Really?" A final shudder and his hypothesis dies somewhere in the crease between his eyebrows. "Just when this arrived I thought I'd figured it out, that this was all a private thing between you two. The word is a name and the names matched up, sort of. Toss Raymond and 'Third Riverside,' which either sounds Indian or makes no sense at all unless you notice the initials and where you live. Third Meridian, riverside. I thought I was pretty damn clever, actually."

"Clever never counts for much by itself, Tommy. Are you gonna print it?"

"It could be seen as inciting public violence, depending how it all turns out."

"My guess is there won't be a turnout."

"Sure there will," says Dewey. We're sitting on the sidewalk curb below the marquee, forty minutes before the mystery event. "People still think there's good value in seeing a smartass get outsmarted."

We're staring at the building across the street. Here and there the weathered orange stucco of the Legion Hall hangs from an emerging underpattern of wire mesh. The place wears its neglect extravagantly, yet neither of us has ever expressed the slightest concern to one another about its state.

"I don't know what you're expecting," I begin, "but if anyone shows they'll be wanting to find out who's in the Coca May. Nothing good can come from telling them you're it."

"Maybe I *was* it, maybe in terms of the original public voice of concern, but I've created an army of Coca May sympathizers. People who know right from wrong and all that."

"People who don't like being made fools of."

"Yeah, that's them."

I note a little more traffic than you might expect up on Main. Passing by, each driver looks our way. A series of half-turns in halftons. Something seems to be building. Dewey's now on the subject of giant fish.

"Sturgeons the size of Volkswagens in Lake Diefenbaker," he says.

"No one can prove otherwise."

"But they never catch a fish that big. Not that everything you believe has to brought up to the surface—to be philosophically accurate about it—but you'd think someone would bring the right gear along and go after a fish like that."

"Maybe they do. Maybe it just stays close to home." I keep an eye out for my own truck to float by. I've lent it to Perry for the evening in exchange for his promise that he won't show up here at the Palace. "Is there anything playing tonight? You still got last week's bills up. Don't you ever read the marquee?"

"Why should I change it? No one ever pays attention to the thing. I'm not even sure people in this town *can* read. What sort of skills you teach at that school?"

"It looks like someone thinks otherwise." I point up to the marquee. Dewey stands and cranes his neck, takes a few steps out onto the street to get an angle on the board. Something like wonderment comes across his face. The sign reads:

i as here

gledth

"It doesn't make a lick of sense. Who's gledth?"

"'gledth' is just what's left over. 'i as here' is what you're supposed to notice. Whoever scrambled that was limited by what you had up there."

He looks down at me and then up again, just on the verge of

nodding as if he understands. "Just some of the usual summertime crap. 'A Sheer Delight,' a teenage romance flick." Back down at me. "But I don't think I get it."

"What's to get? Just a little public mischief."

He sits back down beside me. Up along Main Street Zinvalena's Mustang cruises by the intersection and allows her a two-second appraisal of the scene. One month out of school and already she's learned cunning. She'll now circle us and approach from behind and in a minute pull in across the street and roll down her window and pretend not to know what's up. That much I can count on.

"You know what? I'm flattered," says Dewey. "I think that's just great. Wish I'd thought of it, actually. I oughta thank this gledth person."

"Probably just some kids."

"I really think that's great."

"You said that."

"Well."

When Zinvalena appears Dewey grants her a paid night off and she confides she'll drive out to Blair's farm and spring a surprise visit. I tell her this is the first I've heard about . . . about. . . . "About a thing between us?" she helps me out. "Yeah, about a thing, a romance-type thing," I say.

She says, "Then you must've been even drunker than I thought at the dance, 'cause you came to our table and went on for about ten minutes on how happy you were for us both and how you guessed it was out in the open you'd given Blair advice about me. He was ready to throw you out the door and into the fire but I talked him out of it. You probably owe me your life."

"You don't know what you're accusing yourself of."

"But we're even," she says. "Dad changed his mind about my going to university. He said he'd been thinking, but that's not like him. So anyway, thanks. I wish you'd be around to look out for me the rest of my life."

And then—I didn't feel this coming—I'm suddenly choked up. I can't say a thing. I can't say, I wish I could be with you too. I can't say it was my pleasure, or tell her that her dad just wanted to do the right thing and had no idea what it might be.

It's an awkward moment.

Dewey gets up and goes to the car and asks what he owes her. She tells him and he pulls from his pocket a thick-clipped fold of bills and pays her.

"That's way too much," she says.

"Use it for books," he says. Then he very formally offers his hand and she shakes it.

At that moment we all know this is the last time we'll be together here, though only Dewey knows *why*, and saddest of all, for me, is knowing that Zinvalena knows it too. She doesn't say anything more. But she gives us a slight smile and a small nod and then drives off, and it almost kills me to watch her go.

In the next several minutes no fewer than seven pickup trucks park along the street just opposite us. A few men emerge and huddle together over there, careful not to look at us directly, but I manage to catch Eldon's eye for a moment and he winks at me, which could mean anything but I hope means I'm still okay by him.

Things are bound to get complicated so, if anything needs saying to Dewey, this feels like the time to say it.

"I'm sorry about trying to shoot you."

"I'm not. You believed me enough to actually blast away."

"I might not've fired but Perry tackled me and the gun went off."

"No matter. You believed. Thank you."

"I was drunk."

"That's enough"

"Okay."

At about 7:25 up along the sidewalk comes Karen, her sandals moving purposefully beneath a long floral skirt. She sees how the camps have formed and without so much as a hello to us veers over and across the street to the men whose numbers continue to grow. I count twenty-one cars and trucks. She exchanges words with Eldon and waves a hello to those nearest him, eight or nine guys from the Bucks. Then she crosses to our side.

"Eldon asked me to go home. He said this might not be any place for a woman tonight."

"That's the spirit," says Dewey.

"Dewey," she says. "I think maybe you should leave."

"Nonsense."

"I mean it." She looks to me. "Toss?"

"He can't leave. He's scripted all of this."

"You just keep your mouth shut," he says to me. "Don't you worry, Karen. I can handle it."

"Handle what?"

"Sorry. We're dealing with a 'need to know' restriction here."

He gets up and swings wide the red Palace door and jams the little stopper into place.

He says, "I just wanna say, I couldn't think more highly of the two of you." Then, no doubt sensing that everyone's watching him anyway, he adopts a stentorian voice and calls out to the townsmen, "The meetin's in the theatre, genties!" and disappears inside.

The crowd's size turns out to owe something to the cancelling of ball practice and a closing of Honkers, Eldon and Roger being two of the town's leading retributionists.

"I know he's your friend," Eldon tells me, "but he's making clowns and monkeys."

The two of us are among a small group pressed in behind the candy counter to make room in the lobby as the mob files in. The inner door to the theatre is closed and locked. Karen's over behind the ticket window but I can't see Dewey anywhere.

"I don't think that's his intention, Eldon."

"Then what is it?"

"I don't exactly know, but it sure has brought us all together, hasn't it?"

We're all pretty uncomfortable now, due as much to the unCanadian lack of order as to the crowding. People keep coming in though there's obviously not room for them.

"What the hell's the matter with everyone? Why don't some of 'em just wait outside a minute?"

"Pressing need," I say.

Eldon calls out, "Why the hell don't some of you just wait outside!"

"Shut your trap, Eldon. We're not your shitty ball club."

A mix of laughter and grumbling, objections of ballplayers. The room grows loud.

I catch Karen's eye and string together a few charades to suggest she get the key from under the cash tray in the till. She has trouble opening the till but someone near the glass talks her through it and, just as a scuffle and shove start up near the outer door, she finds it. The key is then passed man to man to whoever's up near the front of things. About the moment I decide to sneak a bag of licorice, the door opens and, scufflers subdued, the group comes forth.

Karen and I are among the last to enter. The lights are down but the screen's lit up to reveal, by way of a transparency drawing, the head of Clyde, the Mayford Wolf. We know it's Clyde because a balloon trails from his fang-crammed mouth containing the following words:

I don't exist but you know me as Clyde.
Who the hell are you?

At the bottom of the screen, outside the balloon and presumably in Dewey's voice, are the words "For all you need to know, break the Bad Luck Apple."

The men have wandered down the aisles about half-way to the screen, a few have taken seats, and a few, like me, peer back at the source of the beam, but there's no one visible in the projection booth. For a brief moment none of us moves, no one says anything. Then some old guy's voice up near the front of the group makes a pronouncement. He says, in a tone of utter disgust, "Damned jokester!"

And they're off. Karen and I step aside as a stream of truth-starved and cursing men tweaked one too many times rushes past us and back into the lobby. In seconds the projection booth is all aflurry and Clyde is yanked from the screen in a general air of bread-riotousness. Then the beam is killed and the theatre falls dark as several figures rush blindly back into the aisles. One of them trips on something and—judging by the sounds reaching Karen and me, now seated safely out of the way and waiting for our eyes to adjust to the dark—others spill to the floor. I offer Karen a licorice stick but she ignores me, completely involved in the play. We can't see much yet, but it occurs to me that this must be what one of those slapstick silent pictures would sound like if it had sound. Whatever's happened out there, it sounds painful. I guess I'd prefer the usual piano music.

Someone cries out, "The fuck off me!"

Others call for the lights.

One of them finally senses clear ground and breaks for the exit sign off to the right of the screen. The idea is that Dewey must have escaped out the back and that some good will be done by running after him, as if he hadn't left eight or ten minutes ago. And, naturally, locked the door behind him. Which occurs to the guy rushing for the exit door at about the time his full stride is broken by the door itself. There is only the thud. He recoils a half-step and falls over cartoonishly. We've just seen a man knock himself out.

"Oh Jesus," Karen observes.

I half expect someone to throw a bucket of water on him. A revolving circle of stars to rise above his head.

When the lights came up, the loser by knockout was revealed as Randall (Floorboard) Wright, one of Two-Four's cousins. Two-Four collected him, loaded him into his truck and set off for the hospital. No one said much. It was pretty embarrassing.

At the moment we're mulling around on the street outside the Palace. Everyone except Karen is looking briefly at one another. She stands beside me with a neutral expression, looking slightly above everyone's head and tugging at my elbow. She can't say as much right out loud, but she seems to think I or both of us may be about to take a fall here. But it's such an odd moment in this town, I can hardly leave. Especially since doing so would only confirm our guilt for those who suspect us as part of some conspiracy.

For a few more seconds nothing much happens. Given the sudden quiet, you'd almost mistake what is surely a marshalling of bile for a moment of reflection. It's a time of real community. Adding to the general sense of betrayal is the obvious fact that quiet resolve, the very stoicism we imagine we're famous for, it just won't do a bit of good here.

Someone finally calls out, "We're gone to his house." It's Harvey (Mother) Hubbard with his brother Little Mother. Both of them are adenoidally blunted of facial features and forever overcompensating for their lack of expression by uttering threats. "You come or not. We catch him we won't need no help." They climb into a truck and squeal away.

"Ah hell, you better go along," Eldon tells a few of his players. It's understood that he means his players should keep Harvey and Little Mother from punching up Dewey's house when they don't find him there. Somewhat reluctantly, the whole starting outfield piles into another truck and takes off.

"Anyone here belong to this Coca May outfit?" asks Roger.

"I been meaning to join," says Mel Dubois, standing next to the old guy who said "jokester" in the theatre and who, I now realize, must be Mel's dad, Roland. I haven't seen Roland in years.

He's come to resemble someone perpetually suspended in the moment before a sneeze.

Eldon turns to me.

"So when did you find out?"

"Yesterday," I say.

"Find out what?" someone asks.

I lead us over to Eldon's pickup and hop up onto the bed to give myself a platform.

"I didn't know what he had in mind tonight, but I found out yesterday that.... "

"That what?"

"That the Coca May and Dewey . . . they're really on the same page about things."

"What does he mean, page?"

"My friend Dewey, he's been arguing with himself all along."

I look down at a couple of dozen faces, each clicking once. I'm hoping they'll be angry. I couldn't bear seeing so many moments of defeat.

"So this is all between him," Karen speaks up, longshotting.

"Like hell" is the response. "He thinks we're a buncha idiots and losers."

"I don't think so."

"Well fuck you too, Toss."

"Whatever."

"Let's break that Bad Luck Apple against Beyer's skull!" someone shouts.

A cheer rises. Eldon nods.

As they start up the street to Honkers I call out, "Just remember half of him is on your side!"

A few weeks ago Dewey and Karen and I sat here at our table under Lenny discussing history and truth, which led naturally to the history of truth, and of big truth, which landed us in religion. It was one of those conversations wherein people wax on about things they haven't thought through and don't really care much about as if they're revealing the guiding principles of their lives. Or I thought that was what we were doing—it was what I was doing in complaining about the narrow-mindedness of local church congregations, and what Karen was doing in recalling incidents from her prairie Catholic upbringing that first revealed hypocrisy and what she now considered "tribalism"—but somehow we ended up very near Dewey's heart. For once he spoke plainly, directly, and in a quiet voice I hadn't heard before. He said he believed in the value of foxhole conversions. He said he was certain that for some people religious faith actually connected with something outside them that could alter their circumstances in miraculous ways. He said the best way to think of God was the way you did as a child, as a bright and shining grandfather type, and you should pray at least as often as you brushed your teeth, though you shouldn't necessarily pray like a kid—it was something you had to grow into and find your own methods for. Then his proposition that the cruel lessons of humility work the same as cattle prods and we must all decide whether or not we can trust painful coercions. There is another side to faith, of course. If you are prodded in a dark room, how can you be sure who holds the prod? Is it a celestial taskmaster who has your good in mind, or a demonic rancher sending you to slaughter?

The question stands before me just as certainly as do the townsmen who've walked up here to Honkers from the Palace. Roger opened up for us but only after making it clear he didn't want anyone breaking his apple. He reminded us that it was the only thing he'd taken from his first wife in the divorce. Apparently she was a collector of crafted fruit and this was her favourite in the native produce category, something she picked up down in Ontario and had shipped out at great expense.

"Alot of hard feelings get put in their place here," he says, tapping the apple with one hand as he pours bourbon into a line of shot glasses with the other. The hard feelings are his own and everyone else's too. In the last ten years or so, dropping two-dollar bills into the apple became an entirely local superstition we could all share, men and women, farmers and bankers, Conservatives and socialists, old-time Protestants and Catholics (if not charismatics) alike. Drained resources, unheeded protests, lost government contracts—decades of grievances against Ottawa, Toronto and Quebec were represented by those rust bills, once rare in the west. All our troubles were reduced to a small space you could fold up, tape shut and flick away. But there was more than politics attached to the bills. If a two-dollar bill was bad luck, it must come from the same place all our personal and shared misfortune come from. And wasn't it true that about the time two-dollar bills started flooding the west, the drought set in?

The drinks are passed around, the first one to Karen. On the way over I asked her to go home but she said I was less likely to get beaten up as Dewey's stand-in if she was with me. And I'm here partly as a potential voice of reason and partly because it still isn't clear how I could carry off an exit without triggering a lot of judgements.

Other reasons are put forth as to why we should not break Roger's apple. Arthur Morissette, a farmer who has kept afloat only because he has steady work as an agricultural insurance adjuster, points out that doing so would spill years' worth of bad luck onto the floor.

"That's a superstitious thing to say, Arthur," says Lane Boland.

"That Boland's a real asshole," Karen whispers. In fact, Lane is a self-righteous young family man who inherited huge tracts of land from his dad and has weathered the drought because of a diverse investment portfolio he'd be happy to tell you about.

"You don't fear superstition and you don't have to worry about it," he concludes.

"I say we dump the money on Lane there," says Stew Gates. "He's used to it."

"Now now," says Roger.

“Let him break it open then,” says Stew. “It’s ten years’ bad luck he’s got coming.”

Keith Sidoryk moves us along with “Why the hell should we do what Beyer tells us? Fuck ’im, I say.”

Quite obviously we’re trying to come up with justifiable cause for cracking the thing open. Whether we do find cause or not, the apple will break before long, we all know damn well.

“I think we’re displacing our anger here,” says someone standing in the back row near the entranceway. Before you can say “Where the hell did that come from,” the crowd is parted to reveal Dick Pully. Dick is one of the quietest guys in town but was rumoured to be quite intelligent, and was sometimes referred to as Still Waters. Then his wife enrolled him in an adult-ed psychology course at the school over in Goose Lake so he’d have something to do after driving her to her five-pin league night. Now every so often he spouts snippets of things he picked up there. Still Waters turns out to be a boob. The crowd closes again and he disappears.

In the rearrangement of faces I see Bob Panaway. Bob was a friend of my father’s. They were schoolkids together, became drunks and then reformed drunks together, supported each other as each lost a wife. Bob even has the same greyish wolf eyes that Marius had. Since sobering up twenty-five years ago he’s been a paragon of quiet rectitude and sound judgement, with an instinct for serving the higher good. Bob delivers even pleasantries on the street with an air of square dealing. I have no idea why he should be here among us young fellows all caught up in a silly public spectacle. He is one of the last remaining town builders. He is well-spent blood and sweat. He’s all the reason anyone would need to feel piercing despair at the death of this town.

He sees me looking, looks back, nods. It’s then I realize Dewey can have all the sport he wants with young yahoos like me, but I won’t have him diminishing the best of us. For all the troubles wrought by an ever-expanding generational gap, without the Bob Panaways we’d all have turned our noses up, put our palms in our pockets, and run off to the cities long ago.

"You have a loon?" I ask Karen.

"No."

I get up and ask Eldon for a loon. He hands it over without diverting his attention from Carter Shay, another farmer saying his piece.

I walk over to the pool table and insert the loon into the coin slot, and the balls come tumbling down to the side tray. I take two in hand and walk over to the bar. Roger sees me coming, knows what I have in mind. Carter stops talking.

"What do you say?" I ask Roger.

He hesitates a moment, then moves aside the mickey bottles and with both arms slides the huge apple front and centre on the bar.

"It's had its day, I guess," he says.

"Fine then," I say. I turn to the room and announce, "If there's any hard luck in here, let it be on me. But don't expect any solutions to come tumbling out." And with that, I raise up the balls and bring them down on the terracotta.

The apple shatters and a thousand bitter wishes surge out and shower to the floor. They carry with them a small white envelope, folded tightly but untaped and so blooming open as I snatch it from the bills at my feet. I turn to the group and open it up. There should be some drama here, but the men are murmuring at the sight of so much strapped cash just lying there.

I read the note to myself.

"What's he say?" someone asks.

"I guess he says, 'Game over.' I guess he says, 'Goodbye.'" I hand the note to Roger and collect Karen by the elbow. We make our way to the door as Roger reads aloud Dewey's version of all we need to know: "Speak Large or Vanish."

Karen and I walk along the town line on our way to a late-night visit to Dewey's house. Perry spots us and pulls my truck over. He fills us in on the goings-on over at Harvest Lane. It seems traffic there has been steady all night. A group of ten or twelve vigilante types (he recognized among them Eldon's dad and Old Norm's son, Young Norm) have already been by three or four times, and they seem to have an arrangement with Old Norm that he'll get on the phone if Dewey shows. Perry offers to drive us but I tell him to go home. He says he will, but adds, "Mom thinks we're both crazy, you know. She doesn't care I agree with her."

When he's gone I ask Karen if she thinks I'm crazy.

"Of course you are. The question is, does anyone here appreciate craziness enough to let you get away with it? I would say the night's events suggest they do not."

"This year I can handle anyone else's opinion. I'm only worried about yours."

"Well, I think you're out of your mind on a local scale. I told Mother your plans and she just thinks you're desperate. She thinks you must blame her for my leaving."

"So what if I do? We all have our guilty consciences. I hope you pointed out to her that my plans for a colony give you both a practical reason to stay."

"That's the first time I've heard it described as practical."

When we get to Dewey's we walk a flashlight beam up from the rear and slide into the garage before Old Norm wakes from whatever pull-action dreams he's savouring in his lawnchair across the way. Dewey's truck's not here. We take the concealed side entrance. The place is dark.

"There's no one here," says Karen.

"He could hide in here for as long as his food held out." I lead us over to the pool, lit blue by the moon through a skylight.

"It's empty."

"I didn't think he swam," she says. "He told me he has drowning premonitions."

"No, I mean the bottom's been cleared out. This was his spot. He had his mattress in there, his books and clothes."

"He slept in the pool? Don't you find that a bit odd?"

"I guess I never questioned it. I just wonder if he hasn't packed up and moved off. He must've had time to get his stuff together."

"I bet he did his packing before the Palace episode. They were flanked out pretty fast after the Honkers thing."

"We better check out the rest of the place, maybe he just changed rooms again."

We find his suite in the basement shooting gallery. The furniture's lined along one wall of the narrow fire zone. His mattress is under the target clipped to the electronic clothesline device. The clothesline is hung with clothes. Karen pushes the retrieve button and we collect several shirts and two pairs of jeans before the target is visible. Approaching us is another rendering of Clyde. He arrives abruptly. The dominant feature is not, as Dewey would have intended, the overstuffed and multidirectional fangs, but rather the ears. They're too large. They look like mule's ears, not so much pinned back as flopped over from their own weight. The eyes, meanwhile, are somehow placid, perhaps because the eyebrows curve into one another and look exactly like any preschooler's version of a bird in flight. The whole thing is meant to be menacing but it comes off inexpert and goofy.

I reach up and pluck the drawing from the clip. Beneath it is an envelope with a note scrawled across it: "You probably think I'm leading somewhere with all this. And you a history teacher."

Karen's draped the clothes over her arm. She's staring at them. "I thought maybe he left town, but why would he leave his clothes?" Her voice echoes.

"I could have told you nothing had . . . *become* of him."

"It's pretty obvious *some*thing became of him, but whatever it was, it happened before we ever met him." She turns and marches away on up the stairs.

I'm left holding the envelope and Clyde, the unsuggestive wolf-mule. He doesn't seem worth pondering. And anyway, I'd rather follow Karen.

21

I SUPPOSE there's a note in this envelope too, but I hesitate in opening it. Should Dewey be gone from our lives, then maybe he's best left here, in this moment, as an unanswered question on a dark night. How did we ever get ourselves in the position of wanting him, of all people, to explain himself? Not only is he an unreliable booster of community spirit but I now know he's living by the wrong adage. It makes no difference whether you speak large or small, you'll vanish just the same. What became of Mulwray's Richard Wallace, of the nations he claimed to have the goods on? And what of Eugene and his traceless life? In this land, in this time of disappearances, the only thing that might save you is to tell the hardest story you can tell, the one you think you'll never give up because it's too complicated, too hard to reason through and, anyway, you come off in a poor light. Speak large all you want, but what's at stake is whether or not you can speak true.

Of course, I open the envelope. The second note of the night reads simply, "Play tape in player in kitchen."

Karen's waiting for me at the top of the stairs. We'd best keep the ground floor dark, but by the light of a slightly open fridge door we create a kind of false dawn in the kitchen and discover two chairs facing the oven as if it were a tv. On the stove sits the cheap, portable tape machine.

Karen says, "You two didn't stage all this just to get me to spend a night with you, did you?"

"No, but you might consider that God has staged it for that very reason."

I fetch us two beers and in short order we're set up for the next amusement. I hit the oven light and the play button and we sit there staring at a rack through the glass. A repose hangs over the scene. We look briefly to one another in the soft light, a light for opening up, a storytelling light, and Dewey finally begins telling his story.

"You ever heard of such a thing as a burrowing owl?" It's Dewey.

"No, but they sound like a good idea."

"Who's that?" Karen asks.

"It's Murphy, I think, the shortstop."

We hear a few pauses and background noises as they settle in for the conversation. The sound of an ice tray torquing, a few cubes tumbled into their glasses. Dewey finally resumes.

"I used to work all sorts of jobs around the west, mostly Saskatchewan, and in the last few years I caught on as a hired hand with two farmers, an old guy outside Regina with the business sense of a duck who went from wheatking to welfare in a kind of blasted mallard freefall, and then a farm couple, Lorne and Dianne Mills, north of Pridemore, where I rented a house from them in change for my work and about four hundred bucks a month. There wasn't alot of work in the fields—there *weren't* any fields—and so I did what I could around the yard and helping Lorne haul a mobile grain-cleaning outfit here and there to keep some cash coming in, but there wasn't much demand for that either. He should have let me go by midsummer when it was clear there wouldn't be crops, but he didn't, I guess because it wouldn't matter anyway—Lorne's debts were a week or two from becoming the bank's problem.

"Lorne and Dianne were a typical middle-aged farm couple, with a few big disappointments they never complained about. For one, they wanted kids but couldn't have them and settled for a sabre-toothed German shepherd named Rex they kept tied up next to the house. And two, they wanted to work their farm but were going to lose it. They didn't ask for much and they didn't get it.

"Lorne's last chance was applying for help from the province, and one afternoon the government's man came around to size up our chances at ever seeing black again if they propped us up. I was out checking an owl's nest beside a road bordering the last quarter-section when Lorne drove up with this guy in his truck. I knew who he was right away. A kid just out of university who looked like he hadn't broken a sweat since toilet training. Lorne introduced him as Tim Spires. He said hello and I didn't. I asked Lorne if maybe we shouldn't report this nest to authorities somewhere. Then I said, 'What about you, Mr. Spires. You're official. Is it any good to tell you there's a nest here?' He stepped up and looked where I pointed, at the mouth of a drainage culvert, and it's what I could see and he couldn't, it's that image that stays with me, the picture and everything it's ever made me think of. Fanning in a half-moon away from the culvert was what looked like thirty or forty short pieces of string all dusted over with drifted soil, because it isn't the bodies you notice in the earth—they lose their shape—it's the tails. Spires just looked at Lorne and asked if we could get on with business.

"Ten minutes later the three of us and Dianne sat around the kitchen table and pretended to study numbers. I mostly looked at Dianne. She was a kind of worn beautiful and she must've known I thought so because I usually acted up around her like a twelve-year-old. She mostly looked at Lorne. He was this huge, balding man with glasses and a wide mouth that just grew wider when he smiled or lost himself in thought. Lorne looked at the numbers and tried to think of something to say. Spires glanced at Dianne and must've known the numbers had said their piece before he ever arrived. Other than that he didn't look at anyone eye to eye. I asked Spires what it took to do his job, and he said some formal education and some farm experience. 'And some balls,' I said. Lorne took off his glasses. He told Spires, 'There's been something moving around in the yard the last few nights. It's been making the dog howl. I thought if I didn't take it as an omen then it wouldn't be one, but it turns out that's wrong.' I got up and headed for the back door as Dianne asked Spires if he'd like to stay for dinner. I paused to hear him say, 'No thanks' before I went outside."

Dewey falls quiet for a few seconds. He apparently tends his drink and we can hear him ask Murphy if he wants more ice. There's no audible reply.

"Are you picturing this?" Dewey asks.

Murphy says, "Yeah."

"This is late summer, I'm standing out in an old farmyard surrounded on all sides by rows of windbreak trees."

"And it's hot," Murphy adds.

"Hot as a fresh-dressed axe blade and so dry your spit would evaporate before it hit the earth. Same old colourful-description kind of hot."

"And dry. Dry as a nun's—"

"That dry."

"And burnt brown."

"Well no. The place is scorched but here's where things change. Things turn green in a hurry. I'm standing out in the yard, midway from everything, when Spires leaves the house. I see Dianne watching from the kitchen window, and she must have seen it coming before Spires did.

"I once knew a guy who claimed to have telepathy with dogs, which he said he never told people about because everyone thinks they have that to some degree, but he could tune into dogs he'd never met, even when they were in the next room. He said they have a lot of intentions but not much in the way of language, so there was no way of explaining their thoughts, though often they came to him as sort of colours. He said, in dog terms, green is deadly. I've always remembered that, and I swear I had a flash of green myself when I saw Spires scrambling for his car to get clear of Rex, the shepherd. But his car was locked—you understand he didn't leave it that way—so he jumped in the back of Lorne's truck and hunched behind the spare fuel tank. Rex sprang up and cleared the tank enough that Spires could land a forearm shiver to the throat and send him tumbling back to the ground without so much as a whimper, and then he scurried around the tail and took Spires from a better angle. Neither of them had much traction, but Rex got hold of his shirt collar while attempting what was no question meant to be a jugular kill, and he pulled Spires over frontwards. About the time the dog's teeth got into Spires' shoulder the guy flopped over the side and the two of them fell to the ground. Rex was in final approach when a single head shot felled him for good.

"Spires lay there, not able for a long time to take his eyes off what was left of Rex, the top of his head creased like a hatchet wound and the back blown clear away. Dianne ran out to Spires. Lorne was standing just outside the doorway, holding the rifle, cursing to himself. I was still standing there, mid-yard. Eventually Spires sat up and looked around. Lorne and Dianne both knew he'd been set up but they didn't know whether or not he knew it. Dianne kneeled over him and asked him questions in a voice so calm...you wouldn't have to answer a voice like that. She began to tell Spires about the dog. She said, 'You know, Mr. Spires, we've had Rex for six years now and he wasn't always like this.' He said his name was Tim. She said hers. Then he asked if the dog had had his rabies shots and she said he had and he told her he was off to a hospital to have his shoulder looked at but he wouldn't trouble them any more. She just nodded. I walked over to my truck and left the same time Spires did, and there was Dianne still standing over Rex with her arms crossed."

For a few seconds there's no sound, then Murphy asks, "Is that all? Then what?"

"Well, there was a falling out. That particular world was lost. The Millses moved on. We all did. But it's hard to stop wondering just how I ever got connected to Lorne's omen, that thing moving around in the dark farmyard. Or at least in the darker parts of poor Rex."

We listen for a few minutes more as Dewey explains his getaway strategy, then he signs off by saying, "Toss, I think you and Karen could make some interesting noises together. I hope I get to hear them some day."

Later, I walk Karen back to her house. The town has stilled itself and doesn't invite commentary, and I can't think of a thing to say. I'm a little angry at Dewey for having left, a little sad for him, too, though I don't think his story by itself explained as much as he might have hoped it would.

I ask Karen what she's thinking.

"I'm thinking I'm ashamed of myself. Dewey tells us his farm tragedy and I feel . . . reassured by it. I mean, I thought all this hooting and gunplay was just men being boys."

"You feel better that Dewey's not just amusing himself? That he's actually been damaged?"

"It's terrible, I know, but yes. I do."

22

YOU HAVE to believe that even this far along when something comes to you out of the blue, you're given part of another man's life, there must be a reason for it you might find in looking where you yourself have come from. Yet take fifteen years of Dewey's life and play it backwards, it sounds the same: that's here then Pridemore then Central Butte, Amazon, Sceptre, Ituna, Swift Current, Dafoe. He remembers these places as a series of fresh opportunities for manufactured dramatics, but only at the last of these stop-offs, the Mills farm, did he learn what dark creations his overlarge imagination was capable of.

The lesson of the broad stroke, one I learned long ago: remove the saving ambiguities in your actions and you see in exaggerated behaviour that it's you these actions are about. They're exactly and pointedly and only about you.

Somewhere around nine-thirty on another dustbake morning I stand on the riverbank, thinking about Dewey and watching a light current lift itself against the passenger side of his truck. Before his sign-off wish that Karen and I "make noises" together, Dewey explained that I'd find the truck half-submerged in the river about three miles east of my place. He said he wanted me to call enough witnesses so that theories would form (I've called Eldon, and Harrison Lee is bringing his tractor over). Dewey said people would assume he'd just been scared away rather than killed, and the consensus would be that he'd had a proper sendoff. He predicted, "Everyone will feel a little bad and a little better at the same time. Meanwhile, a car belonging to Ballplayer Lacousiere's girlfriend, Miss McKeegan, will have gone missing, along with my friend John here. They believed he'd gone out to get beer for the three of them at the offsale. The car will be found at the Saskatoon airport within several hours. John's uncle has a turfing operation down in Mesa that I can be a big part of. I'll call in a week."

I hear Harrison's tractor about a quarter-mile off around the bend in the access road. It turns out he's holding up a convoy of spectators. Besides Eldon are a few of his players and three or four trucks full of recognizable faces from last night at the Palace, and one who wasn't there—Perry. And in behind these is Corporal Hall in his police cruiser.

The line stops itself along the road. The men wait for Hall to walk on ahead, then they emerge and follow.

"Morning corporal."

"What have you got here?" He's wearing drab civilian clothes but he brims with official capacity.

"Well, there's the river. There's a truck. Something doesn't fit."

"Why didn't you call me?"

"It's not your truck."

"If this is an accident, I should be called. If it's a crime scene, I should be called. Have you looked in the truck yet?"

"No. But it's empty."

He ignores me and walks to the water's edge. Then he starts taking his shoes off. I turn to the men and shake my head.

"I only made two calls," I tell them. I knew two would be enough, of course.

Hall wades in and I pull my boots off and follow him. The men move closer to the bank.

The front end of the truck is nosed a little deeper than the rest but the cab is mostly out of the water. Hall looks in the driver's door and I look through the opposite one.

"Where is he?"

"You want to check the glove compartment? He's gone."

"His clothes and things are still at his house."

"Go ahead and take what you want, corporal. Now can we dry this thing out?"

We crawl ashore and as Harrison backs his tractor into place Eldon tells Hall his theory that Dewey's getaway car was likely the one his American shortstop stole from the other American's girlfriend.

"American?" Hall asks, distracted, perhaps worried we've got an international incident on our hands here.

"Yeah," says Eldon.

"But how does that explain the truck here?"

"It's a diversion," says Eldon. Then everyone turns and looks at the truck again.

Perry and I wade in and run a crude stability test that involves rocking the truck from side to side to see if it might drift. When it stays put I duck under the surface and loop the chain around the rear axle. Though most people don't realize it, there is nothing like the feeling of cold river mud sun-drying in your hair and on your face. When we secure the chain and climb back onto the bank, Harrison hits low gear and tows the truck with uncomplicated ease until it sits twenty feet from the water, draining and looking somehow relieved. The lot of us just stand staring at the rescued truck as if it's some sunken treasure brought up from the deep.

Hall walks over and opens the driver's door, makes one last check of the thing.

He asks, "Do any of you men know what went on here?" No one says anything. "Well, then, go on home." There is a general air of disappointment, but the show is over, after all, so people start to clear off. Perry is eyeing the truck and I know what he has in mind. I ask Harrison to tow it into my yard. He waits for the others to leave, then gives Perry a perch on the step, and hauls it off.

Hall looks defeated.

"You think he's gone for good?"

"I hope not, but yeah, looks like you got your wish."

For a moment his face grows clouded, and I wonder if he isn't off somewhere in what he thinks of as a simpler time in his life. I can't help but think that he's lost the game to Dewey, and it's a loss I feel close to myself.

I say, "It's good of you not to press charges."

"It never wins me much." He starts off to his cruiser.

"By the way," I ask, "do you still think I was trying to dynamite my neighbour's house?"

He turns and regards me impassively.

"I knew it was your cousin in the truck that night. I was just seeing if you couldn't do some good."

"Sorry, but things took their own course."

I'm a little afraid to ask him the next question. Certainly there were other consequences waiting there at the end of Dewey's story, ones he didn't tell us about on the tape. He never explained, for instance, what had happened between him and Alvin Hall back in Pridemore.

"Did you know a man at your last posting named Lorne Mills?"

"Yes," he says levelly. "You know that story then?"

"Not all of it. That's why I'm asking."

Hall walks back towards me, turns to the river and answers my questions while looking out at a small island near the south side. He says that Dewey had worked for Mills and rented a house from him in town. One day the house burned down and it was evident to Hall, though he couldn't prove it, that Dewey and Lorne Mills had decided to collect the insurance money. When it became clear there was no way of proving arson, Hall called the Mills farm and accused Lorne, a man he'd never spoken to or known in any way, of being a coward. There was no reply. The next afternoon when his wife was in town Lorne Mills took his rifle out behind the machine shed, got into the cab of his combine, and made a gesture. Dewey found him.

Hall describes the rifle. I wonder why for a moment but then realize the details are important to him, and knowing that Lorne used a lever-action 30-30 with a twenty-inch barrel leads you to a pretty accurate picture if you want an exact sequence of final events.

"Your friend Beyer knew about the phone call. He told me he'd torched the place and Lorne Mills had nothing to do with it. He just wanted to get them some money." He turns and looks at my truck sitting down the road in the shade.

"Did he blame you for what happened?" I ask.

"He blamed himself, but he wanted me to take a share I guess."

Because I have to know, and though I feel a traitor, I ask, "Do you know if Lorne Mills was in trouble with his farm?" And if he had a wife named Dianne? And did he shoot his dog and does the name Spires ring a bell?

"He was going under, yes."

I leave it there. Then I ask him if he's ever told anyone the end of the Mills story before. He just shakes his head.

"Do you feel better?"

He glances at me before looking out at the trees along the river. A light breeze lifts off the water and moves in the high reaches heading east.

"No. I feel like hell."

"Good. That's probably good."

"But I refuse to be just another sad son-of-a-bitch, like your friend."

He looks down at the wet, clinging pantlegs, and pinches the fabric and pulls it away from his thigh.

I say, "I guess Dewey is sort of a junk heap of faulty defence mechanisms, but I don't think his regrets are tracking him down." He peers up to give me a listen. "It's more like he's tracking them."

My day proceeds between shifts at Cora's house fending off the growing number of get-well wishers who've begun to make it hard for her to get the rest she needs. I make some effort to organize the time ahead of me, something I'm not used to doing. In the last few days before she and Kate leave for the coast, I hope to spend as much time as I can in the company of Ms. Shaulter, a few hours of initial planning, schedules and phone strategies and such, then placing enquiries and securing dates for a few face-to-faces with small-gallery and fine-arts people, to extend invitations and thereby secure references for grant applications. Somewhere in there we'll drive Kate out to the hills where I know just the spot to take measure of the now twice-acquired family land and where we can picture freshly coated buildings, skylight modifications, a few flatboard cabins, a handful of men and women in practical dress taking in the full light and one of them pointing up in our direction, where deer bound freely, safe with the knowledge that they are in season but in no one's range but mine. Upon leaving we'll take with us a great sense of promise. Very likely, the wild grass will look greener and not quite so patchy. Then to town again where the three of us will pay a call to Cora, who will renew acquaintances with Kate while Perry and I discuss building plans and make estimates on the generous side, adjusting them to the particular needs of studio construction as insisted upon by Karen. Soon Cora will retire to rest again and I'll drive Kate home and she'll tell me this Vancouver move was logical until I turned out to be such a good fellow. Then I'll return the truck for Perry, who will disappear with a promise to keep his good senses in responsible order. Finding ourselves alone, Karen and I will grow surprisingly tentative and quiet and will make busy by way of a chili dinner for four. As she stands at the chopping board I'll come from behind and nudge her into a little hug and she'll pretend the onions are to blame for the tears. When Cora next rises she'll find that we've broken into a Cabernet Sauvignon and lament she can't have any because of the painkillers she's on so we'll offer to put away the wine if we can have Percodan too. Karen will ladle some chili into one of the old sealer jars Cora keeps for crabapple jelly and walk the few blocks to her house where she and Kate will have the same meal as Cora and I, though not eating together will allow everyone to talk openly about how sensible and well suited to each other we all are. Before sunset Karen and I will meet on the lawn across from the Anglican church and stroll the last streets in every direction, which will take about an hour, and without announcing any intention to do so we'll end up at the museum, in the Pioneer Bedroom, re-enacting moments from everyone's past.

"Where are you exactly?"

"At the Flyway for lunch. Cora's sleeping and Perry's home to relieve me for an hour so I thought I'd not hang around. But I have to see you later. I have a gift."

"I can't just close up and leave for the day. You make the calls yourself. It's not like you can avoid the real work of making contacts."

"It's not the work I'm afraid of—"

"It's that you don't know what you're doing, or why, even."

"I know why. Why isn't the problem. But this might be more complicated than setting up a truck pull. I can't ensure success with a few wet t-shirts or a paying gallery for the nude sessions."

"You can't humour your way through this one. Look, let's do a little test. Do as I say. Go outside and wait for something to catch your eye, then tell me what it is."

Having just entered the motel restaurant, I leave the counter and walk back out the front door. I consider how the world appears. Then I go back inside the Flyway and pick up the phone.

"A pink Cadillac."

"What was it doing?"

"It came in from the west and it's just cruising down Railway."

"What did it make you think?"

"The way it moved, without hesitation, it didn't look like it had any intention of stopping to do business."

"Did you think of a shape, maybe a bird or animal, a memory?"

"Animals in general. Animal experiments and cosmetic testing. People get cars like that from selling makeup."

"There's always this economic thing with you."

"Profit is one question, but simple viability is many. I just don't want to turn into one of those poor suckers whose capital problems become respiratory ones. Besides which, I'd have to make these calls from Cora's phone, which has a dial. Phone dials hold a high position in the order of my irrational-response triggers. I never make important calls from Cora's phone."

"Do you really want me to know that about you?"

"Well, there's your pioneer underwear thing." Then nothing. Presumably I was kidding about the phone dials. I pretend it's important I get a bowl of lentil soup du jour before it's all gone.

The food arrives all at once, beef dip and soup, lentils afloat. I find myself staring at the little plastic saltshaker in the likeness of a cowboy boot. Here comes that rare state of mind wherein little things bother me that no one else notices. I once spent a whole day in bed all but paralysed by the materials of my existence, especially the many kinds of summertime plastics. But then I was hung over too. It's a state of nonthought that I don't want just now, so instead I start into the food and contemplate the staggering density of trash we import to our lives and use to construct battlements of crap that surround us, that configure us, that we can never get beyond unless we are willing to risk terrifying ourselves into paralysis. And what is beyond these productions, these false borders of consciousness? What exactly is the fierce outland we only see if we meet with disaster—if, say, we are transported by tornado to the heart of a sad story? Another time or another country? No. We find almost everything in our lives, all the externals and much of our understanding to be irrelevant. All we have is our physical and emotional selves navigating as best we can through our element like reptiles in warm mud. Whatever else is true in general terms, or whatever we hope is true, mutual concern and the better applications of reason, the only common denominator is the physical fact of our existence, something many of us would frankly rather ignore, given that it's the root cause of so much pain and anxiety, and eventually runs its course. Whereas some of the crap lasts centuries, well beyond the worryfree period before planned obsolescence kicks in.

All I'm asking for is a fucking art colony.

Heading my way are Wayne Walker and his sister Shawna and her two pre-teens. It will take some concentration not to speak like a booby-trap.

"Hear you found his truck," says Wayne.

"Yes. He seems to be gone from us."

"Only 'cause he was your friend I'm not saying any more about him," Wayne says. We sort of nod at each other.

"And we hear you made a little purchase yesterday," says Shawna, grinning. Wayne affords me a smile too from under his UGG cap. Of course they've heard, probably ten times over. The kids look like snivellers.

"News travels."

"You really think you can haul in painters?" Wayne asks. "It's the sort of scheme just wouldn't occur to me."

"I'll see. There's a lot of work to do before it could ever get off the ground."

"Well, if you need a hand..." says Wayne.

"Perry and I will do most of the work. We don't know what kind of material expenses we'll have so we're trying not to hire out much."

"Yeah but that's not what I meant," he says. "You need a hand just give a call and I'll put in these." He holds his hands out and wiggles his fingers. "Shawna's Bill too, prob'ly."

Shawna explains, "He likes that sort of thing, long as you don't go overboard on the drink."

"Those are the sorts of provisions we've already accounted for." I laugh. The kids look like fine children. "I guess it would help to have someone who knew what he was doing. Maybe I'll take you up. When's a good time?"

"Whenever. It's not like harvest is gonna ask a lot of us this year."

"Hey, did you ever get that sun deck built off your kitchen?"

"Sure did."

"The wood turn out okay?"

"I made damn certain of that. You be careful the same way with those guys down at the lumberyard. They'd sell warps to Noah if they could."

Wayne sends Shawna on ahead with the kids. She hesitates a moment as if she expects Wayne to say something dumb to me. Then she waves bye and moves the kids away and on out the door.

"People appreciate you being the one to break that apple," says Wayne. "Your bad luck begin yet?"

"I used it up this last year," I say. "What's happening with the money?"

"It's not even two thousand dollars. Nobody really has a claim to it. If they ever get the tape off they'll just throw a party in the Legion Hall in a few weeks. Take everyone's mind off there being no crops at harvest. Listen, Toss?"

"Wayne?"

"People are saying Beyer took off to the airport with Murphy. You know if that's true?"

"Might be. You know, he didn't mean any harm to anyone, except maybe himself."

"People took it different."

"Well, they took it wrong."

Shawna calls from the doorway. Wayne nods to me again—he was hoping for more answers than I've given him—and leaves me to my lunch.

Later, thinking of Wayne and Shawna while heading back to Cora's, I wonder how it is I've lost the knack of recognizing kindness when it advances on me. In bad need of therapy, I perform a little diagnostic test. Driving west I pick out a few distinct clouds above town and try to imagine what they remind me of. All I come up with are ink blots. White photo-negatives of ink blots. This is plainly unsatisfactory so after I've pulled in at Cora's I try harder, singling out one cloud in particular that seems familiar. Then it comes to me. Hudson Bay. I say it out loud, "Hudson Bay." My mother's birthmark. I say, "Hudson Bay," and for a moment a small part of my lost history is returned to me.

23

KAREN CALLS me at Cora's with the news that the few grants we might qualify for are considerably smaller than we'd imagined. The application forms are on their way but from what she understood after phoning both provincial and national arts councils, the startup money is nominal. If I can run the colony for a year or two, they'll help out later, but the provincial fund is more likely to go to something that has a family angle, a project to keep people from moving out of province. She explains that at one point the term "nuclear farm" came up. She says, "Language like that gives you some indication of the depth of our problem." I'm taking all this in with remarkable clarity for the moments following a half-hour of attempted introspection in Cora's living-room that left me feeling that everyone's sudden abandonment of me must be all my fault. Yet somehow I've skipped any re-entry phase and find myself here with two feet on the ground dealing with cash worries. I make Karen promise she'll come down to see me at the river after supper, then make a call of my own. When Pinch comes on line I explain the matter straight up, knowing he has a nose for bullshit and hoping he'll appreciate my avoiding it.

"What I'll need is about twice as much as I'm in line for from the other sources."

"Assuming you get the grants. Assuming you get all you ask for."

"Yeah, assuming that. But it's not like I'm building a theme park here, Pinch. And if it comes to it, and it won't, I've got collateral."

"Collateral doesn't mean anything in these times. Insurance is more or less removed from the picture."

"So tell me."

"I'll sound it out, though I'm not required to, of course. But here's how it might read: you need money for a venture of questionable viability; you plan to spend most of your cash assets in setting up so there's no bumper from our viewpoint, except that you have a steady income, except rumours are that either you're about to quit, which I know you aren't, or you're about to get squeezed out, which I wouldn't know about."

"Is anything on my side?"

"You are well liked by me but...but generally thought to be capable of making a mistake of disastrous consequences. I'll get back to you."

I'm still waiting for Pinch to get back to me when Cora emerges from her bedroom in late afternoon and shuffles into the kitchen. She finds me talking with her friend Miriam Lake, who's come by to put in a shift.

"It's good you showed up," says Miriam. "Toss and me were discussing the future, and that sort of thing could go on for ever."

Cora moves up to her usual chair and says, "I'm just going to sit down."

"You sleep okay?" I ask. She waits for me to fetch her a glass of water and her pills.

"I've forgotten how your dreams are different when you're sick. It can be an ordeal. There were all sorts of animals, I'm not sure what they were, but herds of them, running on a plain, and I was floating along above them. It was...I felt very strong. But then it was as if they just ran off the edge of the world and began falling. And I fell with them. I thought, 'We'll hit the bottom soon and then it will be over,' but we didn't, and then I realized there was no difference between the flying and the falling. We weren't earthbound any more, is all, and falling was just the thing we were."

Diving under the axle this morning reminded me what fun can be had from simply mucking around in a river. I told Karen we'd go swimming tonight and as she comes through my front door with a tired countenance and a concerned sounding "Hello, Toss," she appears very much in need of some play time.

"That's Dewey's truck out there?"

"Yeah, Perry comes down when he can to try and get it running."

"And you haven't heard from him."

"He said he'd call in a week. It's not a week yet."

"Right," she says dismissively. "You know, I've decided I'm truly, seriously angry with that man. You should be too."

"Maybe when I get more time."

"Uh-huh," she says. She understands I don't want to talk about Dewey. "Pinch Martin called me."

"He was supposed to call me."

"He wanted to know how the grants worked. But even if you get the grants, he can't lend half of what you need."

"I'm going to pretend we haven't started back on this money topic. I'm going to pretend we're on the swimming topic. You go get dressed."

"I didn't bring—"

"That's even better. Then get *un*dressed."

Hooded and wrapped in bathsheets, we pad off for the river through the still evening air, past the remnants of a lawn that Marcie used to tend, past Dewey's truck and the tarp laid out beside it along with the tools of mine Perry's been using to try to revive it, onto the path that leads down to the water. We reach the channel in the form of two dense clouds of mosquitoes.

A few moments of cold, vertiginous escape and I come up with a handful of mud and swim up beside Karen and plop it down on her face, and smooth it over her neck and into her hair.

"What is this stuff?"

"It's silt."

"But what's *in* it?"

"I don't know. Bug repellant."

When we're well caked, we float side by side on our backs and let the small current drift us away from the lowering sun.

"Don't let us get swept into the river," she says.

"Don't worry. As long as this island's on our left, we're still in the channel."

"But you pay attention."

"Shhhh." I put my hand on her belly as it breaks the surface. "Just be here, Karen." I say, "Silt. Water. Be."

This moment has been coming. Insufficiently rinsed, with grains of the river still on us, we sit in our towels and conduct a strategy session with the most far-reaching and personal of implications.

"Either we give up, which I don't want, or we think long-term, putting it all together over a couple years, or we forget the complications of studio costs and turn it into a mud spa."

She will not be amused.

"Sounds like I'm not a part of your backup plans."

"Then let's find some others," I say. Time now to tell her the last chance I see is in approaching the town itself, one reason I wanted Pinch onside from the start. It's just hard to imagine any good can come from leaving myself open to a long line of bad character witnesses.

"And our future comes down to economics?"

"The art is what comes down to economics. You and I don't have anything to do with that side."

"Since *when*?" She actually throws her hands up. I feel I've been given insufficient warning.

"Did I miss something there?"

"All you've ever offered me was the stay or go option. There's never been any consideration that *you* might be the one to follow *me*."

"It's just a setback, Kar—"

"Shut up and listen." I do but she doesn't say anything.

"You getting back at me for that 'Silt. Water' thing?"

"Toss ... I'm trying to get inside your head here."

"Well, I wouldn't rec—"

"Quiet. I think when you look at me you see yet another woman who wants to take you away from your precious family home and out into the wide world where nobody knows who you are or even cares. I don't know that you've ever learned a thing from any of your little troubles." I regard the "little" as somewhat unkind. "And so maybe you're right after all to rule out living anywhere else. Once you leave home you can't always act like you're at the centre of things."

"This isn't exactly the world's navel here."

"But you can *pretend* it is. Living here, you never come face to face with the real size of life. You're never ... adapted to it."

"Well, I admit I never saw the attraction of settling down any spot where waving your arms won't get you noticed or even make much of a shadow. I can't imagine that. And maybe I should be sorry for what I can't imagine, but I'm not."

She bends down and seems to examine her toes. She bites her lower lip. Her eyes have wandered into the pattern on the rug between us. There are sounds. She's mumbling.

"What was that?"

"Winter, I said. Just on grounds of weather this is no place to live. I mean, there's just so many reasons not to be here."

She sits up straight and hugs herself.

"And still," I say.

"Yeah, I know," she says. "Still."

I take her by the hand up to the bedroom and sit her on the bed and show her the shoetree on the windowsill. I tell her what it used to be and how I came to have it. I tell her about Marcie's exit and I point to the brow scar which I believe to represent the sad futility of two people ever making a clean break with their beforelife. I go to the closet and rummage in my travel bag until I find the gift, wrapped in the most colourful page of a newspaper supplement advertising bargains on imported fruit. Then I give it to her and sit beside her on the bed.

"It's hell when your memento is a duck," I say. She opens it and reads the inscription. I explain, "I tried to find something that worked the opposite of a decoy. Besides which, you can trust yourself to look down, not have to worry about all that infinite geometry overhead."

"But 'For cloudy nights in the lead.' What do you mean? How am I in the lead on anything?"

"Don't shake my confidence."

I think she's going to cry. I want her to cry.

"Nice of you to think so. Maybe it's good luck, even." She doesn't cry, but leans over with a kiss and moves her hands along me like a woman recently settled on a toes-in-the-soil outlook. As we explore one another the taste of the river returns to us, the taste of coursing life itself. All this time it's been waiting for us, and now we're there, and now it's here.

VI

THEN

24

I'VE SOMETIMES wondered how the terms of our daily enslavement or passions work their way into moments of free thought. Workplace jargon, the language of tradecraft, sports talk, the figures we find on familiar ground. Pinch once told me he knew a bank manager in another town whose argument by design for God's existence was that the difference between a number and its transposition was divisible by nine. Others have similarly reasoned theories about the invariable mysteries of horse training, successful turnips, and stark coincidence, as when an unfamiliar word finds you three times in a day. It's a matter of attending the proofs you can, then naming what it is you think unifies them, then reminding yourself that if necessary you can indeed say that at least something is true to your experience. Though I don't remember every lesson that evolved the belief, I have learned over the years that when a concern of some importance is suddenly rendered pointless, it is essential to follow through. This is as true in questions of life and love as in sport, shooting the ball anyway though the buzzer has just sounded, and shooting with not a breath's less intensity than if the outcome were yet to be determined. The idea that perfect form is worth shooting for. Here's what I mean.

Though expecting a call from Karen, I've spent the day till now out of earshot, checking out Alan and Wanda's buildings, wandering around their place and wondering how to make good use of all the space, and thinking, of course, about Karen and

Kate's arrival at the coast today and trying to be big enough to want it to go well. Whatever we might say to one another, at least I have some small news bits for them. Not twenty minutes after they disappeared onto Railway Avenue and Sask 44, Blair flagged me down outside the Reliable and showed me the fixings for a martin house he'd finally gathered. For reasons other than sentimentality the two of us spent a half-hour in Kate's yard assembling the thing and positioning and repositioning a concrete stand for the ten-foot pole. I considered it another bad sign of the times that the architecture of back-yard birdhouses had grown so complexly ugly. But there it sat, a miniature aerial condo. Of course mid-August puts us substantially off season, but strictly functional aspects have never much interested me anyway, not that I haven't been by each day since to keep an eye out for claimants.

The day of the sendoff Karen went downtown to fill up the car and left me with Kate for a few minutes. We were standing around the living-room with nothing to do, and she was fretting.

"We must be forgetting something," she said.

"I think you're all ready. I'll send anything on if you think of it."

She'd left most of the house intact—she wasn't about to ship things off until the spring, when she'd have a place picked out for herself, so until then she'd stay with Karen. I was looking at a print of an oil painting hung beside the Dali. A ranch set below huge yellow hills, in the distance a few men on horseback amid cattle on a low slope.

"Doesn't it remind you of here?" she asked. "I ordered it from the States, they send me catalogues. The artist is Australian. I think it's supposed to be in Australia somewhere."

She sat in her favourite chair, an orange floral rocker, but she sat forward in it, and folded her hands, and looked down at them.

"I've lived all my life here in Mayford, except a few years during the war when I worked for the British Admiralty in

Connecticut, and most of the friends I have left live here still." She took an audible breath and looked up at me. "And you know what, Toss?"

"What's that, Kate?"

"I don't think I could tell not a one of my friends how I feel about leaving."

"Karen said you two aren't to leave before noon. She said some people are coming by. Maybe you'll get a chance then."

"Are you pretending you don't understand me?"

"Yes, I guess so."

"There's no one else I can say this to. Maybe because I'm not close to anyone your age."

"You have some advice, Kate?"

"Leaving here at my age, I'm leaving my life. I don't mean leaving the place where it happened, I mean the whole thing—*me*. It shouldn't be that way, maybe Vernon and I, we should have travelled more, learned how to be comfortable in other places, but we didn't. And now.... "

"You think I should leave while I'm young?"

"I'm just saying, wherever you live, if you choose to live here or there, don't spend all of your*self* in a place."

Through the picture window I saw Karen pull up outside. I realized then how much I wanted the two of them to be happy, whatever that meant, even if their happiness excluded mine. A moment of charity and regret.

"Now you promise me you won't tell Karen a word of what I've just said."

"I promise." I took her by the elbow and helped her up. "And if it's any solace to you, Kate, I'll look after things here while you're gone. I'll tend things. Your life won't fall apart without you."

And she laughed, and I thought there was a chance that, somehow or other, this woman would get her life back.

When Karen had Kate set up in the car she led me back inside the house and stood me in the living-room. She faced me and took my hands in hers, and her eyes flickered up to mine.

"This feels worse than it is," she began. "The bad part's when Mother meets the city."

I nodded. I said, "You could tire yourself dead if you keep worrying about her."

"I *am* worried about her, but just right now.... Can you think of anything that needs to be said?"

"I don't have anything prepared. Do you?"

"Yes, sort of." She dipped her head and leaned it into my chest. "Toss, in your weaker moments, I don't want you thinking that my leaving was a way of telling you something I couldn't just say."

"You mean like 'This isn't working and I need to get the hell away'?"

She looked back up at me and, I thought for a second, tendered her most earnest expression.

"That is so definitely *not* what I'm saying by leaving. Do you understand that?"

"I do as long as I can be sure you'd tell me that if it were true."

"I don't . . . you're making this complicated." She squeezed my hands. In her concern I'd been hoping to detect signs of misgivings but, plainly now, her doubt encompassed so much more than just us two.

"Listen," I said. "Last summer I drove the same route from here to B.C. for reasons I didn't understand. It turned out I was scared of my life. I'm still not sure it wasn't my sanest moment."

"You think I'm scared of my life?"

"I think you're smart enough to be scared sometimes by what you can imagine. You're scared for Kate and your daughter, and for yourself. But you have to be willing to believe the better things you might imagine too."

She seemed to think about that.

"Am I imagining you?" she asked.

"No, but imagine yourself, driving away in a minute, and what you'll be thinking of. That's where I want in."

That almost did it—nothing beats a great exit line. She didn't exactly break into tears but her jaw clenched and her head nodded wildly three or four times.

Then she gave me a long hug, and she held it perfectly, and no sooner did she release me, it seems now, than she was gone.

The other news for Karen and Kate is that most of the world I can see from the front-room window is now mine, if only legally, here at the end of my summer of sobering first anniversaries. I was on my way yesterday morning to drop in on Darrel and ask if he'd heard anything from Alan about clearing out his house when a moving truck passed me on the road, going the other way, so I swung around and followed it to the Nash yard. The movers were from Calgary, a husband-and-wife team, Rod and Sheela "with two e's."

"You the one's moving in?" asked Sheela.

"I'm who bought the place."

"Well, we'll be out of here by sundown, though technically we got till midnight."

"I'm not the kind to call you on technicalities."

"That's good," said Rod. "Some people are, though, so we don't leave ourselves open." Sheela had a key and was already in the house, assessing potential complications. She carried the itemized list of their responsibilities. I wanted a look at that list.

"I give you a hand?"

"Not necessary, thanks. We sort of know each other's moves."

"Of course. I guess it's like dancing." He nodded, stood there. My presence was holding him up.

"You go on then," I said. "There's some angles inside I'd like to check once you clear some space, if you don't mind. I bought this place on memory. I didn't feel right inspecting it without the owner around. You know him?"

"A voice on the phone. Look, I don't mean to be a prick but I don't know if we can let you in. You're not the one we're under contract to. This is the sort of thing Sheela says we can't be so dick-ass about—"

"I understand. There's plenty of time for my work after you two clear out. I bet you're not so professional you'd turn down a cold beer around noon."

"We're both on the wagon."

"I see. Cokes?"

"Brought our own, thanks anyway." Then he saluted and went inside before I could suggest home-baked cookies. I went home and phoned the number on the side of their truck, adopted my best Rod voice. "This is Rod. There's stuff in this place we don't have listed but I can't find this Nash guy's number. You have it?" The man on the other end said, "What if I wasn't here? This is exactly what I mean when I say dickass." Then he gave me the number. Area code 604. British Columbia. Alan only eleven digits away (and closer to Karen than I am).

But I couldn't bring myself to call just then, not only because I wasn't sure what to say but also because a year ago the lack of forethought wouldn't have mattered to me, one reason the damage got out of hand. I could have told him I'd packed up his Uncle Cole's collection and returned to the earth both the authentic and the forged by way of an abandoned and nearly inaccessible badger hole, but this was for someone else to uncover on his own, and if no one ever did then so much the better for enigma avoided. Then again, I might just have wished him good luck.

Dewey called when he said he would. This morning marks a week since he left.

"How's Arizona?"

"Does it make you angry, thinking of me in Arizona? Or maybe you miss me a little."

"You wouldn't want me to hold any but complicated feelings for you."

"Now you've got me. Guess what?"

"You're not in Arizona."

It turned out he *had* gone to Arizona, and even met Murphy's uncle, but the first day of work he felt small and ignored and came to believe the heat down there would likely kill him, so he hopped a bus and headed north. Nothing caught his eye. At Lethbridge, Alberta he decided to bear east. He got out on the highway, hitched into some hamlet and got a room from a bartender, shortly after which, because, he said, he missed "having a project to work on," he left in the middle of the night and wandered out to a highway, and not two hours later he stole into Mayford under diminishing cover of night. He thought the safest place would be the Palace, and that's where he was calling from.

"I'm tired of candy," he said. "And I'm guessing I need an escort before I can re-emerge."

Perhaps nothing is to be learned from Dewey, but if anything can be learned *about* him, it's that expectations will be defeated. Yet the reason I wasn't as angry as Karen at his leaving, I now realize, is that I expected his return. I wonder what it means for Karen and me that she had no such expectation.

On the drive to town, a small "spell" not unlike the one I had the morning last summer when I couldn't remember details about Marcie and somehow as a consequence ended up making a spectacle on Main Street. I was thinking about my swim with Karen and all that I'd said to her in the last days about my not being able to imagine a life elsewhere, and about wanting her to imagine *her* life elsewhere, namely here, and I was staring out at the familiar long views of the dead prairie, and I felt suddenly disoriented. For just a moment I was afraid and hopeful that I could lose my sense of direction here in the place I feel most located. I simply couldn't say for certain where I was. I couldn't. And of course there was no one to say it to anyway (which may have been why I felt lost). And then I heard voices, or rather, I *invoked* them from the somewhat severe available light. I asked Alan for his view of my part in the troubles but he wanted to know how I got the number so I admitted having misrepresented myself and he said that's the first thing, that as of the night on the island he was honest and I wasn't, and then he said he hoped I'd get clobbered by an oar some day and he left with the comment that he didn't give a shit why I bought his house. Marcie said she was "bemused," a strange word for her to use, and asked me not to do anything "freaky," one of Karen's westcoasterisms sneaking in. She said something in Spanish I didn't understand. Cora said only that these sorts of fancies are silly and that now I was misrepresenting *her.* Perry regarded my state of mind as proof that he'd made a bad investment. Dewey noted the cartoon nature of my imagining such conversations. It's also childish, or at least he talked to himself in many voices as a child. Eugene and Marius refused to take part.

I passed the field where Marius rolled his truck when his rhythm section packed up, this year a field of mustard, stunted and burnt and more black than yellow, a field of subtle undulation and not a lot of rise and fall. What should have been topsoil was caked in a quarter-inch shell, lineated in a tight but irregular crosshatch broken only by crevices formed by the deep contractions of the land. It struck me as a hell of a place to take note of in hopes of deciding your life instead of having the world decide it for you. I slowed to a stop and waited for the slight vertigo to subside, for sitting again to mean sitting still, and the hard lines of time and space reasserted themselves.

The quarter I was looking at is part of the flats that extend a few miles east and tilt enough to the river that they could be drained to make farmland. Closer to the river the drainage resulted in the ditch. If there was another search area for the burial ground it would be there, though it hadn't occurred to me until, due to some lateral thought or another, I watched Dewey's truck being hauled out of the river. The lands here weren't drained until after Eugene left, which means the grave might now be on an island or underwater, or, as I choose to believe, simply washed away.

I got out of the truck and stood on the road a minute. My one thought was that the land here is so perfect for our passing through and forgetting that if we try just standing still and remembering, the place can seem a beautiful adversary.

The Palace in noon light looks a bit washed out and tired as an old farm building, not at all a locus of colourful, exotic, entirely foreign stories. I park across the street in front of the obelisk war memorial outside the Legion. There's no one here on the lower part of Fourth but a block away the Main Street intersection accepts the traffic of shoppers, bored kids, mere passers-through.

At twelve sharp the town siren begins its lone, towering wail to signal what is called around here the "dinner" hour, just as it signals the six p.m. "supper" hour and the nine p.m. who-knows-what hour, the sirens being a local oddity we're happy to keep, though they serve no purpose and no one knows when or why we started them. As the howl turns over to its descent, the theatre door cracks open, pauses, then swings wide, and Dewey steps out, squinting and holding our bottle of whiskey. He smiles broadly. His hair is unruly and the film on his unshaven face suggests he's been caught in a real duster.

"You look like you broke out of jail," I say.

"Buses," he says.

We begin at the Flyway. He needs food first, he explains, and we might as well get the public appearance over with. There are a few cocked brows as we come in from the parking lot, but the real test is ahead.

I say hi to the hostess, Bonny, a woman whose manner usually implies she's seen it all, but she apparently hasn't seen anything like the returned Dewey. She stares at him a minute like maybe he's here to buy trouble and not her soup 'n' sandwich special. After a moment she hands us menus and, still saying nothing, disappears into the kitchen, leaving us to seat ourselves.

The place is crowded—it's the dinner hour after all—and noisy as we enter, but it falls nearly silent as we walk through to take a table along the far wall, the only voice being that of Eddy Chapdelaine, who has his back to us and is caught up in his own hee-haw story about how some dog got the name "Pussy." As we pass him, the story is cut short. It's a minute or so before the new topic gets everyone going again.

I fill Dewey in on exactly what happened the night he left, trying to remember the names of those most offended. He keeps wanting to talk about Karen.

"She'll call today," I inform him.

"Well I have news about her."

"How could you have news about her?"

"You're right, but I have news just the same."

Before he can lead me any farther, we're interrupted. Of all the regulars there in the Flyway, any of them might have come by to have a word with him, but due to some understood sense of propriety, the pleasure is granted to Two-Four Wright. His concussed cousin, Floorboard, has recovered, but he'll be picking up the cheque on bad jokes for the rest of his life.

"Toss."

"Two-Four."

"Two for what, exactly? I mean, what kind of name is that?" asks Dewey.

"What the hell you mean?" asks Two-Four.

"Does it bother you you're named after a case of beer?"

Two-Four looks to me for an interpretation. So does the rest of the room.

"It could be worse," says Dewey. "You could be named Crock, I guess."

We hang there for a few seconds.

"What's he expect?" Two-Four asks me. He wants to do the right thing here.

"I guess he expects you to get it over with."

And like that, Dewey gets socked in the teeth and knocked from his chair.

"Shit!" says Two-Four, standing straight again. "I shouldn't of suckered him. I'm sorry I suckered you."

Dewey lies on his side, holding his hand to his face—we all have reason to be worried now—and slowly gathers himself and gets right back in the saddle.

He mutters, "No problem. Wouldn't have it otherwise. My best to your cousin."

As Two-Four walks back to his table, people resume their lunches, presumably feeling a little cheerier and with something fresh to talk about. A minute later, Dewey holding a wet paper napkin to his face, Corporal Hall walks in for his daily slice of Key lime pie. When he sees us he almost turns around, but Dewey waves him over.

"Say uncle," says Dewey.

"I was hoping you'd gone off with the shortstop."

"Why didn't I think of that?"

Hall glances my way. He lowers his voice to address Dewey.

"Look, Mr. Raymond here asked me what happened"

"That's enough, corporal," I cut him off.

He shakes his head almost imperceptibly.

"All right." He spots his pie waiting at his usual table near the door. "Let's all just start over then." And with that he walks away.

"I think we had a narrow escape there," I say.

He ignores my observation. "There's no explaining," says Dewey. "Don't expect any explaining."

The rest of our lunch is without incident. At the till on the way out I arrange with Bonny for the kitchen to cook up two chicken dinners and deliver them to Cora's refrigerator around five. Cora and Perry are due home in the evening from her check-up in Saskatoon and they won't feel like cooking, especially since Cora will be exhausted from haranguing Perry about his driving now that she's conceded to let him have a go at the Delta 88.

Dewey rides along with me to Cora's so he can shower and pick up his truck, (Perry's got it back up and running) and go on with the rest of his business—trying to get his job back and his house in order.

"You were saying about Karen?"

"Well, *I* didn't say anything about Karen, but I *heard*, or I guess *read* something about her."

"I'm bursting with anticipation." I remind myself to get some vegetables from Cora's garden and leave them on the kitchen table.

"It was last night, in this little town I don't even know its name, and I'm lying in a back room of this bartender's house, and it's like I'm being *called* to get out of there, so I get dressed and slip out and go behind the house and there's this field, just dirt really, and I just start walking in this field in the starlight, out towards where I think the main highway is. And what do I do?"

"Is this a monster story?"

"I look up. It's like someone's tapping me on the shoulder, and I look up and see this...dis*play*, all these stars in final burnout, taking their angle on our little world—"

"It's called a meteor shower." Out of nowhere I think of Mulwray. Stars, when they fell.

"Except there wasn't anything random about these stars, or at least I got the sense it was some higher kind of randomness that I could tune in to, that was... meaningful."

"And how does Karen come into it? I'm afraid to ask."

"Well, I picked up a world of information, and one little bit of it is that she'll be back. Early spring."

"Well that's great news." I'm hoping Perry left the keys in Dewey's truck, I don't want to cart him around all day.

"Anything else you want to know?"

"There's your truck."

I pull in behind it. Dewey jumps out clutching his whiskey and runs to his truck, starts it up and listens, shuts it off. He takes a walk around it inspecting the rust damage.

"Your cousin does good work," he says.

We head upstairs to find him some clean clothes—the only close fits might be my baseball sweats and undershirt—and he skips jauntily into his shower.

In Cora's garden I appraise the burn damage. The irregular waterings have barely greened the pathetic harvest. A few salads, a pie I'd rather not eat, maybe two or three new sealer jars for the basement shelf. What misery is vegetable gardening. The point of the exercise seems to be some vague lesson about savouring delayed gratification, but the best you can hope for is a jackpot of roughage. Of course almost everyone here feels elsewise and I don't question them. Maybe I should take up growing things.

I wander along the rows and inspect the leaves, pull a few carrots which turn out to be larger below the soil than their tops suggest. I rub the dirt off with my hands. In a moment I find myself staring hard at what I'm holding. This is like something, I think, or else it's the same as something. I'm facing north. So what? Seconds later I've lost it. I've become aware of myself standing in a garden staring at a carrot in my hand and I know I'll never recover the original wonderment, but when I'm back in the kitchen washing them it comes to me. I'd been standing in that very place in one of the tornado dreams I told Cora about, and the twister had been the long, attenuated kind, remarkably like the shape in my hand. Though I tell myself this is nothing to be spooked about—unlike red potatoes and rhubarb, carrots are not a naturally eerie vegetable—the coincidence holds in me. I confess the tornado dreams scare me, in fact I always feel a lingering dread well into the following day, but now they seem a little ridiculous.

I leave the carrots on the table beside a note telling Cora and Perry about the chicken in the fridge and explaining why Dewey's truck is gone.

In my clothes Dewey all but disappears. As we walk out to his truck he rolls up the sleeves so high they look like blue waterwings under each arm.

"You don't want to see me to my door, I guess." He attempts a beseeching expression.

"Look, I'll make you an offer. You pack up and get the hell out of that ghost trap and move into my neighbour's house. It's mine now."

He maintains himself for a few seconds before his face disassembles itself and his eyes begin lighting all over Cora's yard.

"I don't...that's about.... What's the setup then?"

"You can stay there free on condition that you don't spread lies and piss people off. If you do piss them off then it's, what, three-fifty a month."

He considers the arrangement.

"I can't afford that...Two seventy-five."

"Three hundred."

"Deal."

He climbs in his truck smiling much less theatrically than usual, and so more earnestly, I assume.

"I tell you, Toss, she's coming back."

"Right."

"Shouldn't you be down there waiting by your phone?"

"Better I just go about my day. We'll connect." The truth is I'm trying not to want her too badly, though the trying's not working.

He starts the truck and looks out over the wheel. A car passes and someone, I can't see who, cranes over her shoulder to get a load of Dewey. He takes no notice.

"I don't suppose the stars said anything about my getting this colony going."

"I don't think it came up." He finally looks at me. "But what if it doesn't go?"

"I guess it depends if Karen's here. Maybe I'll sell the buildings. Someone can haul them off. Then, I don't know. I think I'd just like to *raise* something."

He looks back over the wheel and down the street.

"That's my kind of thought," he says, just before pulling away.

I'm about to leave too when I hear Cora's phone ringing. I break from canter to trot towards the front door and, once inside, scurry into the hall and around the kitchen corner, lunging for the thing and bashing my knee into the stool at the little phone nook.

"Is this Mr. Raymond?" A young woman's voice.

"Zinvalena?"

"What? You wanna try English?"

"Who is this?"

"I'm calling Wesley Toss Raymond. The one number nobody answers. This was the second number I was supposed to try." The background is anonymous, voices and clatter breaking up, re-forming. "I'm at the end of my break so I don't have much time. And Tony, my boss, he thinks this is local."

"I'm sorry," I say. "This is Toss. I just wondered who I was talking to, but I think I know now."

"Mom said I'd take you by surprise but I wanted to meet you, I mean talk to you. She says we know the same amount about each other except I haven't seen a picture. She says you're not over-homely. Why would you let her leave without a picture?"

"I'm pleased to meet you, Wendy."

"Sorry? She said you get formal like that around strangers, and you'd be nervous so your voice might crack."

"I said it's nice meeting you."

"We aren't meeting, really. Everyone says we should though. Gramma says I'd like you. I asked if you'd like me and all she ever says is, Everybody likes you, dear, which isn't true at all. Like you already think I'm too forward, maybe. That's what's been said before."

"Forward's my favourite direction. Is your mom there?"

She laughs Karen's laugh.

"You make me sound like a three-year-old with that question. No, I called her and she gave me these numbers for you and said to tell you she'd call later, maybe tomorrow. So when are we going to meet? She says I should put the pressure on and don't worry if you get awkward."

"I don't know when we'll meet, Wendy. I honestly don't."

"That's all? Look, my break's almost over so we can't talk much longer. You'll know when it ends because Tony'll walk behind the bar, where this cord goes—we use the hallway to the bathrooms to talk—and he'll just disconnect us. That's the kind of guy he is. So don't think I'm rude. Unless you think my question's rude. When are we going to meet?"

"I don't think it's rude."

"Shit, there goes Tony and you haven't answered me. We'll talk again soon. This is then. Nice meeting—"

"...you." Not "this is then." The end. This is the end, though we didn't get our end, of course, and almost missed our beginning. I sit staring at the phone dial in the abject stupor of wondering where things come from or disappear to. There are no bigger questions, and none of more consequence to the history of most places you can name, or that sends us into more fruitless pursuits or varieties of trouble. But, as Dewey would say, there's no explaining, beyond knowing that hope exists not in clean endings, or happy ones—neither of which we really expect to meet with, except in movies—but in our imagining them. This is no small thing, given that, quite obviously, we can change our future through imagining it, and perhaps less obviously, even change our past in small but important ways somewhere up ahead.

Three women on the coast keep me in something other than a picture. It hadn't occurred to me to find one for Karen, and anyway, I have yet to see a good likeness of myself, and who wouldn't rather be evoked against the sweet resistances of the mind? Better to leave Karen photoless, with whatever watery images survive, lifelike, in memory.

I get up and start walking—my knee hurts but I really don't mind the pain—walking out of the house and into mid-day at season's end. And then I'm out of the yard and still walking, waiting for what I know *will* come to me, the small, sustaining miracle of a simple moment impossibly composed. It could be anywhere. A spray of gravel fixed into a patch of paving tar on the street. The sound of a tailgate shut hard.

Two boys fly past on their bikes and take aim at a veil of water where a jammed sprinkler head has stopped revolving and overshoots the hospital lawn. A woman—a patient? a nurse?—looks down from the sun-room window, smiling at the sight of them. The dark shape of a man appears over the sprinkler in the diffused, raining light, and crouches to make repairs. There, a certain line of trees along the residential part of Main standing the same way all my life as if time stopped. A town at the speed of light. The boys pass through laughing and now the woman's turning, gone. Both of us aloft in the thought of a full, loving, and everlasting home.

© Susan Carr

Michael Helm is the acclaimed author of *The Projectionist*, a finalist for The Giller Prize, and *In the Place of Last Things*, a finalist for the Rogers Writers' Trust Fiction Prize and for a regional Commonwealth Writers' Prize for Best Book. He studied literature at the University of Toronto, and has taught at colleges and universities in Canada and in the United States. His writings on fiction, poetry, and photography have appeared in North American newspapers and magazines, including *Brick*, where he has been an editor since 2003.

Born in Saskatchewan, Michael Helm has lived most recently in Michigan and Toronto.